# Kill Abby White! Now!

C.B. Huesing

**Kill Abby White! Now!**
Copyright © 2020 by C.B. Huesing

Library of Congress Control Number: 2020918803
ISBN-13: Paperback: 978-1-64749-247-2
Epub: 978-1-64749-248-9

All rights reserved. No part of this publication may be reproduced, distributed, or transmitted in any form or by any means, including photocopying, recording, or other electronic or mechanical methods, without the prior written permission of the publisher or author, except in the case of brief quotations embodied in critical reviews and certain other noncommercial uses permitted by copyright law.

Although every precaution has been taken to verify the accuracy of the information contained herein, the author and publisher assume no responsibility for any errors or omissions.No liability is assumed for damages that may result from the use of information contained within.

Printed in the United States of America

GoToPublish LLC
1-888-337-1724
www.gotopublish.com
info@gotopublish.com

# Chapter One

*Chicago 1929*

"What happened? Where am I?" Her speech was slurred, and her eyes barely opened as she gazed at a figure in white standing next to her bed.

"You're in Samaritan Hospital, in Chicago. You were wounded," said the nurse who was adjusting the bed covers. "I'll tell the doctor you're awake."

The patient turned her head slowly from left to right and tried to focus on the bottles hanging on stands and sprouting tubes attached to both her arms. She closed her eyes and dozed.

Dr. Ambrose, a fiftyish balding man, arrived minutes later with the nurse and gently awoke the patient.

"Sorry to wake you, young lady, but I need to see if your concussion left any after-effects."

"Am I dying?"

"Oh, no, Miss. Please just try to relax. I'm Dr. Ambrose. You were shot three days ago. Fortunately, the bullet struck you in your left rib area and missed your vital organs. It passed through after nipping a rib bone. You must have been on a step or some elevation to hit concrete with such force when you went down."

He put his fingers softly on the side of her head, moving aside her blond hair. "This looked pretty bad when they brought you in, but the swelling has gone down. Your skull was x-rayed. No fractures. We put you to sleep as a precaution. You lost a lot of blood from the bullet wound, so you had your second transfusion yesterday. Are you up to answering a few questions? I need to assess any damage from your concussion."

"Yes, I think so. But I don't feel so good. Awful headache, and my shoulder and side hurt. Where are my friends?

"All right, later on that question. What is your name?"

"Abby White."

"How old are you?"

"Twenty-two."

"How many fingers am I showing?"

"Ah, three."

"Now how many?"

"Two."

"What is the date today?"

"Don't know for sure. Last of February, I think, 1929."

"What do you do, and how do we contact your family?"

"I'm a student at Northwestern—a senior in my last semester. My parents are on a tour in the Far East. Hard to reach."

Fleeting images of her parents passed through her mind. *If only you could be here now.*

"Okay. I think your brain survived that hit. Your cognitive skills are good."

"It's all kind of a blur to me. What happened? Where are my friends?"

"Well, Abby, the police have been waiting to talk to you about that. We'll phone them, but you need to rest until they get here. You're a strong young woman—you'll be fine"

"I'm so thirsty."

The doctor nodded, using his thumb and index finger to indicate to the nurse how much water to give the patient. "Now try to rest."

Abby raised her head slightly and looked toward the door as the doctor and nurse left. She saw a uniformed policeman sitting on a chair just outside. *What's he doing there?* Abby wondered. The drugs, still in her system, sent her back to sleep.

About an hour later, a ruddy-faced, heavyset, older man with a bad shave and rheumy eyes nudged her. He smelled of cigarettes, and his rumpled suit needed a pressing. He flashed a badge. "Miss White, I'm Detective Nino Masconi of the Chicago police. Can I sit down?"

"Yes. Where are my friends?"

"We'll get to that. What were you doing at that place at Clark and Dickens streets?"

"Working. All of us are interns for a Chicago newspaper. Now, where are my friends?"

Masconi took a hard look at her. There was enough thrust in her chin to hint that she had a mind of her own.

"Jeez. A stubborn cuss. Just like my daughter! Okay, but you're not gonna like what I tell you." He pulled out a spiral-bound notebook from his breast pocket and began flicking the pages.

"Here we are. You were wounded. So were Esther Frankel and Daniel O'Gara. One person escaped without injuries, but two were killed outright. We have the names of the deceased as Harold Hubble and Carol Martin."

"Oh, no," said Abby softly. She stared at the detective, her eyes filling with tears. Masconi made notes as Abby struggled to regain control.

"Sorry, Miss." He paused. "The fellow who escaped major injury was one Karl Kruger. He was pulled inside by a homeowner. After he came out of the house and saw all the carnage, he passed out and went into shock. The docs got to him fairly quickly, and he seems to be okay. Now it's your turn, young lady. I need more details."

"I don't feel so good. Think I'm going to be sick."

Masconi shuffled as fast as his big frame could carry him and found the nurse. She held a pan under Abby's chin. It was mostly dry heaves since she had not eaten anything solid since admission to the hospital

The nurse set down her pan and stood with her arms folded. "Sorry, Detective, but that's enough for today. This woman was seriously hurt and needs her rest. Come back tomorrow."

Masconi sighed, folded his notebook and slipped it back into his coat pocket.

"Okay. Miss, I'll see you tomorrow." As he left, he murmured to the policeman at the door "Sit tight. Don't leave for anything."

Sometime during the night she awoke, struggling to breathe. Something heavy was pressing down on her face. *It's a pillow.* She tried to raise her arms to pull it off, but couldn't. There was a heavy weight on her body. *Someone is sitting on me!* She was beginning to lose consciousness when her hand felt the cord to her call button. She pressed it frantically. A bell rang in the hallway. Seconds passed, and Abby stopped breathing. She didn't feel the weight come off her body as someone rolled off her bed and moved quickly through the door.

The night nurse heard the bell and saw the red light for Abby's room. Moving swiftly around the corner, she started running when she saw a figure fleeing through the exit door at the end of the hall. As she turned into Abby's room, she let out a yell, pulling the pillow off the patient's face. She pulled the emergency alarm cord and began giving Abby mouth-to-mouth resuscitation. The night physician ran in with another nurse, and together they managed to get Abby breathing again.

"Where's that policeman who's supposed to be on guard?" the night nurse asked as they reattached the dangling intravenous tubes. Just then, the policeman came into the room.

"What happened?"

"Where were you?"

"Had to go to the bathroom. Only gone for a minute."

"Well, it was time enough for someone to try to smother this woman with a pillow and pull out all of her tubes."

The doctor examined Abby thoroughly, then turned to the nurses.

"Bruises on her arms. Somebody must have used his knees to hold her down." He paused and looked at the nurses. "Her responses seem normal. I don't think she was without oxygen long enough to cause brain damage. Her heart rate is back to near normal. We'll have to watch her closely the next forty-eight hours. The wounds on her side and back need to be bandaged again. They were reopened in the struggle."

He shook his head. "This young woman has had terrible things happen to her in the last few days. I'm calling that detective again. This is attempted murder."

Though Abby was semi-conscious, she heard the essence of what was said. *Someone is trying to kill me—again! How can this be happening to me?*

Dawn was breaking over Lake Michigan when Detective Masconi arrived an hour later, huffing and puffing, his tie loosened. The night doctor told him what had happened. Just then, Dr. Ambrose came through the door.

"If she hadn't punched her call button, she'd be dead now," said the night doctor.

"Who would want to kill this poor woman now after all she's been through?" Dr. Ambrose asked.

Masconi lowered his head and mumbled. "The mob. They must think she and the other students saw too much. They don't like witnesses who could send them to the chair. We've got to make other arrangements for her as soon as she's able to be moved."

Masconi continued. "In the meantime, I'm posting my most reliable men at the door. Two at a time, around the clock. There'll be a man on the main floor watching the elevator and stairs. Another man will be at the elevator on this floor. Doctor, this woman and the other students could be key witnesses to a major murder crime. They *will* be protected." He spoke to the floor. "Certainly better than they have been so far."

Masconi didn't tell them that the first policeman had already been arrested on suspicion of bribery. *They'll get him as an accomplice to attempted murder. That's even heavier stuff*, thought Masconi.

It took two days after the attack before Abby's condition stabilized, and then Masconi returned.

"Miss, I don't suppose you heard or saw anything when you were attacked here in your room?" Masconi asked.

"Nothing. I was asleep when I felt enormous pressure on my face and body. It must have been a big man because I couldn't get him off me before I passed out." She paused. "What about Esther, Dan, and Karl? Where are they?"

"They're safe. We put them under more protection after your attack. Your own protection has more than doubled."

He paused and once again flipped open his notebook.

"Let me tell you what we think you young people saw," said Masconi. "Maybe it will help refresh your memory. We think you kids were standing on the steps of a boarding house across the street from the warehouse at Dickens and Clark streets. There were multiple murders in that warehouse. Did you hear gunshots?"

"Yes! We all did. It sounded like machine guns, then single loud shots. It went on for quite awhile."

"Why didn't you run?"

"Well, we were curious, I guess. We're reporters looking for a good story, and we thought we'd found one."

*Looking to get killed*, Masconi thought. He shook his head and motioned her to go on.

"We stood speculating about what was happening. Then it was quiet. We climbed up on the porch of the house for a better view—it looked like nobody was home. About a minute later four men came out of the building. The front two men had their hands in the air. They were being guarded by two uniformed policemen holding machine guns. Harold said that we should interview the cops after they put the guys in the car."

Abby's fists clinched as she remembered. "The policemen looked our way and stopped cold. One man said something to the other and to their prisoners. The policemen turned and starting shooting at us. Can you believe that? Policemen shooting at us! I was hit, and that's all I remember."

"Well, that adds up so far," Masconi said. "You all must have got a good look at them for them to shoot to kill. We think they fired left to right, hitting you, Frankel, Hubble, Martin, and O'Gara. The lady in the house opened the door a crack and pulled Kruger inside."

Masconi continued. "They fired a few more rounds at the boarding house and then ran to their stolen police car. The car was found later about five miles away. The boarding house lady was a real heroine and saved Kruger's life.

"Miss, you and your friends probably got a good look at the faces of the mobsters who killed seven men in that warehouse. The policemen were phonies, pretending they had captured the shooters so that they could get away safely. You are all key witnesses."

Abby shook her head slowly. "And we had to be there."

"Okay, now tell why all of you were there. It doesn't take six people to report a story."

She closed her eyes. "Sir, I'm suddenly very tired. All I can tell you now is that we took a holiday from work and school on St. Valentine's Day and decided to follow a gang member to see if we could get a good firsthand story."

As if on cue, the nurse came to the door. "Okay, chief, all for today."

Masconi grumbled and then used both arms of his chair to hoist up his 250-pound body. He lowered his voice. "I'm working on a transfer for you, Miss. Top secret. Be back soon."

The next morning, he was back. "Doc Ambrose said you're well enough to move if we're careful. Tomorrow is the day, and it won't be any too soon. Your names appeared in the newspapers. Somebody from the police leaked them. A new, green reporter added them to the story right before print time. Everyone is very upset over that. The *Tribune* wants the mobs shut down and the killers found. People are really up in arms about the murders of unarmed students." He paused and sat. "There's more.

"There were strangers at Northwestern snooping around dorm rooms, looking for you and your friends. I guess they thought they would catch one of you back in school. Other students chased them out. Police crews have taken all you victims' personal possessions from your dorm rooms. They'll be returned to you and the others in due time."

"Where are you moving me?" said Abby.

"Not for you to know right now, Miss. But I think you're a smart lady. Let me give you some perspective on all of this. Al Capone's Italian gang from the south side of Chicago is suspected of murdering the seven men who were all associated with Bugs Moran's North Side Irish gang. We think they were lured there by a promise of sharing a stolen shipment of whiskey provided by Detroit's Purple Gang. Bugs Moran himself missed the party because they say he was running late. 'The Saint Valentine's Massacre'—that's what the press is calling it.

"Oh, quick question. Which gang member did you students follow?"

"I don't remember."

Masconi pulled out his notebook and started reading names.

"That's the one, Albert Weinshank" interrupted Abby. "Harold Hubble was talking to one of the crime reporters at the reporter's desk, and he read Weinshank's name and address upside down."

"Okay. He was a clever boy! What a tragedy for you kids."

He leaned over Abby's bed. "Be ready to go at nine o'clock tomorrow morning. Don't tell your nurse, doctor, or anyone about this. I don't trust anyone in this town anymore. Now let's look at some mug shots to see if they look familiar."

Masconi passed one photo after another to Abby. "Take your time, Miss. Try to put a policeman's cap on them."

Abby sorted through a dozen shots, finally handing two photos to Masconi. "This one was in a policeman's uniform, and the other man was right ahead of him with his hands up. I couldn't see the faces of the other two. They were on the other side"

"Good. This guy is Frank Burke, and the other guy is James Ray. They have been known to wear police uniforms on their robbery sprees. We'll see what your friends, Kruger, Frankel, and O'Gara, come up with." He whispered to Abby, "See you at nine in the morning."

Masconi arrived in the morning, accompanied by a medical doctor and two policemen in medical garb. The day nurse on duty came running from her nurse's station. "What are you doing?

"We're moving her to a safe place. This place isn't safe for a person under police protection. Dr. Ambrose said it would be okay if we were careful." The nurse sighed, shook her head, and then helped them lift Abby gently onto the gurney.

"Thanks, Nurse, you've been very kind," Abby said as they rolled her down to the elevators.

Masconi had an ambulance pull up to a back dock and block the view as they rolled Abby's gurney into the back of another ambulance. Masconi climbed into the ambulance and took a seat next to Abby's gurney. He instructed the ambulance driver to drive around several blocks and alleyways to ensure that they weren't being followed. Masconi was constantly checking the rear window of the ambulance. No one seemed to be following—that he could see.

# Chapter Two

*Athena, Michigan*

Abby's ambulance headed east, then north. Abby turned her head on the gurney to see Masconi's weather-beaten face. He was rubbing his eyes. "You look so tired, Detective. Are you getting enough sleep?"

Masconi shook his head. "As if this job isn't enough, one of our little ones got sick during the night. I took turns with my wife watching him. I think he'll be okay."

"How many children do you have?"

"Three from my first marriage—my wife died in childbirth. I married Teresa, and we have two of our own."

"What a handful," Abby said.

"That's what Teresa says almost every day. That and, 'Nino, you've got to lose that weight or you're going to croak right here on the kitchen floor, and I'll be left with all your bambinos to raise.'" He chuckled, "I don't know what I'd do without her."

After an hour they pulled into a large, upscale nursing home in the small town of Athena, Michigan. Abby was preregistered as Mary McNamara. The ambulance drivers wheeled Abby's gurney to a room overlooking a small lake. Masconi followed and then patted her hand. "Here's my phone number. Call me anytime. You'll be safe here. And there's a doctor on the staff here. I'll be checking on you.."

Abby's wounds from her attack at Samaritan Hospital needed more time to heal. She lay in her bed thinking about what had happened. *Poor Carol and Harold. All they wanted to do was graduate and get on with their lives.*

*All I wanted to do was to be a good journalist, enjoy some travel, and have some good adventures—not this misadventure where people are shot and killed.*

She passed time reading books and working crossword puzzles from the local newspaper. The St. Valentine's Day shooting was still front-page stuff. According to one reporter, the word on the street was that Capone was steaming mad at his boys for shooting the students. An editorial speculated it put a lot more pressure on Capone from the police and public then ever before. Another related article said that Capone had more than 400 people on his payroll, including politicians, police, and even hatcheck girls.

At the Chicago police station, Masconi heard from a snitch that the men who did the shooting told Capone and his lieutenants that the tall blond girl, Abby White, had had the best look at them. According to the snitch, Capone had yelled, "Kill that Abby White! Now! And find those other kids who lived and finish the job, you goddamn idiots, or we're dead meat! And make it look like Moran's boys did it."

Abby's location was close to Esther's and Dan's rehab hospital near Lansing, and Karl was on the Michigan State campus in a student resident hall.

The Chicago police department had notified the parents of the surviving students that they were under protective custody. That didn't stop the parents from calling almost every day. Abby's parents had returned to Indianapolis from their tour of the Far East, and her father, John White, had made several trips to Chicago to talk with the police. Masconi handled most of the calls and visits. As part of his protective custody assignment, he had obtained information about the parents from Northwestern University's registration office after getting authorization through a court order. For the most part, they all appeared to be well-to-do people. Masconi was impressed. *If the mob knew about these kids, they might have kidnapped them for ransom instead of shooting them,* thought Masconi.

Two more weeks went by, and Masconi again called the doctor at Athena. This time there was a positive note. "Abby has healed nicely and is walking the grounds with ease," the doctor said. Masconi's other calls found that Esther's leg wounds and Dan's arm wound had also healed, and Karl was restless in his campus room. Masconi made the rounds again and told all four that he would pick them up the next Wednesday for a picnic and outing. He said they would talk about what they had seen at the crime scene and clarify obscure points. He needed to get updated recorded statements by the end of the day for the District Attorney's office.

\* \* \*

Masconi drove an unmarked police car and picked up Abby, Dan, then Esther, and finally Karl. The students hadn't seen each other since that ugly St. Valentine's Day. They kissed and hugged and chattered away. They cried for Carol and Harold.

"We couldn't even go to their funerals," sobbed Esther.

It was a chilly, cloudy day in April as they drove into a deserted campground some ten miles north of Lansing. The entrance sign said WELCOME TO HAPPY HOLLOW PARK—TAKE YOUR TRASH OUT WITH YOU. "It's quiet here, especially since the kids are still in school," said Masconi. He pulled the car up to a small clapboard and tarpaper building. "Not much to look at, but this is the community building for the campgrounds. You kids open it up, and I'll bring the food from the trunk. Karl, can you help me?"

Dan built a fire to ward off the chill while the girls wiped off the wooden picnic tables and spread the paper table cloths that Masconi brought. "Okay, while you eat I gotta find a telephone in town and make a couple of calls. I've got a tape recorder in my car to take your statements when I get back. You kids have fun. Back soon."

The hungry students devoured the ham and cheese sandwiches, chips, and soft drinks he'd brought them. Dan and Esther sat across the picnic table from Abby and Karl. They stared at each other for a long minute. "How did we get into this mess, Abby?" said Dan.

"Well, don't you think it started around the first part of January when Harold told us at lunch that he had an uncle who could get us into a speakeasy?" said Abby. "Everyone thought it was a grand idea, you'll recall. Harold, bless his soul, had regaled us with the reminder that we were all seniors, ready to graduate, and had not yet been to a Chicago speak-easy. 'It is high time we celebrate!' Harold had said. All six of us agreed."

"You girls looked very chic that night," said Karl as he finished his sandwich and took a swallow of cola. Karl then went on about that night in January. "I could describe you well in German, '*Scharf Madchens,*' but not well in English. Let me try. You flappers all looked sexy and worldly."

"What do the German words mean?" asked Esther.

"Hot girls!"

The girls laughed and a "Wow!" came from Dan. He stood and threw more wood on the fire.

# Chapter Three

*Chicago—Two Months Earlier*

The speakeasy, Ollie's, was down long steps in front of a big brownstone. At the landing at the bottom was a recessed, heavy-looking oak door. Harold rang a bell, and a narrow slate was slid opened. Small bloodshot eyes stared at him. "Well?"

Harold almost fumbled the password his uncle had given him. He blurted "Uncle. No wait, cousin!" The door guard, dressed in a cheap tuxedo, opened the door a crack. His eyes looked all six of them up and down. He noticed that the girls looked great with their bobbed hair and knee-length dresses with dropped waists and pearls. He winked at the girls.

"Okay, genius, bring in your friends." He opened the door just enough that the party could slip in one at a time. A wall of cigarette and cigar smoke and stale beer odor hit them in their faces. They were ushered over to a round table big enough for the six of them.

A waitress came by their table; her enormous breasts leading the way and also providing support for four steins of beer. "Be right back." She served the beer to the next table and came back. "Whatcha want, kiddos?"

They had decided beforehand. "Beer all around," Dan said. The beer arrived—four steins atop the waitress' breasts and two more carried by an underling. "Reminds me of a Stuttgart beer house," Karl said. They lifted their glasses in a toast to the last semester of their senior year and good friendships. Clinking glass all around, Harold and Karl almost broke their steins in their exuberance. A six-man jazz band played on a stage above a dance floor. Abby finally got Dan off his chair to try the Charleston. Dan caught on quickly, and the couple won deserved applause from their group. Carol and Karl had a bit of difficulty, and Karl soon retreated to their table and his beer. Esther politely refused Harold's offer to dance.

When the band took a break, Esther voiced her opinion of their internship program at the *Tribune*. "It stinks!" she said, as she sipped on her second beer. "Granted, I've learned some good things about the newspaper craft, but I think they treat us as children. I do know when and where to bring coffee to the old guys in the newsroom. When I complained, one of them told me that we have to pay our dues like they did when they started." Esther was the smallest of the group. Her dark eyes had danced around the room, viewing everyone and everything, like a small bird thoroughly checking for predators before eating.

Abby nodded. "Yesterday they had me sitting for hours next to the girl who writes wedding announcements. I'm almost brain dead."

"Okay, I hear you," Dan said. "We are the 'Wildcats,' and we will not be denied! Let's meet for lunch next Saturday at Sandy's Coffee Shop on Orrington Avenue in Evanston. That's near the campus for you day-trippers. Think you all can find it? I've got a plan brewing. But we have to be cold-sober to consider it."

\* \* \*

It was near zero degrees that Saturday early in February, with a stiff, paralyzing wind blowing in from Lake Michigan, but they all showed up at Sandy's.

Abby opened the discussion. "We're writers and journalists, not 'cubs' or 'copy boys' or 'stringers.' The *Tribune* doesn't quite agree. I went to Edgar, our boss of interns, and asked if we could shadow reporters on crime scene assignments.

"Edgar said, 'It might be too dangerous, and we would be liable if anything happened to you young folks.'

"'Well, sir,' I argued, 'This internship is supposed to cover all aspects of newspaper journalism. That includes finding stories out there on the streets and reporting them to the public. We would waive our rights and relieve you from any liabilities.'

"Edgar just smiled and said, 'Abby, you make good points, but the higher-ups at Northwestern would have our hides if we put you students in harm's way. Sorry.'"

"Abby, you did your best," Dan said, and they all nodded. Dan put down his fork and looked thoughtful. "I'm trying to remember Dr. Samuelson's lecture on journalism. It went something like this. 'You can't just sit behind your desk and write about whatever comes over the transom. You have to get out there and find good stories to report. That means you must be aggressive and get to the source of the action before it happens, or as quickly as possible after it happens. That's how you get the scoop before the other newshounds.' Remember that, classmates?"

"I remember reading what a young Winston Churchill said when he was a war correspondent in the Boer War," said Abby. "To paraphrase it, 'Go as far as you can, as quickly as you can, must be the motto of the war correspondent.' Now Chicago is at war with the mobsters."

"That's what we need to do," Carol said. "We've got to get that experience. Great writers started as reporters, like Hemingway. He bummed around Europe, was an ambulance driver in the Spanish civil war, and then became a foreign correspondent for the *Toronto Star*."

"Yeah, that's what we need to do, something exciting!" Harold said.

"Here's my idea, my fellow Wildcats," Dan said. "The gangs in Chicago are always going after one another. Like Capone's south side guys shooting at Bugs Moran boys and vice versa. The press writes about it way after it's over, glorifies it, and uses questionable eye witnesses as sources. What if we, as a fine group of talented writers, got to the scene at the same time it happened?"

"Oh, sure, Dan," Carol had said. "How could we possibly do that?"

"Ha! Got your attention! We follow one of the gangsters when he leaves his house. We can use my car and follow at a safe distance. When he parks, we park, and then we follow him on foot."

Carol laughed. "What? Six of us walking down the street following this guy? It would look like an Easter Parade!" She paused. "I get it now. Who would suspect a laughing, joking group of young people as being crime reporters?"

"We'll submit our story under all of our bylines," Dan said. "If the guy does nothing, we will try another day, or follow another guy. Okay, Wildcats?"

# Chapter Four

***Back to Michigan—Happy Hollow Park***

Abby looked around the picnic table and eyed Dan. "Well, Dan, does that answer your original question? 'How did we get into this mess, Abby?' How soon we forget."

Dan threw another log on the fire. The clapboard building leaked cold air like a sieve.

"Hey, what happened to our super hero, Masconi? He should be back by now," said Dan. "And look, he took his yellow pad and briefcase. Why would he do that?"

"I think I hear a car now," said Esther. Esther was always on the alert, like a feral cat. While she had not experienced or sensed any anti-Semitism from her fellow Wildcats, it was always in the back of her mind—a sixth sense that kept all her other senses alert.

Dan pulled back the front window curtain slightly. "It's not Masconi's car. They're parking back near the woods. Look, Karl, they're getting out of the car, carrying some things. It looks like one guy is carrying a machine gun, and the other one has a rifle or shotgun."

"Did Masconi sell us out?" asked Karl.

Esther made a low moan. "They're going to kill us! They're going to shoot us again!" Her tiny body was quivering. Abby held tight to her.

"Okay, Wildcats. We stand firm." said Dan. "Do what we have to do. First, close all the curtains and turn off the lights. We can't do any thing about the fire light now. Let's turn the picnic tables on their sides and drag them over to the left of the fireplace. Leave enough room between the tables for all of us to lie down." They worked fast. "Okay, now pull the chairs to each end of the tables and then lean them on the ends of the tables to close them off after you get in."

Just as they finished their makeshift defense, bullets began ripping through the flimsy walls. Window glass exploded and bullets hit the heavy picnic tables and lodged there. Some shots ricocheted off the stone fireplace and struck the backsides of the tables and chairs. Esther was sobbing even though Dan, Karl, and Abby protected her body. Finally, the shooting stopped. Dan crawled to a window and peeked out. "Damn, they're walking this way, reloading!"

"Okay, listen closely." Dan softened his voice as he lay near the broken window. "Abby and Esther, stay between the tables. Stay quiet and don't move. Karl, get two pieces of firewood that we can use as clubs." Karl picked two good pieces out the stack of firewood. "Now crawl to the left side of the door. I'll take this side. They'll blow through that door, ready to finish us off. Wait 'til both heads are visible, then swing as hard as you can. They are killers, and we can't let them get up again. Okay, Karl?"

Karl nodded and crawled to his position. "I'm ready."

The two gunmen kicked in the door and waited, listening for sounds. "We may have got 'em already," said one of them as they walk through the doorway. Dan and Karl hit them hard, and they dropped like stones, their guns rattling as they hit the concrete floor.

"Girls, it's safe! Come out and help us find their car keys. Blood was oozing out of cracked skulls as they rooted around in the gunmen's pockets. "I've got them!" said Abby.

Dan gathered the group together. "We can't trust anyone. We'll take their car, pick up our personal stuff, and then start driving."

"Where to?" asked Abby.

"Out of this area first. We can talk as we drive."

They ran to the black sedan. Dan opened the trunk. "More guns and ammunition." He pulled on gloves that were in the trunk and dumped the cache on the ground. He kept a .38 caliber revolver and a box of ammunition.

Dan drove well below the speed limit to each of their rehab places and Karl's dormitory building. They hurriedly packed their things, and within the hour they were on their way driving southeast toward Detroit with a tank full of gas provided by the mobsters. They dipped down into Ohio, then across into Pennsylvania. It was dark when they pulled into a motel. Its sign was flashing a red vacancy. "Are you sure about this place? It looks seedy," said Abby.

"The seedier the better. We want a low profile," said Dan.

# Chapter Five

*Pennsylvania*

Dan and Karl each took a cabin using false names. The night desk clerk looked at them suspiciously, and then asked for cash upfront. Karl whispered to Dan, "We'll flip a coin to see who sleeps where and with whom."

"In your dreams," said Dan.

The women took one cabin and the men the other, and then they walked a short distance to an all-night diner. "Well, we made it this far," said Karl, after they ordered their food. "Now what?"

"We've got to get out of the country," Abby said. "You know what we learned in Chicago. Capone and O'Bannon have connections all over the Midwest and East Coast, certainly in New York City. We are sitting ducks wherever we go. Our car will be spotted soon. It was probably stolen by those gunmen."

There was a pause. "You're right, Abby." said Dan. "I've been thinking. Try this on for size, friends. My father in Ireland has been working with a Boston bootlegger to get Irish beer and liquor into Boston. I think the big shot's name is Frank Kenny. I'll cable Dad about our situation. Maybe he can have Kenny get someone to prepare false papers with new identities for all of us. Our family has a large vacation cottage near Tralee and Dingle Bay in southwestern Ireland, which is usually empty. We can sail to Galway and then lay low for a while at the cottage. But where can we stay until we put this all together?"

Talk ended when the waitress brought the food. "Where you folks headed?" she asked.

"We're going hiking on the Appalachian Trail." Abby said quickly.

"I hear tell there's still a lot of snow up there. Stay warm!" she warned.

Karl perked up. "I have some German friends in Atlantic City, New Jersey, who will put us up for a while. It's a large house on the beach."

"Are they trustworthy, Karl?" asked Esther

"They're a little bit shady, like we've become. We'll be okay."

"We've got to find out what ships go to Irish ports from New York or New Jersey ports," said Esther.

"We'll have time to do that. There are several travel offices in Atlantic City," said Karl.

"So you've been there, Karl?" asked Dan

"Oh, yes. They are my friends."

"Okay, good. Sound okay, Wildcats? Then let's do it!"

"Wait a minute, Dan," said Esther. "You, Karl, and I are all from across the water. Abby, you should catch a bus at the next big town and get back to Indiana. I'm sure you have friends or relatives where you can stay until this is over."

"No way, Esther. We have stuck together this far, and I will not leave you. Besides, the mobsters are most likely watching our house and our relatives' houses.

"What *is* important is we need enough cash to make this happen," said Abby. "When we get to Atlantic City, I'll call my father collect in Indianapolis to have money sent from my account to an Atlantic City bank. I'll tell him we are still running but are safe. Our whereabouts will be safe with him."

After finishing their meal, the women retreated to their cabin and the men to theirs. All of them were exhausted from the near-death experience and the long drive. The night desk clerk waited until their cabin lights went out and then walked quietly to their car and wrote down their license plate number. In the morning, he noted the direction they were heading.

# Chapter Six

*Atlantic City, New Jersey*

"Dan, I want to stop in the next town and find a gun shop," said Abby. "I want a gun to protect myself and Esther. I think Karl should have one also."

"I don't have that much money," said Karl.

"I'll loan you the money," said Abby."

Dan briefly took his eyes off the road ahead and looked at Abby. "Do you know how to use a gun, Abby?"

"Dan, my father is a hunter, and he taught all three of us girls to handle a gun, including pistols, when we were in high school. There was a firing range not far from our house."

They found a gun shop after they crossed into New Jersey. Dan went in with her. After shopping a bit, Abby bought a Beretta, a small, palm-sized Italian pistol that held nine rounds. She tested it in the in-house firing range. It was the same type of gun that Abby had used at the firing range with her family. Karl had declined Abby's offer of a loan to buy a gun. "I'm a foreigner. They would probably deport me if they found a gun on me."

They made their way slowly across New Jersey in a hard rain. The weather had improved when they stopped to refuel at a service station that had a small, wooded park with picnic tables. After gassing up, Karl pulled into the parking lot of the park while Dan was paying for the gas. Abby and Esther came back with sandwiches, cokes, and a New Jersey map.

As they settled at a picnic table, Abby saw a car pulling in behind theirs in the parking lot. Two men in leather jackets started over toward their table. Their hands were in deep pockets. *Oh, not again*, thought Abby. She pulled her Beretta out of her purse with her back to them, pushed the safety off, and put it in her coat pocket. Dan came out of the service station and saw the men. He reached into his waistband and pulled out the gun he had taken in Michigan from the mobsters' car. He came in quietly and quickly behind the two men just as they were pointing their guns at the trio at the picnic table. Dan dropped one with a shot to the head with his revolver, and Abby shot the other in the chest as he turned his gun on Dan. The station attendant came out of his door when he heard the shots and then retreated back inside. "Okay, let's get out of here!" yelled Dan. Dan had to carry Esther—she had fainted this time.

"The station guy will call the police. They should be able to piece together what happened. They'll find the mobsters with guns drawn," Dan said they pulled away. "Let's hope these cops are not on the mob's payroll too. Karl, pick out some side roads on the map to get us to your friends' place. That damn motel operator sold us out. Probably got our plate number and knew who to call."

Esther recovered after a few minutes. "Why don't we just stop at the next town and get protection at their police station. I can't take this anymore!" said a sobbing Esther.

Abby reached over to the front seat and tapped Dan on the shoulder. "Dan, we need to stop at a safe place to regroup."

They eventually saw a sign marking the entrance to a county park and pulled into a remote parking and picnic area. A warm breeze gave a hint of an early summer as they walked and half-carried Esther to a picnic table.

"I know I should be brave," Abby said. "But I just killed a man." Then she burst into tears.

Dan and Karl consoled her as Esther continued to sob. They were all in a state of shock. "This has been a nightmare," said Dan. "Let's join hands and pray."

After a silent moment, Abby got herself under control and said, "God, please help us. We know why this is happening to us, but enough is enough! We have to kill to protect ourselves. Tell us what to do. We are weakening and need your divine help to save us. Amen."

"It's like being in a war," said Dan. "We have to stop them before they kill us."

He paused. "Okay, let's take a vote," he said. "All in favor of turning ourselves in, say 'aye'." Esther's was the only "aye."

"Esther, I don't think we can trust *any* police after what's been happening to us," Abby said. Esther ran to the car and slumped down in the corner of the rear seats.

It was another hour before they pulled up to a large oceanfront house in Atlantic City. Karl introduced Hans Strasser and Peter Farben, stocky young men who both had military haircuts. They accepted Karl's explanation that they were on a much-needed holiday from their university work. Abby studied the two men. Peter was a nice-looking man who appeared confident, but Hans, she thought, had a face that resembled a frog's, and his mouth kept opening and closing like a goldfish's.

"Let me show you around the house" said Peter. At the front bay window they were enjoying the view of the Atlantic when Hans put his hand on Abby's back and moved it down to her bottom. Dan grabbed his arm. Abby pushed Hans and yelled, "Stop that!" Hans made a move as if to fight Dan, and then broke into a smile.

"My mistake. I see you're taken," said Hans.

"Listen, I'm not 'taken' by anybody, and I will not be pawed by anybody," said Abby. "Dan and Karl, we've been through hell, and now this? I want to move on."

"Hans, apologize to the lady, you animal!" said Peter.

"I'm sorry, Miss."

"I accept your apology, but I must warn you that I carry a gun. Stay away from Esther and me."

"A bad start. Please stay. It won't happen again," said Peter, glaring at Hans. "It is as much your place, Karl, as ours. We have plenty of rooms, thanks to our German government." He stared at Hans again. "There will be no more of that, I promise."

The four visitors moved off to a room near the front of the house and closed the door. "That sickened me. How can Esther and I sleep soundly at night?" said Abby.

"I agree. That was unbelievable," Dan said, and then he paused. "The problem is we have no place to go right now, except a public place where we could be spotted. Okay, hear this: Karl and I will take rooms between you girls and our hosts. On the positive side, it looks like they have room in their garage for the car. If the mob still finds us, Peter and Hans should be of help. How does that sound, ladies?"

The girls gave reluctant nods.

"Karl, why does the German government have a house here for you men?" asked Abby.

"It's no big secret. We are part of the Friends of New Germany organization. We're forming campaigns to promote support for nationalism in the new Germany. We feel that our leaders betrayed us by signing the Armistice at Versailles to end the war in 1918. Our army was far from being defeated, and the reparation penalties have wrecked the German economy."

"So that's what you've been up to on your mysterious absences from campus. Why didn't you tell us if it was no secret?" said Abby. Karl just smiled. "You had no need to know."

Later that day, Abby was able to make a phone call from a post office phone booth. "Oh, Abby, it's so good to hear your voice again. Are you all right?" said her father, John.

"Dad, we're still being followed by the gangsters. We are in Atlantic City, New Jersey, and plan to go to Ireland and hide for a while. Dan O'Gara's family has a family cottage there. We can't go to the police. We hear that New York and New Jersey police are just as bad as Chicago's. We've had a couple of close calls already."

"Incredible, Abby. Can I do anything?"

"Yes, can you wire two thousand dollars from my bank account? I'm sure glad you're a cosigner on my account. I opened an account at the Atlantic City Bank and Trust near here." She gave him the account number. "I think it's safe to be in my name, unless bankers are gang members too. Wouldn't be surprised! I'll need the money to buy false papers and steamship tickets. We don't want our real names on any ship's passenger list. And I don't know what kind of expenses I'll run into overseas."

"One more thing, Dad. Can you find out if Masconi is still with the Chicago police department? We think he sold us out."

"What? No! Somebody has got to clean up that city! I hear the federal government may step in."

"Is all well with the family? How is Mother?"

"She's fine. We're all very worried about you."

"I'll be okay. I think some of Grandmother Cass' toughness is coming through."

He laughed. "Good!"

"I will call you this time next week. Mum's the word. Thank you so much, Dad. Love you."

\* \* \*

The seniors from Northwestern settled in the house on the New Jersey shore. After tasting Hans' cooking, the girls decided to lend a hand in the kitchen.

"Women with guns are dangerous," Hans whispered to Peter. "Stay away from Abby for sure. But these girls are good cooks, so I'll tolerate it."

Dan's father was successful in getting his business contact in Boston to find a forger in New Jersey. Dan called the forger and met him in a church in Atlantic City. The cash deal was done in a week, and the students had new identities.

Karl and Dan decided to confide the true situation to Peter and Hans. "Unglauelich!" said Peter. "Unbelieveable! We'll help you get away safely."

Abby's father, John, sent a cable in care of the bank telling Abby that he had transferred the money. He added that Detective Masconi was recovering in a hospital from a severe beating and torture. A police detective told John that Masconi had multiple cigarette burns on his body.

The people of Chicago were horrified. An editorial in the *Tribune* read: "No one is safe. The mobs are now torturing our policemen."

The Chicago police were in a quandary. They knew the students were somehow able to overcome mobster attacks based on the trail of bodies from Michigan through Pennsylvania. They didn't want to draw attention to the students' whereabouts, so their press releases said that the deaths were from Capone's boys battling Moran's boys again. Another press release said that the students were still under "protective custody."

Abby told her friends the news. "Poor Masconi must have held on a long time before telling them that we were at that campground. A brave man. He did it for us. At least we got a couple of them in return. I hope it was the same two gangsters that got Masconi."

Abby drove to a travel office in Atlantic City and bought steamship tickets on the SS *Bremen*. It would sail in a week from New York City with stops at Galway, Ireland, and Southampton, England, before docking at their home port at Bremerhaven, Germany. Karl declined to go, saying "I will be safe now with my friends, and I want to complete my work here."

Before leaving their lair, Abby was returning clean linen to Hans' room when she noticed a copy of *Mein Kampf*, written by Adolf Hitler, on his desk. She had learned from Karl that he was a rising political figure in "The New Germany." Next to the book were maps and notes in German, but she noted American names on maps and notes, such as Great Lakes Naval base, Maine Iron Works, and Norfolk Naval Base. There were some photographs also. As she moved for a closer look, Hans grabbed her from behind. "What the hell are you doing, going through my things?"

Abby pulled her Beretta out of her pocket and slowly backed out the door. "I told you not to touch me. Change your *own* dirty linen, you turkey!" she yelled.

\* \* \*

It was a pleasant late spring evening on their last night in Atlantic City, and they all joined together on the deck overlooking the beach. Peter raised his glass of beer to wish them a safe voyage, and all joined in the toast. Hans was quiet, ready for the people to leave. Just then, Peter looked down on the beach to see three men coming up the sandy trail to their house. "In the house, now!"

Dan and Abby ran for their guns. Esther ran for her room and hid under the bed. When Dan and Abby returned, Peter and Hans both had machine guns in their hands. They opened the patio door and sprayed fire over the heads of the intruders who had pulled handguns from vest pockets. The mobsters realized they were outgunned and ran down the beach.

"Someone must have seen the car when we went to the grocery yesterday. We should have waited until Peter returned and taken his car." said Abby.

"Well, somehow they found us," said Karl. "They'll probably be back with machine guns. It's getting dark. Get your things together. I'll drive you up the coast to New York in Peter's car. Okay, Peter? I'll find a place for you to stay near the ship's berth."

Abby looked at Peter with concern. "We'll be okay," said Peter. "Take my car. Neighbors have probably called the police. The cops can't all be crooked. Hans and I have been well trained if the police don't show up and the mob does. And we have a special place to stash our weapons if the cops do come. Get moving now!"

Karl sped northward toward New York City, looking in his rearview mirror for followers, but after a while he told his friends, "Relax, I think we made a good getaway." It took another hour before they pulled up to a small hotel on the Hudson River near the docks. Karl helped them get their luggage to the lobby and made sure they had rooms available. He made a telephone call back to Atlantic City. Peter said they had no further attacks by the mob. He hung up the telephone and turned to Abby and Esther.

"Well, I kept looking out the rearview mirror and saw nothing, but they are pros at following without being seen."

"Keep your guns handy, Dan and Abby," said Esther.

Karl bear-hugged each of his classmates. "Remember when we started our little experiment to find a big story on St. Valentine's Day? Who would think it would lead to this. Now we really have something to write about. Be safe."

# Chapter Seven

*Atlantic Ocean—Aboard the Bremen*

The SS *Bremen* was a new, fast steamship that could cross the Atlantic in four days. Abby had bought first-class tickets for each of them. They decided to stay in their staterooms, Abby with Esther, as much as possible to avoid mingling with other passengers. Abby created a code for knocking on each other's door: three knocks, count to five, then four knocks.

"I feel like *we* are the gangsters hiding out," remarked Esther.

The ship was barely out of the harbor when the ship's speaker system ordered all passengers to their lifeboat stations for an abandon ship drill. "So much for hiding out," said Abby.

After reaching their assigned lifeboat station, the ship's captain spoke. "This is Captain Dieter speaking. Sorry for the inconvenience, but this drill is now required by international maritime laws. I want to assure you first-timers that our route is well south of any possible icebergs. And, unlike the *Titanic*, we have more than enough lifeboats. After more instructions from the crew, please return to your cabins and enjoy a wonderful cruise. Thank you."

"I think he said too much," said Esther. "With gangsters chasing us, I forgot about the *Titanic*."

On the first night, they pleaded sea sickness and had food delivered to their rooms. The next day they waited until the dining room hours were almost over and then went together. Dan thought it was safe to go out on deck after dark. Esther decided to stay in her stateroom. "Every time we think we gave them the slip, there they are. I'll stay put for now."

Dan and Abby found a two-seated cushioned chair on the deck, sat down, and wrapped themselves in blankets to keep warm. They watched the lights from a ship passing by heading to New York. The ship's lights shimmered in the sea spray and slowly disappeared over the horizon. The *Bremen* had picked up speed as she hit open water. Now the darkness was only lighted with small running lights on the side of the ship's bulkhead. They could see no one else on the deck. Abby snuggled up to Dan, and he put a protective arm around her. Abby knew the terrible experiences of the past weeks had a lot to do with it, but she also knew she might be falling in love with Dan.

"Dan, I feel so safe with you that I left my gun in our room."

Dan laughed. "Well, I've got mine, but somehow I feel we are okay now."

"I love your Irish brogue, Dan. Did I ever tell you my mother was a Dugan from the old country? She was raised in a small village called Skibbereen on the southwest coast. Mary Dugan, as Irish as Paddy's pig. We had Irish immigrant 'greenhorns' in and out of our house for years when I was growing up."

"No! I've passed through Skibbereen as a young boy, a pretty place. Now I know why I care for you so much. You're more that just a pretty, smart girl—you're at least half Irish!"

What about you, Dan? You're not the usual red-headed, fair-skinned Irishman."

"Yeah, my mother told me her side of the family was descended from so-called 'Black Irish' who were Norman invaders from France. That's why I look different."

"A handsome difference, I would say."

"Abby, we never had much of a chance to talk at Northwestern. We were all busy with classes. I'm glad we interned at the same time," said Dan. He pulled Abby close and kissed her and then kissed her again. Abby didn't resist at first, but then she held him back a bit.

"It's getting chilly, Dan. Let's go back to our cabins." She'd had one regrettable experience when she was a freshman at Northwestern and was now very cautious. She remembered Grandmother Cass' advice to her three granddaughters: "Don't give yourself to any man unless you feel this is the person you would like to be with for with the rest of your life. Make sure he loves you as much as you love him. Save yourself until then."

*All right, Grandmother, I won't make that mistake again*, Abby thought. *At least I'll try harder not to.*

* * *

The next day the ship was going through a rain squall, and passengers were staying in their cabins. Esther and Abby were playing cards in their cabin when Dan joined them. Esther paused and asked, "Dan, why did you leave Ireland for America and Northwestern? Ireland and England have all those fine universities."

"Always with the questions, Esther. Okay. You and Abby will remember about the IRA—the Irish Republican Army—fighting for their independence from England. My father hates the English, and I do too. And I love any country that's broken England's oppressive yoke. The United States revolted and threw the English out bodily. India achieved independence from the English through passive resistance. We tried and were only partially successful. Northwestern Ireland is not freed yet."

Dan's Irish lilt was sweet on the ears, and Abby and Esther listened closely in silence.

"The English almost taxed my father's small business out of existence. He was an active member of the IRA and fought with what they called the 'flying columns.' They were small groups of guerrillas who could attack suddenly and disappear. British troops were ambushed at random. They raised havoc for years. Then Dad was seriously wounded and had to stay home. My uncle John, Dad's brother, was killed. Both my mother and father were afraid the British would seek revenge on them and the family."

"How old were you when your father was shot?" asked Abby.

"Old enough to know what was going on—about ten. My mother had relatives in New York State, and they sent me there to be safe. My aunt and uncle were very kind and generous. They got me into good schools where I was able to make friends."

"What happened to your mother and father?" asked Esther.

"They were harassed for a while, but since he was severely wounded, they left him alone. The British finally conceded and freed the southern part of Ireland, and our family brewery began to grow without the heavy British taxes. Father sent money when I was able to qualify at Northwestern. So here we are. Ha! He will soon know all about how safe I was in the United States. Let's play cards."

"Hold the cards," said Abby. "I want to tell both of you what I saw and heard while we were at the Atlantic City house." She told them about coming upon notes and photographs of American military installations in Hans' room when she was changing linens. She also saw a copy of *Mein Kampf* on his dresser. Hans had chased her out and was really upset. Also,

Peter and Hans didn't know that Abby understood German, and Abby told them she overheard Peter telling Hans that he must get closer and clearer pictures of the ships located at the Norfolk Navel Base.

"I think they're spies for Germany, but why *now* when Germany is weak and we are at peace?" Abby said.

"Never a better time to load up on intelligence while there is peace, I suspect," said Dan. What is your take on the Germans, Esther?" said Dan.

"I know that Hitler's book blames many of Germany's problems on the Jews. The Orthodox Jews are an easily identified group with their beards and black clothes. They are the first to be singled out—good scapegoats. That's what I learned from Jewish friends in Evanston who'd fled Germany.

"I didn't feel comfortable around Peter and Hans. They gave me the creeps," said Esther. "Nothing we can do about it now, though, so let's play cards."


As they spent more time together, Esther could tell that Dan and Abby were growing close. She decided to give them more time alone and wandered around the first-class deck during daylight hours. She came upon a handsome young man about her age leaning over the rail, watching the ship move through the water. Esther moved over next to him at the rail. "What are you looking at?"

He turned and looked at her. *A pretty one, at last,* he thought. "Nothing very exciting. Trying to figure how I would calculate the coefficient of friction as the ship pushes through the water, and then relate that to the speed of the ship."

"Are you a scientist or engineer?"

"Studying to be a scientist. A way to go yet. How about you?"

"Just finishing a degree in journalism at Northwestern University."

They chatted for a while, exchanging names. "I'm Jacob, Jacob Bernstein. Come meet my family. There're just up the deck."

The Jewish family was returning home to Berlin. "That's my father. He pointed to a man trying to read what Esther thought was a prayer book. He held on to his yarmulke in the stiffening wind, smiled, and motioned them over. She introduced herself as Esther Frankel. She couldn't bring herself to lie to these people about her name.

The Bernstein family planned to get off the ship in Liverpool to travel to the University of Cambridge. Cambridge had made a scholarship offer to

Jacob, who had just finished undergraduate studies in physics with highest honors at Purdue University. His sister, Ruth, about two years younger than Jacob, was petite and pretty. She and Esther looked like sisters.

"We heard that there were seasick students in first-class. Was that your group?" asked Jacob's mother, Sophia.

"Yes. But we're much better now, thank you."

"Jacob, at last someone your age. Why don't you take Esther into the lounge and play some darts? And there is a piano in there; you can play some pieces for Esther."

"I can play too," said Esther. "Should be fun!"

"Did you go to any football games when Northwestern played Purdue?" asked Jacob while he played a Chopin nocturne.

"I do remember one such game. I think Purdue won that one. I was too busy with studies and other things to go to games"

Esther played a ragtime tune, "Frankie and Johnny," and then they went out on the deck to play shuffleboard.

Esther and Jacob had hit it off quickly, and she was the happiest she had been in weeks.

\* \* \*

On the third night at sea, Abby told herself that her feelings for Dan were genuine, but that any feelings they had for each other were based on the terrible experiences they'd been through together. Abby wanted to have some time with him in natural surroundings like ordinary people, not being chased by killers. She told him that as they huddled together on the boat deck. Dan reluctantly agreed.

"I guess you're right... I'm still having problems from having to kill those gangsters. I've never killed anything in my life. It's like a bad dream, but it really happened. Has it bothered you?"

"Yes," said Abby. "I'm trying to deal with it too. But remember, you saved our lives at the park building in Michigan, and you and I stopped them at the picnic grounds in New Jersey. They would have killed us all in cold blood. I know Karl helped in Michigan, but it was you who told us what to do. We all are grateful to you for saving us. Everything we did was in self-defense."

Esther walked the deck after an innocent rendezvous with Jacob, and as she passed Abby's and Dan's blanket-covered bodies, she heard laughter and the sound of kissing. She smiled and went on to bed. She punched her pillow a number of times before going to sleep.

The next night was the last night at sea for Abby, Esther, and Dan. The traditional Captain's Dinner was held to say farewell to those passengers disembarking at Galway. A first-class officer found a tuxedo that fit Dan, and the girls had on their best gowns. There hadn't been any time to shop during their escape, but Dan thought both Esther and Abby looked beautiful.

Before dinner Dan talked it over with the girls, and they decided that if mobsters were aboard, they would have shown their hand by now. They would begin to use their real names and their true identifications, but Dan and Abby would carry their weapons just in case.

It was a wonderful seven-course meal with a string quartet providing soft background music. The dining room was immense yet elegant with beautiful crystal chandeliers and overstuffed dining chairs covered with the finest fabrics. The room easily seated the first-class passengers. Even the waiters were dressed in vested formalwear. Each carried a white cloth over his left arm.

Abby, Esther, and Dan were seated with an elderly couple returning to Ireland after visiting relatives in New York. The Shanahans were from the city of Cork, but they knew of Patrick O'Gara of Kinsale, Dan's father. "A brave man he was with the 'flying columns', one of Michael Collins' top men. How is he now, young man?" asked Mr. Shanahan.

"He finally recovered from his wounds and seems to be doing well, but with a little limp, he writes."

"Dan told us of the fighting that went on. It must have been terrible," said Abby.

"That it was, my dear. I would have joined them in the struggle if I had been younger," Mr. Shanahan said. Mrs. Shanahan tilted her head and sighed. "Mary is cynical, but I surely would have been there if it wasn't for her and the children."

As was the custom, the captain of the ship made the rounds of all the first-class tables, introducing himself, asking the passengers' names, and wishing the passengers a safe journey after docking. Captain Dieter was tall and square jawed with a noble nose, and when he removed his cap to make the rounds, his thick black hair was unruly. He looked too young to be the captain of a large ship, but his gold-braided dress uniform and confident demeanor gave his passengers comfort.

When Captain Dieter got to the students' table, they exchanged names, and then he smiled broadly. "I heard that there were seasick students early on our voyage. The ship's doctor gave me a listing of passengers who were reported seasick. He pointed out the ones who were students. You are much better now, it appears." Then he paused. "There seems to be some differences regarding your names on the ship's manifest and what you are telling me now."

Abby spoke in German, which surprised the officer.

"*Nun ja, Captain. Wir Schriftsteller und Journalisten. Nur so zum, haben wir uns entschieden unsere Schriftstellernamen zu benutzen wenn wir unsere Tickets gekauft haben. Wir sind traurig, wenn es so ein Problem.*"

"That explains it then," the captain said. "Enjoy the rest of your dinner and the voyage. It's a pleasure to have all of you aboard the *Bremen*."

Esther was invited to have her dessert at the Bernsteins' table. They set a chair next to Jacob.

"We understand you are of the Frankel family who has a lovely gem company in Lyon. Is that right, Esther?" asked his mother, Frieda.

"Yes, it is. I'm anxious to see them again after a brief holiday in Ireland with my friends. Mother and Father just visited with me when they came to Northwestern in December."

As the conversation turned away from Esther, she leaned over toward Jacob. "Jacob, tell me about your family."

"Father has a company in Berlin that specializes in real estate, mostly large business buildings which he owns. He is encouraging me to join him in the company. I'm not sure about that. I'm very interested in physics. Einstein's work has opened up an incredible field of opportunity. I hope that I can get on at Cambridge for graduate work."

Back at their table, the Shanahans had left for their cabin. "Our bedtime," Mary had said as they excused themselves.

"Okay, Abby. First, what did you tell the captain?" asked Dan.

"I spoke in German to try and throw him off a little. I told him we are writers and journalists, and for fun we decided to use pen names when we purchased our tickets."

"You're always full of surprises, Abby. I knew you understood a little German, but how did you learn to speak so well?"

"The usual way, I guess. My German is still not that good. The captain was gracious in not correcting me. I had four years of German in high school, and it was my minor course after journalism at Northwestern. Much like what Esther did in learning English," she said as she nodded toward Esther at the Bernstein table.

"What really helped me in conversational German was working at a resort near Milwaukee during one summer. The owners were from

Germany, and they gave jobs to immigrants from their homeland. They wanted to learn English quickly, so we workers practiced our language on each other as we worked and at a nearby lake where we swam and relaxed on our days off."

"My mother and father believed that my sisters and I should make some of our own college expense money during the summer. I'm glad they insisted on that."

"I wish my parents had suggested I learn a second language," said Dan. "Speaking of them, I forgot to tell you that, for sure, my father will meet our ship tomorrow and drive us to the cottage. He wired me this morning to confirm things. Mother is at the cottage now."

The orchestra started playing, and suddenly Captain Dieter appeared at their table. He bowed to Abby. "Will you excuse me? May I have this dance, Miss White?" he said. He also looked at Dan, who nodded a reluctant okay.

The captain waltzed beautifully. "You've had experience at this, haven't you, Captain?" said Abby.

He smiled. "It is a custom on my ship that on the last night at sea, the captain gets the first dance with the most beautiful passenger on board. And you certainly are that, Miss Abby White. And you speak German to boot! May I ask, where is your final destination?"

Abby felt herself shiver a little. *Okay, Abby, control yourself. He has to be ten to fifteen years older than you—but what a handsome, charming man!*

"Well, for now, I'm vacationing with my classmates in Ireland to celebrate our graduation from college. After that, who knows? I'm looking for an interesting job in journalism." Then, for some reason, she added, "My family home is in Indianapolis, Indiana." *You never know about things,* she thought. *Why not leave a trail?*

The orchestra finished their long piece, and Captain Dieter escorted Abby back to her table. "It has been a pleasure, Miss White. I hate to have this end, but I must return to the bridge. I hope our paths cross again some day."

Dan had a bit of a frown on his face, and Abby smiled and asked him to dance with her. Dan was a good dancer who knew all the latest steps. It was a wonderful evening, and Abby glowed with excitement.

They finally got up from the table. "It looks like Esther is in good hands," said Dan, taking Abby by the hand. "Let's take a final walk around the deck. I want to show you something."

They walked to the fantail in the semi-darkness and looked over the guardrail at the propeller wash. It was alive with sparkles.

"That's from the iridescent plankton disturbed by the propellers."

"It's beautiful!" said Abby as she squeezed Dan's hand.

Over the soft, rhythmic sound of the propellers, they heard footsteps behind them. They turned to face a man with a gun.

"Jump into the water, or I will kill you both now. I'd rather not fire shots or make a mess on the deck, but it's your choice. Either way, you're going in the water. You were lucky to get this far from Al."

He was a short, thin man dressed in black, wearing a Yankee baseball cap. His eyes were steely and unblinking. He held the gun steady. He moved closer to Dan and Abby. "Now, get up on the rail, both of you, and jump."

Dan put his foot on top of the rail as if complying, and then sprang backward, knocking the smaller man down. The gunman's head hit the steel deck with a thud, and his pistol slid down the deck. Abby picked up the gun and threw it over the side into the water. She pulled out her Beretta and quickly took the safety off.

The gunman recovered, got up, and ran at Dan who sidestepped him and grabbed his belt in back. He lifted the little man over the rail and threw him in the ocean. They saw him disappear into the sparkling waters without a sound.

Dan hugged Abby. "And I thought we were done with those people. I wonder where he was hiding all this time," said Dan.

"I don't remember seeing him before," Abby said as she put the safety back on her Beretta and put it back in her purse. "I brought my gun this time, thank goodness."

"He had the drop on me. I'm glad you were prepared to shoot."

Abby looked around the deck. Nobody could be seen. Nobody to shoot.

"At least we don't have to explain this to anyone. No body, no shots, no blood." She paused, horrified at what she'd just said. "I can't believe how blasé I've become in such a short time. Are you all right, Dan?"

Dan looked at her wryly. "Couldn't be better! What a cruise! We'd better go check on Esther."

Esther answered their coded knock on her cabin door. "What's the matter?"

"Oh, nothing," said Abby. "We just wanted to make sure that you got back to your cabin okay."

"Thanks. Jacob walked me back. Dan, your tuxedo looks awful. What happened?"

Dan smiled. "Clumsy me. I slipped on the wet deck. Didn't hurt anything except my pride."

They moved away from Esther's cabin door. Abby said, "If we told Esther what happened, she wouldn't sleep for a week,"

Dawn brought a ship's attendant knocking on the doors of passengers getting off at Galway. "Good morning. Prepare to disembark, please."

The *Bremen* slowed as Captain Dieter navigated it into Galway Bay. A small tugboat nudged the much larger ship toward its assigned dock space. The students leaned on the rail and saw a group of people waiting on the dock.

"I think I see my father. He's the one in the yellow straw hat."

The captain put his propeller screws in reverse, and the *Bremen* eased into the dock "with the touch of a soft kiss," as Dan had said. Lines were thrown over fore and aft, and dock hands secured the ship. A gangplank was slipped over the side to the waiting dock crew.

Esther said goodbyes to the Bernstein family and offered her cheek to Jacob. "Jacob, I wish you luck at Cambridge."

"Thank you, Esther; in any event, I want to see you again. Here's my home address in Berlin. If I make it at Cambridge, I'll send you that address."

Esther quickly wrote down her home address in Lyon on a slip of paper and handed it to him.

They turned to go down the gangplank. "Wait a minute, Esther," said Jacob. He held Esther tenderly and kissed her on the mouth. His father chuckled, and his mother frowned.

# Chapter Eight

*Ireland*

Dan led the way to his father, Patrick O'Gara, who was dressed in a light blue seersucker suit and a jaunty straw hat. He had a smiling Irish face, light skin with freckles on his nose. Patrick was in his fifties, but he looked older and careworn. Aided by his silver-topped walking stick, he walked toward them with a decided limp and a joyous grin on his face.

Dan hugged his father and introduced him to the girls. Patrick doffed his straw hat and bowed slightly. Then he shook Abby's and Esther's hands gently. "Welcome to Ireland, ladies."

He looked at Dan. "How is it you ended up with two pretty girls? The luck of the Irish is still with you! I'm having my driver retrieve your luggage. Dan gave me your names in his last wire. Let's walk to my car."

As the shiny black Duesenberg moved slowly away from the seaport, Esther squeezed Abby's hand and smiled. *I think we're safe now*, was the unsaid message.

They travelled south on Road 18. "It's the scenic route," said Dan.

"We'll stop in LimWarrenk for a little lunch" said Patrick. "It's about a two-hour ride to the cottage. Can't make much time because of the narrow roads and wandering livestock standing in the road. In Ireland, that's okay. We get a chance to wave to friends and see what changes they may have made to their properties. Life is slow here, except when we fight for our freedom. You can see from the limp in my walk that freedom is not free." His audience seemed more interested in the rolling countryside, so he changed the subject.

"Now, I want to hear all the details about how you managed to escape those gangsters."

"That you will hear, Dad," said Dan.

"It was on the wireless and in the *Cork Dispatch*," said Patrick. "The Chicago police say you're still under protective custody. Ha! Since I'm now protecting you, I should have a Chicago police badge, don't you think?"

That brought polite laughs from the girls and Dan.

Patrick had his audience back. "The newspaper also said that federal agents are now active in Chicago, trying to get charges brought against the gangs, especially Al Capone's. So the mobs may have enough to do without tracking you. The article said Capone has more than 300 gangsters on his payroll. It also said there are a bunch of police and politicians who take his money to look the other way."

"Didn't I tell you my father was a talker?" said Dan as Patrick rolled his window down to wave to friends.

"The O'Donnells, back there, are the salt of the earth," said Patrick as he leaned back in his seat. "But poor John O'Donnell felt the pain of a British bullet in his chest and never made it home alive. He was in the same skirmish as me brother, John, who took a bullet to the brain. Didn't know what hit 'em, they said.

"O'Donnell's son, God blesses him, stayed home and stayed alive to help his poor mother work the farm. You know, this thing, 'The Troubles,' is not over yet. There's a major political effort afoot by a large faction of Irish to take back the British section of Northern Ireland. What a mess! There were even differences among the IRA that led to the assassination of Michael Collins, a brave leader, a few years back. It was an awful peace settlement that gave the British a big piece of Northern Ireland."

The car had to slow down to a stop several times for sheep and cattle in the road. The animals moved out slowly as if it was their road, but they might make an exception for an automobile. At one such stop, Patrick got out of the car to talk with an old friend while his driver nudged his way through a flock of sheep.

By the time they made it to LimWarrenk and Foley's Olde Pub, it was high noon and they were all famished. Patrick recommended his favorite, the Lamb Shank Lunch Special. "Excellent," said Esther, after she finished her meal. They all had a pint of Shamrock, the O'Gara brewery's best-selling beer, to wash down the food. Patrick had two. "I'm not driving. Sean is. I asked him to join us, but he wanted to visit with an old friend from his home village. He's bringing the car out front."

After they'd gotten back in the car, Patrick said to his driver, "Sean, my lad, would you drive down south on Road 69, along the Bay of Shannon? I want to show the lassies a few pretty villages." Patrick then took a nap along the way.

"It's lovely, like a fairyland. Look at the beautiful colors on those cottages," said Abby as they drove through Foynes toward Tralee. They turned north at Tralee and traveled up a hillside road. They were almost to Ballyheigue when Sean turned into a driveway leading to O'Gara's place. He stopped and got out to open a large wrought iron gate. Tall hedgerow bushes of hawthorn and blackthorn spread left and right from the gate. It was the first time Abby and Esther got a good look at Sean, their driver. He was a big man about their age with a mop of curly red hair and a serious look on his handsome face. Esther looked at Abby and raised her eyebrows in interest.

Sean honked his horn on the way up the drive to alert Dan's mother.

"It looks like a small castle, not a cottage," Esther whispered to Abby. The house sat high on a hill overlooking the beautiful Tralee Bay that opened to the Atlantic.

Darcy O'Gara walked down the steps from the door and greeted Dan with kisses and hugs. She held on to Dan and looked in his eyes.

"Oh, my son, it's so good to see you again! We were very worried about you," she said through tears. "Your eyes have seen a lot, I can tell. You're not the same lad who left here three years ago after a school break."

Darcy was in her mid-fifties but was still young-looking—tall with straight black hair, high cheekbones, a straight nose, and full lips. It was no wonder that Patrick looked at her with love and pride.

"And who might these beautiful ladies be?" She smiled as she moved away from the men and toward Abby and Esther. "My dear ladies, welcome to your home away from home."

Darcy seemed such a stately and elegant woman that Abby and Esther found themselves curtsying slightly before her.

"I'm Darcy. Let me see if I can remember Dan's telegram. Abby White and Esther Frankel? You must have been through some terrible times. We know just a little from news reports."

"I'm afraid so," said Abby. "Thank you for having us."

"Please come in. You're just in time for tea. It's a tradition which the English stole away from us," she laughed. "But first I'll show you to your rooms so you can freshen up. You've been on a long drive. Sean has taken your bags to your rooms. Sean is our driver since Patrick was wounded in 'The Troubles.'"

They had their tea in the sunroom, and Darcy introduced their staff, Cormac and Sally. Sally, forty with graying hair, served their tea, and Cormac, a huge man about sixty, made off with a bow and a "welcome."

\* \* \*

The *Bremen* had been in port several hours, loading fresh provision, taking on fuel, and readying the cabins for new passengers, when Captain Dieter was summoned from his cabin. A man in a black suit was with the Officer of the Deck. "Captain, this man said that he is missing a fellow police officer." The man flashed a Chicago police badge, saying his name was Sergeant Joseph Brandish. He was short with a big torso riding on stumpy legs.

"My partner, Fred James, didn't return after a walk on the deck last night. I've searched all over the ship, except the boiler room. He's short and was wearing a dark suit like mine. We're on duty."

"What is *your* duty on *my* ship?" said Captain Dieter.

"Well, we're after several students to bring them back to Chicago under protective custody."

"Why didn't you identify yourselves to us when you bordered the ship in New York? And are you carrying weapons? Don't you know international law regarding such matters?"

"Hey, we ain't lawyers, we're cops. Damn right we carry guns, we're cops, remember?

"Again, why didn't you identify yourselves when you boarded in New York?"

"Uh, we wanted to do things quietly and not bother your crew and passengers," said Brandish. "We were in second- class."

"All right, we'll look for your partner." He nodded an okay to his second officer. "This is a big ship, so it may take awhile. We leave port at 1700 hours. That's five p.m. We must leave regardless of the outcome of the search. In the meantime, take a seat, please. I need to confirm this with the Chicago police department by cablegram."

Captain Dieter left to go to the wireless room located mid-ship. It didn't take more than twenty minutes to get an answer from Chicago.

"There are no such names with the Chicago police, and we know of no one from other agencies assigned to your ship," the reply said. "They may be using stolen badges. Ask to see other CPD papers they should be carrying. They could be armed gangsters, so be careful."

Captain Dieter returned to the bridge.

"Where is that man?"

"I turned my head, and he was gone," said the Officer of the Deck.

"Well, he's a phony. Probably a gunman after those students. Arm our men, and find him and his partner."

The man calling himself Joseph Brandish was already at the end of the dock, flashing his badge at the dock hands and taxi drivers. He held a ten-dollar bill in his hand.

"Did you see a party with two young ladies that left the ship?"

"Is that my money if I tell you?" said a chunky taxi driver puffing on a cigarette.

"Yes, but you better be right." He motioned the taxi driver over to the side.

"There were lots of young girls that left that ship, but I think you're talkin' about the Patrick O'Gara group. I was talkin' quite a while with their driver, Sean something, while we waited for the ship to dock. He said there was students coming, and, oh yeah, they were going to O'Gara's vacation home near Tralee."

"Okay, here's the ten dollars. Now, how much to drive me there and back? I need to put those ladies under protective custody." He pulled out a wad of bills held together by a gold money clip. The taxi driver's eyes grew big as saucers.

An officer from the ship ran down the dock to the group of dock workers and taxi drivers. "Have any of you seen a short man in a dark suit from our ship asking questions?"

"Yeh," said one man. "Flashed a police badge and took off in Billy's cab headed to Tralee where the O'Gara family has a cottage. We heard most of it. Had a wad of money on him, he did, and I saw a gun under his jacket on his heart's side."

"He's a phony, boys, and not a cop. He may be very dangerous. If he comes back again, call the police station. I mean your Garda station."

Telephone lines were strung to the ship when she docked. Captain Dieter called the Galway Garda station.

"All right, sir. I'll try to reach the O'Gara house, and I'll also alert the Garda in Tralee."

Billy and his passenger arrived in Tralee where Billy had to ask for directions to the O'Gara house. Darkness was closing in when the taxi pulled up to the gate. Billy started out of the car to open the gate.

"Wait. I'll do it myself and walk up to the house. I noticed a pub back there, not far. You drive back there and have a pint. I will have them call you at the pub to come pick us up. Here's forty dollars. There'll be more when we get back." Billy had never seen such money at one time.

The gunman waited until Billy left him. He was not the smartest gangster in the world, so he stood there rethinking things. *Wish I had Fred along. Wonder what happened to him on the ship?* He knew he had to do what Al Capone wanted done: eliminate the witnesses to the St. Valentines Day executions. So far, Al's men had failed him. *If I can croak these people, I'll move up a few rungs in the organization. Maybe be Al's right-hand man!*

He waited a few minutes until it was darker and then lifted the gate latch. There was a load creak. "Oh, damn." Then he saw distant lights from the house. *Too far for them to hear the noise.* He moved slowly across the lawn toward a grove of trees. Using the trees for cover, he moved as quietly as possible up the hill toward a large bay window that showed the brightest lighting. His gun was in hand, and another smaller one in an ankle holster. He was on all fours as he neared the window. Peeking over the bushes, he saw a young man and two girls. *That's them!* He had seen pictures of them that were passed around the gang. *Like shooting fish in a barrel!* Just as he raised his gun, he heard noises on both sides of him.

"Drop that gun!" It was a local policeman, the Guarda, with a powerful flashlight in his left hand and a police .38 caliber revolver in the other. Brandish turned and saw another policeman crouched on the ground with his gun leveled at him. The would-be assassin rolled down the hill, firing as he went, wounding one policeman but taking a bullet in his head from the other.

The house man, Cormac, opened the front door. "Call an ambulance!" cried the policeman. He left, and Dan, Abby, and Esther ran to the aid of the wounded officer. He was shot in the arm and the leg and was bleeding badly. Abby ran in the house, and she and Darcy returned with a tablecloth that they tore into strips. Sean followed carrying a baseball bat. Abby applied tourniquets the way she'd learned from her Red Cross class in high school.

The other policeman stood over the gangster with his gun steady on him, as if the bullet in his brain was not enough to stop him.

"Well done," said Patrick O'Gara, as he limped toward the shooting scene. "You got the bastard." He walked slowly to the body and looked down. "You SOB, going to kill my unarmed son and those two young ladies, were you?"

He limped to the students. "You were brave to volunteer as targets for that madman. Thank God we were warned, or terrible things could have happened."

An ambulance rolled over the lawn, and two medics leaped out to tend to the wounded officer.

\* \* \*

Patrick broke out his finest wines to celebrate. At dinner that night, there were many toasts given. Dan told his father and mother about the horrendous chase from Chicago to Ireland. Patrick raised his glass. "To the fair and brave lassies that stood strong against the mobsters and helped bring our son home to the ol sod."

"Thank you, dear ladies," was all that Darcy could express through her tears.

"To a good father and mother who are providing shelter and protection for us. God bless them," said Dan.

When glasses were refilled, Abby and Esther raised their glasses and sang the first bars of "Oh, Danny Boy." "We wouldn't be here without his strong back and good aim," Abby said.

\* \* \*

After breakfast the next day, Patrick wiped his mouth with his napkin and stood. "I hate to say this, but Darcy and I must return to Kinsale to look after our house and business. We will miss you all, but will see you again soon, God willing. Cormac and Sally will look after your wants. The Tralee Garda will be on the alert for any suspicious people in the area. As a precaution, I'm having Sean stay here until things settle down." He chuckled. "He has a double-barreled shotgun now, a better deterrent than that baseball bat. It's been several days since the intruder, so maybe things are over. I have a car and driver coming down today from Kinsale to take us back. Enjoy this beautiful spring. We'll be in touch by telephone. God bless Alexander Graham Bell!"

Patrick asked the Irish police to withhold information about the killing of the mobster so the students' location wouldn't be known. Patrick was a powerful and well-liked man in southwestern Ireland, so the police complied—at least for a while. It would be big news and prestige for their Garda to have killed a Chicago mobster in their quiet little place in southern Ireland.

Sean O'Connor, the chauffer and now also their protector, seemed to come out of his shell. Even when Dan was there, Sean told them of his responsibility.

"Mr. O'Gara told me to protect you, that I'll do. Let me know if you want to go for a walk, and I'll hang a bit behind. If you want to go out in the car, I'll drive. Dan, I know you and Abby have handguns, but my shotgun is a great equalizer if we need it. Mr. O'Gara also gave me a handgun."

Abby looked at him. "May I ask how old you are?

"I'm twenty-five and been hunting all my life if that's what you're wondering about. I can shoot."

"Good. We're pleased to have you with us, Sean."
Esther rose to her full five-feet and offered her hand. "We are delighted to have you as our protector, Sean."

# Chapter Nine

*Ireland—Skibbereen*

Abby wanted to see the little coastal town, Skibbereen, where her mother was born.

"They have a parish dance every Friday evening," Sean said. "It's fun and there's lots of good Irish music."

After they parked the Duesenberg on a side street, the four of them had to walk single file along the narrow stone sidewalk to the church, St. Alphonso. Some of the shops were still open, hoping that the extra hours would bring in a customer or two. Abby and Esther stepped into a soft-lighted shop that sold Irish linens and laces. A gray-haired lady smiled but did not get up from her chair as the girls browsed.

"We'll have to come back here," said Esther. "When we can shop without men."

At Dan's suggestion, they walked down a block to the fishing boat docks next to the fish factory. Men with weathered faces wearing slick rubber waders and wool sweaters were using a winch to hoist fish in a net from a forty-foot boat. It set deep in the water from a good day's catch. They swung the net over to a large open factory door, then one fisherman pulled a line that allowed the fish to fall on a wide conveyor. Women could be seen through the doors in the semi-darkness cleaning the fish and putting them on ice. The smell from the factory was enough to gag Abby and Esther, and they put handkerchiefs to their faces.

"You get used to the smell. This is the big money maker for Skibbereen," said Dan.

"Yes, I bet so," said Esther, "Can we move along now? Nobody will dance with us if we smell like fish."

They reached St. Alphonso's auditorium just in time to hear the band finish their warm-up.

Dan recognized the traditional instruments: the fiddle, the accordion, the tin flute, and the frame drum. People were sitting in double rows on straight-back chairs around the periphery of the large room.

The leader of the band stepped out front and made an announcement in a loud but lyrical voice. "We have the honor of having the Kennedy sisters from Cork's St. Philip's parish to show us a bit of their championship form they had in winning a cup in last month's step dancing competition."

Four pretty teenaged girls went to the center of the floor and stood shoulder to shoulder, their arms stiffly at their sides, waiting for the music to start. Their long curly hair was held back by matching tiaras with fabric crowns. Colorful dresses with short skirts, white calf-length stockings, and black hard-soled shoes completed their costumes.

The music started in the classical Celtic folk style, and the girls danced in perfect unison. They stiffened their upper bodies while performing quick, intricate footwork. The hard shoes made a clatter on the wood floor in time to the music. It was a warm room, and the girls soon showed perspiration on their foreheads and the rosy cheeks that true Irish natives often get. They received resounding applause from the audience, and a big "thank you" from the band leader.

Dan scanned the audience. The Friday night dance was a community affair with young children mixed with older women and men dressed in their Sunday-best dresses and suits. He eyed a man standing along the wall near the end of the room who didn't seem to fit in. His suit had more of a continental cut to it than those worn by Irishmen. Dan thought he looked Italian.

The band started with a slow waltz to get dancers onto the floor. For a long minute, nobody seemed to be brave enough to get up to dance. Finally, one man moved to the dance floor with a young girl who was probably his daughter. That was enough to start the ball rolling. A very old man walked slowly over to Abby. "Would you care to dance, young lady?"

"Why, of course," said Abby, and off they went, moving slowly to the music. The man was a graceful dancer, surprising Abby. She told the man just that.

"Well, thank you. I should be after seventy years of practice!"

Dan was seated next to Sean, and he ask him to find out if the man in the corner was a local person. Sean nodded and got up to ask around.

"Nobody knows him," Sean said when he returned.

"Damn it, not another one," muttered Dan. "Keep an eye on him, Sean. We may have to take him out later. He doesn't look that big, but he's probably carrying."

Abby could see concern on Dan's face when she looked over her partner's shoulder. *It couldn't be jealousy, could it?* The old man was not shy and pulled her to him as the music stopped.

"Thank you, sir."

"My pleasure, I'm sure," as he led her back to her seat.

Sean offered his hand to Esther as the music started again.

"Anything wrong, Dan?" said Abby.

"We may have another mobster following us. He looks Italian." He turned to where the man had been standing, but he was gone. "He's left. Not a good sign."

Abby remembered what Masconi had told them about the European Mafia and the Union Siciliana with their close ties to Capone's Italian-American mob. *It's never going to stop.*

Dan motioned Sean and Esther off the dance floor. "But we just got started," protested Esther.

He told Sean to get the car and bring it around to the side door of the auditorium. "Have your shotgun ready."

"Oh, my god," murmured Esther.

Sean pulled up by the door. "Sean, I'll drive. You be ready for anything. Abby and Esther, get on the floor in the back" said Dan. "Abby, have your Beretta ready,"

Dan headed out of Skibbereen toward Tralee. He had been driving in America for the past few years, and it took him awhile to adjust to driving from the opposite front seat on the opposite side of the road. It was a moonless night, and it couldn't have been darker on the country road. He was driving slowly when he saw the headlights of another car in his rearview mirror. "It must have pulled out from a side road. We have a stranger behind us, I'm afraid," said Dan.

The pursuing car pulled close behind and then passed them. It picked up speed, then braked, turned toward them, and blocked the road.

"Okay, Sean, here we go. His headlights aren't turned toward us. I'll turn ours off as soon as he opens his door. When I say 'go', we open our doors and roll out a few feet, then shoot to kill."

"I'm ready," said Sean. "He's coming out now with a Tommy gun."

Dan turned off his lights. "Stay down, girls. Abby, at the ready with your gun. Let's go, Sean."

Just as they rolled out, the assailant opened up with his machine gun, blowing out the front windshield of the Duesenberg. There was enough light from the gangster's car to silhouette the man moving towards them. Sean fired both barrels of his shotgun, and Dan empted his revolver at the staggering figure. The man pitched forward, and his gun banged on the asphalt. Sean reloaded, and they both walked slowly toward the downed figure. The man mumbled, "I'm dead. Sorry, Al." Then there was no movement.

"What did he say, Dan?"

"I couldn't make it out."

"Stay on him, Sean." said Dan. He returned to the car and turned on their headlights.

"It's okay, ladies, we got him. We'll be getting some blankets from the trunk, so don't shoot us, Abby."

Dan rolled the man over while Sean kept his shot gun leveled. "He's dead, Sean. We stopped him, thank god. Let's leave everything as is, except his machine gun. We can't leave it in the middle of the road for someone to take. It's key evidence. We have blankets in the trunk. Let's wrap his gun in a blanket and cover the body with the other."

Abby heard them open the trunk. She raised herself up from the floor and slid the safety on her gun. The headlights of their car flooded the scene with light. She saw them cover the bloodied body with a blanket.

"We'll leave on the lights on his car so nobody will run into this mess," Dan said as they brushed the broken glass from the seats of their car. "It looks like we can go off the road to the right to get around his car and head toward the next town, Ballydehob, I think. Hope we can find a policeman there."

"Stay down, Esther. We're moving out," said Abby. Esther didn't need to see another body. She was trembling so much on the floor that Abby could hear her bracelet rings jangling.

They made statements at the Ballydehob Garda station, and then waited until the police returned from the crime scene. The police told them that the man carried papers identifying him as a Sicilian. He had rented the car in Cork, and had return tickets to Palermo, Sicily.

The police found them a bed and breakfast house in town where they spent a fitful night. Abby and Esther shared a comfortable room with double beds. They were both in shock after this latest attempt on their lives. Ireland was supposed to be a safe haven, even a vacation spot. Instead, two more attempts had been made. They couldn't even go to a church dance without being attacked.

Abby and Esther held hands on the small sofa in the room. Esther was crying.

"I have the feeling I'm going to die without ever really living," said Esther.

"Oh, Esther, that will not happen."

"Don't be too sure, Abby. You know, I'm already under a black cloud, being Jewish. I will never deny my heritage, but I would like to break out of that birth mold. I may never have the chance. In Europe and in my home city, Lyon, there are those who stereotype Jews, unlike in America. You know that Hitler person blames the Jews for all the ills of Germany. He's gaining an audience, and that's fearful. Can you believe that?"

"I think he's just looking for a scapegoat. Saner heads will prevail, I'm sure," said Abby.

Esther stopped sobbing and continued. "I want to be an American. If this chase ever stops and I am still alive, I'll go back to Lyon for a while, and then return to America to work for a newspaper, maybe in the Midwest. Eventually, I want to start that big novel that's lurking in my brain. I'll change my name like so many of the Jewish movie stars in America have done. I want to be an American, not a European Jew."

"Esther, you know America is far from perfect. Remember hearing about the 'Jobs Available' signs when we were children, 'Irish Not Need Apply'?"

"Yes, I hear you. Still, Europe can't compare with the freedom in America. It's not that I will ever deny my birth history, I just want to live *my* life, not one predetermined at my birth."

Abby squeezed her hand. "Esther, I do understand. We will survive this and you will have time to reflect on what you have just said. We are under tremendous stress. You may think differently when we are not being chased by hoodlums."

"Maybe, Abby, but I doubt it." She paused. "Another thing, Abby. Sean whispered to me that we should sleep together for my protection. I know it's a ruse, but I want to have an experience with a man before it is too late."

"It's your life and your decision, Esther."

Abby lay in her bed, unable to sleep after the night's ordeal and Esther's confession of her wants and fears. Abby had her own fears, hope, and aspirations. *Maybe Esther's right. We may yet be killed.*

Abby believed in the old adage: "Life is to be lived, to give love and be loved in the best way you can." She wanted excitement and fulfillment in her life like her Grandmother Cass had experienced, and to try to emulate Cass' wonderful qualities of resourcefulness, clear and decisive thinking, confidence, and bravery. Abby knew that Cass had done some selfish and unkind things in her early life, but in the end, she was a wonderful role model for Abby and her two sisters. *We have been blessed by a large inheritance from her, and I hope I live long enough to use my portion well, and do some good with it,* she thought.

She rolled over in her bed, now thinking about Dan. She liked him very much, but she wasn't sure she was in love with him. *He is one brave, smart man. We'll probably go our separate ways when this is over. Maybe I shouldn't put him off again. I really like the way he kisses…. How shallow I can get? Well, why not? Life can really be short now…* She finally drifted off to sleep.

They made it back to the O'Gara cottage without further incidents. Patrick O'Gara was beside himself when Dan called him about the mobster. "What kind of a police force do they have up there? They were told to look out for strangers, damn it anyway!"

He and Darcy were in disbelief. "Thank God, Darcy, that Dan and Sean had their wits about them. I'm very proud of them again. True warriors."

"Outside of the cowardly assassin, my beautiful car took a beating. I told Sean to take the car to LimWarrenk. That's the closest Duesenberg repair shop."

Sean asked Esther if she would keep him company on the drive.

"Of course, I'll go. That's a long round-trip alone. It's supposed to be sunny and warm tomorrow. We don't need fear any rain without a windshield."

They were off at the crack of dawn eating breakfast rolls and drinking coffee prepared by Sally and Cormac. Sean had placed his shotgun within reaching distance behind Esther's seat.

"Abby, as long as Esther and Sean are gone, why don't we go on a picnic along the coast? I know a beautiful spot that sits above Dingle Bay," said Dan.

Sally and Cormac packed a sumptuous lunch and included a bottle of French Burgundy wine from the cottage's wine cellar. "I know Mr. O'Gara would approve, Sally. It's about time these young people had a day without getting shot at," said Cormac. Cormac was Sally's guardian after her young husband, Cormac's son, was killed in "the Troubles."

Cormac lent them his car, an old Ford that had a tendency to backfire. The first time it backfired, both Abby and Dan thought they were under attack again. As they drove, Dan told Abby about the ocean currents of the Gulf Stream that carried exotic seeds from the Caribbean to the most southwest point of Ireland. "You'll see flowers that will surprise you, my lovely lady."

"No more surprises like real gunfire, Dan." She paused. "Well, I brought my Beretta just in case."

Dan parked the car well off the road and concealed it in a grove of trees. They took their blankets and lunch from the trunk of the car, and started down a hill towards the bay.

"Look at all the beautiful flowers, Dan. I don't recognize any of them."

"My mother took us here several times when we were little. I think the pink ones are Ragged Robins, and the white ones with the gold centers are Dog Rose." The wild flowers continued down the hill to the bay.

"So beautifully different and such fragrances!" remarked Abby.

They walked over to a cave opening in the hillside and laid a large blanket on the ground and rolled up the other for a head rest. Lunch could wait as Abby unwrapped two Waterford wine glasses that were carefully cushioned in the lunch basket by Sally. Dan used a cork screw to open the wine and let it breathe for a moment. They toasted the beautiful day. There was only a slight, cooling wind. The sky was laced with wispy clouds that changed their patterns continuously. High tide was coming into Dingle Bay from the Atlantic, churning the bay waves to sudsy creaming on the beach below. Dan and Abby sipped on their wine and lay back, very happy to be alive on this extraordinary day.

After a while they set their glasses aside and curled up under a blanket. One kiss lead to another. Abby had no hesitation as she took Dan to her.

The sun was setting low in the western sky, casting a rosy glow over the bay and coastline. They finally rolled up their blankets and carried out their partially-eaten lunch and empty wine bottle. Hardly a word was spoken. Both Dan and Abby were savoring their past moments together.

They brought the remnants of their lunch back to the kitchen and thanked Sally and Cormac again and again as they described the perfect day. Cormac smiled at Sally after they left. "I think they left something out," whispered Cormac. Sally smiled and nodded.

# Chapter Ten

*Ireland—LimWarrenk*

Sean and Esther found the Duesenberg shop in LimWarrenk after asking for directions.

"I had the windshield shipped from Galway after Mr. O'Gara phoned. It shouldn't take too long to install," said the garage manager. "Why don't you two take lunch and enjoy our town? Say, are you a hunter? I noticed the shotgun on the rear floor."

"Yeah, forgot it was there. I do hunt. I'll cover it. Do you have a big cloth? We're fresh out of blankets."

"I didn't know you brought that," said Esther as they walked down O'Connell Street. "Do you think there's still a chance of a shooter?"

"Can't be too careful, Esther."

They had stopped at Foley's Olde Pub on the way from the seaport, so they decided to roam the street for another restaurant, poking into interesting shops as they walked. They worked their way to the River Shannon and crossed a bridge to the picturesque village of O'Briensbridge where they found a cozy pub for a late lunch.

"Okay, mystery man, tell me more about you," said Esther. They were relaxing over glasses of Burgundy.

"Not much to tell, really. I was raised on a farm near Drumcollager, about thirty miles from here, with my four brothers and two sisters. We all helped work the farm as kids, then I spent two years at a small college in Cork. Waited tables to makes ends meet. Got a little tired of it and decided to take a break. Got a job at Mr. O'Gara's brewery in Kinsale. He made me a foreman after a while, and then asked me if I would be his driver because of his injury and also help out at their house and cottage."

He ran his hand through his curly red hair and looked down momentarily. "Never did go back to college. Maybe someday I will." He drank some wine and smiled. "But I enjoy my life. Mr. and Mrs. O'Gara are good people—treat me like family." He reached over and squeezed Esther's hand. "Hey, too much about me!"

Esther returned the squeeze and laughed. "You're a lovely man, Sean. Please, one more thing. Do you have a girlfriend?"

"No. Sure, I've had my share of girlfriends, but none right now, too busy."

They walked along the river back to the car repair garage. "See that old castle over there, Esther? Reminds me of home. The family has a three-story, centuries-old castle on the edge of their property. It's a relic that's falling apart. It takes a monkey to get to the top of it. One day, years ago, my older brother, Michael, stuffed some of his old clothes with straw, put his cap on it, tied it to his belt, and climbed to the top of the castle. He waited 'til my father was within earshot, then yelled, 'Goodbye, cruel world' and ducked and threw the dummy over the side. Dad ran like a deer to where he thought was a dead Michael. At first, he was relieved, and then he got as mad as a hornet. Michael had disappeared, and by the time he returned for supper, Dad had calmed down and even ventured a smile with a head shake. The story has become a legend in our county. Its retelling gets the laughing started at every family reunion."

He paused and looked straight at Esther. "Woman, you got me to talk, and now I can't stop!"

The car was still in the shop. The windshield was replaced, and the manager walked toward them wiping his hands on a shop towel. "Do you know there are two bullet holes on the front of the right fender? What kind of war were you in? The heavy steel of the car probably stopped the bullets from blowing out the tire. Don't think Mr. O'Gara would want them on his favorite car. We can fix the holes by filling them with small steel pieces, working them in and then welding them to stay. Then we have to paint, power dry, and polish them so you won't know they were ever there. But the day's almost gone. It'll be late tomorrow morning before it's ready"

"Okay, you're right. Mr. O'Gara would want it fixed."

He turned to Esther. "We'll have to stay over. I'll take my shotgun with us."

"Sean, I found this old gun bag in the tool crib," said the shop manager. "Take it. Hey, there's a nice bed and breakfast about two squares west called Molly's. She's reasonable and minds her own business."

"What's in that bag, young man?" asked Molly.

"A hunting gun, now unloaded."

He and Esther told her the reason for staying over. They called Cormac collect from Molly's phone to tell him they would be back late on the morrow.

"Okay, that'll be two punts upfront. And no loud parties or drunkenness, you hear?"

Sean handed over two bills and got a key.

"First room on the right upstairs."

"What's a punt?" asked Esther as they climbed the stairs.

"That's slang for a pound. Like the American dollar is a 'buck.'"

They had no belongings beside the gun, but they wanted to check the room. It was a large, clean room with a warm, fresh breeze blowing the lace curtains inward. Against the wall was a very large four-poster bed with a canopy over it. Sean and Esther looked at it, then at each other. He waited until Esther smiled, then smiled himself.

"Well, I guess we'll have to rough it," said Sean.

"Yes, well, we'll make the most of it."

They went out for another stroll, and then had a hearty dinner at an old pub near the LimWarrenk racetrack. It was dark when they returned to Molly's.

The bath was down the hall from their room, and they took turns getting ready for bed.

"I only have my chemise for bed," said Esther.

"Well, you'll have to put up with my ugly underwear."

They got into the big bed from opposite sides, and both lay still. Sean turned off the only lamp.

"Well, I guess we can kiss goodnight, Sean."

"Yes, my lady. I'll be right over. Here I come!"

Esther was surprised at her eagerness to be held by Sean. Maybe it was because Sean had been her protector and still was. His loaded shotgun was propped against the wall next to the bed. They finally fell asleep in each other's arms.

Molly served eggs and pancakes with lots of coffee. She even had a smile on her face.

"You folks come back again. You're no trouble. Good luck with your car."

# Chapter Eleven

*Ireland—Sla'n for Now*

When they returned to the cottage, they were chided by Dan and Abby.

"So, you two just *had* to stay over. Whose idea was that?" said Dan.

"If you must know, we both thought it was a good idea," said Esther with a straight face. "Why drive all those extra miles when there was such a pretty town to explore?"

"Okay, I'll buy that," said Dan. "Now, here's some good news, Dad and Mother got a long cablegram in Kinsale from the Chicago police, a Captain Masconi—our Masconi. He's alive and well and has been promoted to captain. It was sent to all the parents of the students who survived the St. Valentine's Day shootings. The two neighbor ladies across the street from the scene decided to speak up, and they've identified the mobsters who came out of that garage. Warrants have been issued for four men. The women agreed to testify in court when the time comes. They are under tight police custody."

Dan held up his hand. "Here's some more news for us. Masconi said one of Capone's lieutenants was arrested on extortion and attempted murder charges. He plea bargained by giving the names of all the gang members who were assigned to find and kill Abby White and the other students. Masconi wrote that Capone had said to his men, "Couldn't even take out a bunch of young kids." Masconi added that one person was missing from the list of men given at the plea bargaining: one Fred James."

Dan had replied to Masconi. "Thanks for all your work. We are happy you survived. By the way, Fred James may have been the short punk that I threw in the Atlantic during a tussle on the *Bremen*."

"Dad thinks there's no real reason for the mob to kill us now," said Dan. "They're cooked meat, now that the ladies are coming through and are under protective custody."

Esther said, "Protective custody, ha! How many times were we attacked while in protective custody? Good luck, ladies."

"Damn good point, Esther," Dan continued. "Masconi also said that the Chicago police, Northwestern, and the *Chicago Tribune* would use our parents for further messages as a precaution."

"I wonder if Karl, Peter Farben, and Ugly Hans are still in New Jersey?" mused Abby.

"Karl will probably hear from his father in Germany," she said. "I bet the mob let them alone after they showed they had machine guns."

The Chicago "Establishment" and most of the people of Chicago had a collective guilt about what their city had become. The killing of young people and other bystanders in the mob wars was the limit. They welcomed the Federal government's "G-Men" to help take their city back from its corruption and the murderous gangs who had taken over their city.

Esther was not convinced after hearing the news. "What if some members of the European mafia haven't got the word yet? Like that Italian in Skibbereen. I've been thinking about this. I'm the only defenseless one in our group. Dan, I want you and Sean to take me to a rifle range or someplace like that, and show me how to shoot. Then I want to buy a small handgun like Abby has. Besides, it hurts when one or two of you jump on me to protect me from the mobsters. I do appreciate that, but my little frame can only take so much."

"Hmm. All right, Esther, I see your point," said Dan. "We know a place in Cork where we can shoot and find a gun for you. We'll run up there before we take you ladies to Blarney Castle to kiss the Blarney Stone. We may need some more luck yet."

The four of them left early the next day. Esther insisted that the other three bring their guns. The shooting range was on a farmer's land near the city of Cork that the police used for a training ground. Esther selected a gun that fit her small hand from a collection that the manager had for sale, and "bought enough bullets to hold off a small army," said Dan. She practiced with her new gun, shot a rifle, and Sean's shotgun. "Not a bad shot for a beginner," commented Sean. Then they all practiced with their weapons.

On the drive to Blarney Castle, Esther smiled and patted her gun in her jacket pocket. "I feel better now."

There were just a small group of tourists at the castle ahead of them as they climbed to the top. There was a castle attendant there who assisted people when they took their turn to kiss the Stone. One had to get on his back and slide a bit out of a hole in the wall, then lean up to kiss the Stone. "Esther, button up your pocket so your new toy doesn't fall out," said Abby.

\* \* \*

They were greeted with more news when they returned to the cottage. Dan's father called to relay another message from the States. "Dad said that Northwestern University officials had met with *Chicago Tribune* owners, and Captain Masconi, to work things out for the victims of the St. Valentine's Day shootings. Bachelor of Arts degrees were awarded to all the victims, all were last- semester seniors. Diplomas were to be sent to the parents' homes including those students who died that day. Compensation for all victims would be made through a joint fund established by the *Tribune* and Northwestern University."

Separate messages were sent to the homes of the survivors. The *Tribune* and Northwestern had developed work offers from their affiliates and newspaper friends in Europe and Ireland. Abby's father cabled that Abby was offered a post in Berlin as an associate foreign correspondent for the *Tribune*.

Dan was offered a position with *The Times* of London, and Esther received a firm offer with the *Lyon Press*, in her home town in France.

"See what happens when you kiss the Blarney Stone?" said Abby as they sat drinking beer on the patio of the cottage overlooking Tralee Bay. "The Irish leprechauns sprinkled us with their magic dust!"

Dan, Abby, and Esther sat around the table mulling over their offers. Dan said, "I'm not happy about going to England, the Irish oppressors. But it's a great opportunity with a world-class newspaper, and I need credentials if I want a career in newspaper work."

"I hate to see us part," said Esther. "I've grown to love each one of you."

Abby nodded and smiled. "Me too. Think, if we had a normal graduation at Northwestern, we would have gone our separate ways without much fanfare. We would be more excited about our new jobs, whatever they might have been, than being sad about our leaving. But our experiences have bonded us in such a way that we will always be close. If not near geographically, we will always be brothers and sisters and sweethearts."

"Look," said Dan. "We can meet frequently. Europe and the British Isles are relatively small and have great train and boat systems. How about us pledging that we will meet in Lausanne, Switzerland, this Christmastime and ski at nearby Gstaad?"

"But I can't ski," said Esther.

"Well, you couldn't shoot, either! Now look at you," said Abby. "We'll teach you to ski, won't we, Dan?" said Abby.

"Absolutely, Abby. Besides, Esther, you're so close to the ground, that you wouldn't be hurt if you fell," Dan said.

"Sean, you can get away, can't you?" asked Abby.

"I'll talk to the boss," said Dan with a laugh.

Abby's and Esther's parents had all relayed the messages they had received from the *Tribune*. Abby's parents, John and Mary, said they would hand-carry her diploma to wherever she would settle. Esther's parents were very excited that she was still safe, and they urged her to come home to Lyon as soon as possible.

After a few hours of talk on the patio, they all thought they would accept the positions if they were as good as they sounded. Their cablegrams gave the names and addresses of their contact persons along with other details. Abby cabled her parents and the *Tribune* to let them know that she would take the position.

Sean sat with them, listening and feeling a little envious of his newfound friends. Because of all their terrible experiences, he wasn't quite a member of their group.

"Well, there are just four Wildcats left—that is, if we can find Karl," said Dan. "I suggest we enlist Sean as a new Wildcat. He served bravely in our last two skirmishes with the gangsters."

"All in favor say 'aye.'"

Dan, Esther, and Abby raised their beer glasses, said "aye," and welcomed Sean to the Wildcats.

"You are our blood brother, Sean, but without anymore blood, we trust," said Abby. "We must exchange our new addresses as soon as we have them. Dan, can we send our addresses to you for relaying to our group?"

"Absolutely!"

Patrick and Darcy drove down to the cottage to say their goodbyes to the now ex-students. They had a grand party, again with many toasts all around. The cottage's fine wine cellar provided several bottles of aged French Burgundy. Patrick was in his best form with his Irish blessings:

May you always walk in sunshine.

May you never want for more.

May Irish angels rest their wings right beside your door.

Dan and Sean drove Abby and Esther to the Irish port of Wexford the next day where they could take a ship that went around the south coast of Wales and England to Le Havre, France. Dan tried to remember other Irish blessings to pass the driving time. "This one is appropriate and timely," said Dan.

May your blessings outnumber

The Shamrocks that grow.

And may trouble avoid you

Wherever you may go.

The dock was crowded with well-wishers and embarking passengers. Sean drew Esther aside before the pair boarded the ship. "Esther, you are a wonderful, delightful person. I will miss you, dear one. I'll be in Lausanne at Christmas, even if I have to swim and hitchhike!"

"Be safe, my lover boy," she said as they kissed. She picked up her tapestry bag and walked to the ramp leading up to the ship.

Dan and Abby also had the opportunity for a private moment at the dock. "Dan, you have been my schoolmate, my intrepid protector, and lover. How can I ever thank you or forget you? We'll meet again soon in Lausanne. Let's face it. What happened to all of us is completely unprecedented, I think, at least in this century. Let's get over this nightmare of experiences, and then see what happens."

They kissed and hugged. "I'll miss you, Abby. I'll wait as you wish. Please be safe; Germany's raising its ugly head again."

Abby joined Esther at the ramp as the ship blew its all-aboard whistle. It was almost second nature as the four of them searched the crowd for possible assailants. They all had their hands on their guns in their pockets, but there was just a sea of nameless faces waving to the departing passengers. The girls went up the ramp and wiggled their way through the crowd to the deck rail. They spotted their boyfriends on the dock and threw enough kisses to last them awhile.

Though they had a roomy first-class cabin to share, they soon surmised that the SS *Waterford* was more like a ferry boat than an ocean-going vessel. Soon after leaving Wexford the ship started wallowing in the

Saint George Channel. Many passengers hadn't brought their sea legs, and soon the decks were slick with the remnants of passengers' breakfasts.

"Let's fight it, Esther. Here are some saltine crackers I brought for us. A crewman on the *Bremen* told me that sailors use these to settle their stomachs after being on land for a while. Somehow they serve to reduce the queasiness."

Esther looked a little pale, and she quickly took a handful from Abby's cracker bag. Esther talked as she snacked on the crackers. "We had none of this on the *Bremen* coming across. I guess it's because it was a much bigger ship."

Abby nodded. "Maybe Captain Dieter found smoother waters. Esther, we don't have to go up front to the dining room. I brought enough snacks to last us 'til we pull into Le Havre tomorrow afternoon. I have a small table puzzle in my bag so we can keep busy. It'll keep our minds off the rolling and yawing."

The *Waterford* always righted itself, and her heavy diesels pushed the ship toward its destination. After awhile the seas settled a bit, allowing Esther and Abby to sleep. They were helped by two canvas belts that Abby found in a drawer. The belts attached to each side of their beds. They wrapped them across their chests to prevent them from rolling out onto the deck. "Cinch it up tight, Esther."

In the morning, they called the dining room and had tea and rolls brought to their cabin as the ship rounded into the English Channel.

The port of Le Havre was busy with ships, both passenger and cargo carriers, going to and from places around the world. Their horns and whistles filled the air.

"Abby, it's so exciting. We're actually going to work for newspapers. I'm ready for a little quiet for a while."

"Esther, call it a hunch, but somehow I don't think it will be quiet for either of us."

# Chapter Twelve

*France*

They caught a taxi for the one-mile ride to the Le Havre train station where they had lunch before boarding the train to Paris. Abby had to transfer to another train from Paris to Berlin, a 650-mile overnight journey, and Esther would take a train south to Lyon.

The train chugged and hissed its way into the Gard St. Lazare in Paris. They hugged as they parted ways in the train station. "Esther, my sweet companion, you're almost home. Stay well, and I'll see you at Christmastime, God willing." They were both in tears.

Esther called her parents in Lyon to ask that they meet her train. In less than three hours the Frankels were hugging their daughter.

\* \* \*

Abby had a porter transfer her luggage to the Berlin train. After settling in her compartment, she made her way two cars up to the dining room. It was evening, and she was hungry and was looking forward to a regular meal after she and Esther had snacked their way to Le Havre.

The dining room was already busy. It was customary for single persons to share a table with others, and the head waiter ushered her to a table where a man in full military regalia was sipping on wine and studying the menu. He looked up as the waiter said, "Monsieur, may the lady join you?"

He stood immediately and gave a slight bow. He quickly looked at Abby and surmised: *Either English or American, no rings, very pretty, tall blonde.* "Of course," he said in English. "Please join me. I welcome your company, mademoiselle."

"Thank you, sir, and *you*, sir," as she thanked the waiter for helping her with her chair and providing her with a menu.

Abby quickly sized up the man opposite her. *Nice face, chiseled nose, firm chin, straight black hair, heavy German accent, late twenties or so.*

"May I introduce myself, mademoiselle? I'm Hauptmann Claus von Fritsch, German Army. And you, please?"

"Abby White, American." She began to dislike him already. *A bit pompous. If he wasn't seated, he would have clicked his heels. But give him time,* she thought.

"Very pleased to meet you." He paused. "I looked at the menu. It really hasn't changed in the four years I've ridden this train. I may be able to help you, if you wish."

"The waiter gave me the English menu, so I may be all right. What is your favorite entree, Captain?"

"The wurst and sauerkraut always suits me. May I share my Rhine wine with you?"

"Thank you, no. I will have a Sauterne from Normandy, if the waiter can find some."

The Captain signaled the waiter. "Mademoiselle would prefer a Sauterne from Normandy. Please see to it."

"Why do you ride this train so often?" asked Abby.

"I'm returning to my family home in Berlin on a short leave. I'm a military attaché at the German Embassy in London. And what is bringing you to Berlin, may I ask?"

"You may. I've been assigned a post as an associate foreign correspondent by the *Chicago Tribune's* Berlin bureau."

"That sounds like an interesting and challenging posting."

"I'm sure it will be for me. I recently graduated from the journalism school at Northwestern University in America and interned at the *Tribune* in Chicago."

"Ah, a good school and newspaper."

Their waiter returned to the table with Abby's Sauterne. She sipped and nodded her approval. They gave their food orders, and Abby did accept the Captain's suggestion for her entree.

The dining car was now almost filled with people. As it darkened outside, the head waiter moved around the car lighting small candles that were in the middle of each table next to a small vase of yellow roses. He then dimmed the car's overhead lamps and turned on soft music. It was a Viennese waltz that Abby recognized, "The Voices of Spring," by Johann Strauss. Suddenly the dining car was transformed into a magical scene that Abby had read about in historical romantic novels. Whether it was from the ambiance from the muted conversations in the background, from the music, the aroma of the roses, or the wine, Abby was relaxed and felt mellow and safe for the first time in a long time. This was the adventure she was looking for when she finished college. The captain across from her now looked dashing and interesting. She had to learn more about the tall German.

"You do know some German, don't you, Miss White? You knew that Hauptmann meant Captain."

"Yes, some. I took German in secondary school and in college. I also worked one summer in a German-speaking business in Wisconsin. I think it helped me get the posting in Berlin. Where did you get your command of English?"

"After the war ended in 1918, my father was assigned to the German Embassy as Ambassador in London, so the family moved there. Most of his work was handling reparation payments to the Allies. I was fourteen years old and took a lot of taunting at my school in London. Like 'Hey, you lost the big one, krauthead! Not so tough after all!' I took a fair number of group beatings before my father found a private school with foreign émigrés. Conditions improved there, and I picked up a lot of English."

"Children can be so mean," said Abby.

"That they can. I got my college training at Heidelberg University. It was hard to find a decent job, so I volunteered for the peacetime army. It was more like a local police force than an army, because of post-war restrictions. I asked to be posted in the London Embassy to be near my family. My duty is primarily to provide protection for the Embassy. There is still animosity against Germany in England after more than ten years. My father finished his tour in London two years ago, and the family moved back to Berlin. He's still involved in government affairs there."

"Are you required to wear your uniform on leave?"

"No. My mother likes to see me in uniform when I come home." He smiled. "She's an old Prussian. I think she would join the army if she could. I will take it off after I get home."

The candle on the table was burning low, and most of the diners had left. Their wine glasses were empty.

"Where does your family live now? May I call you Abby?"

"In Indianapolis, Indiana. Yes, Claus, you may. My father is an architect and builder like my grandfather."

"Mother and siblings?"

"Mother is a teaching nurse by profession, and I have two sisters." She looked around. "Well, it's time to go. I see the waiter looking our way with a frown."

Abby stood and extended her hand to shake, but the captain held her hand and kissed the back of it. Abby almost laughed but smiled instead.

"Perhaps we can meet here for lunch tomorrow before we arrive in Berlin," said Claus.

"I guess that would be all right. What time?"

"I'll reserve a table for one o'clock."

Abby closed the door on her compartment and thought. *An interesting evening. My, I forgot to ask him if he was married.*

They met as agreed the next day. Again, they had a table by themselves.

Claus looked out the window. "We are crossing over the Elbe River. Not long now to Berlin"

"Does your wife and family stay in Berlin or London, Captain?"

"Oh, it's back to Captain again!" He smiled and said, "Not married, Abby. Too busy with my work, I guess, or too boring to interest a girl." He paused and looked into her eyes. "Well, I'll test this premise. Will you allow me to show you around Berlin after you have settled in your position and living space?"

"Testing your premise that you are a bore, Claus? Hardly. I have appreciated your company. You're an engaging dining companion. Yes, I would enjoy that tour. It would also be very helpful to me in a new city."

"See, you have a friend in Berlin already! Here is my card, Abby, with the Berlin family house telephone number on it. Please call me. I am a 'top notch' tour guide as they say. My leave in Berlin is for three weeks."

They parted in the aisle of the dining car with his hand kiss again *and a heels clicking.*

# Chapter Thirteen

*Berlin, Germany*

The train rumbled into the Alexanderplatz station where Abby took a taxi to the hotel where the *Tribune* had reserved a room.

The office of the *Tribune* bureau was close by, and in the morning Abby walked the streets of Berlin for the first time, heading north on Bendler Strasse. This was her first excursion without one of her classmates. She was excited, but she vowed to herself to be calm and confident. The street was busy with workers heading to their offices. The women were modestly dressed, as was Abby. She had seen advertisements in the German magazines that were in the Atlantic City house. The women in the ads had longer skirts than American women and wore vested jackets. Abby had a few outfits like those, but she needed to go shopping soon in Berlin.

The *Tribune* offices were in a large building on Tiergarten Strasse. A number of other international newspapers had offices in the same building. Each staff of the newspapers held breaking news close to them. They didn't want another service to get a "scoop" on them, because then they would be beholden to them or be charged a fee for permission to print the story in their newspapers.

Abby found the *Tribune* office on the second floor. "I am to see Mr. Hoffman," she told the receptionist.

James Hoffman, the bureau chief, greeted Abby. "Welcome to Berlin, Miss White. Did you have a pleasant trip?" He was a short, blond-haired man about forty with an upper Midwestern accent, meaning no accent at all.

"Yes indeed, sir, and the hotel you selected is very nice."

"Good. Now let me show you around the office." He led their way from the foyer to a larger room with a dozen cubicles separated by head-high partitions. The partitions did little to reduce the cacophony of typewriters, teletype machines, and ringing telephones.

"Sound familiar from your intern days on Michigan Avenue?"

"Yes, sir. The office looks very much the same, except much smaller, of course, than Chicago."

"Well, I also interned there some years ago when at Chicago University, and spent three years at that office before they assigned me here."

He walked her over to a window for a view of city landmarks. It was really to speak to Abby confidentially. "The *Tribune* home office sent me a personal message regarding the ordeal you have been through. I don't know all the details, but I congratulate you for your bravery and resourcefulness. Please let me know if I can help in any way."

Abby was introduced to her new fellow workers as they walked along. She guessed there were about a dozen people in the office. At the end of the room there was a glass enclosed office with a door. Mr. Hoffman knocked on the door, waited briefly, and then entered. He introduced Abby to the office supervisor who also served as the desk editor, a Miss Rosenfeld.

"Miss Rosenfeld will take over from here. She will advise you on office routines and our office objectives. We are pleased to have you join us, Miss White."

"Thank you, Mr. Hoffman," said Abby.

"Please sit down, Abby." Miss Rosenfeld looked Abby over with strong peering eyes as if to assess her. *She has a decided New York accent*, Abby thought.

"Abby, please call me Janelle, okay? We Americans aren't as formal as our German friends." She paused. "Our objective is to provide clear, concise, well-written stories to our *Tribune* newspapers in the U.S. and some foreign news services. I assign correspondents to specific stories, give them a reporting time-table, and then I edit their work before transmitting it. Some copy is not sent because of bad writing or reporting, or the story turns out to be not of major interest to Americans as we had hoped.

"I have a helper, Carol Munster, who handles office supply matters, new correspondents, and keeps a daily record of all correspondents' whereabouts."

"Everyone here knows German. *Begrefen?*"

"Yes, I understand and I can speak German, Janelle."

She buzzed Carol and had her take Abby to her assigned cubical. It was fully equipped with typewriter, telephone, and the usual office supplies.

"You'll notice several unoccupied work stations," said Carol as they walked through the office. "Their occupants are out on assignments. Most of our news stories originate in Berlin, but our people will use trains if the story leads them there. If the story is subject to possible error, the correspondent must have the questionable item confirmed with another source.

"Here are your credentials, Abby." She handed Abby some papers and a badge with her name on it, but lacking a picture. "Please go down to Han's photo shop around the corner on Bender Strasse. They will take your picture and fix it to your badge while you wait."

"I'll be by at noon to go to lunch together. Then I can tell you more about how things work here. After that we'll go over to a nearby apartment house that may appeal to you. Two other *Tribune* people have apartments there. It's reasonable, safe, and very clean. When you take an apartment, I'll help you get your bags from the station lockers and help you get settled. That's part of my job."

After a delightful lunch at a small Tiergarten restaurant, they strolled through the park. "It reminds me of Central Park in New York," said Carol.

"Yes, and a little of Lincoln Park in Chicago to me," added Abby.

"Some inside advice, Abby. Don't take any defective work into Janelle's office. I've seen seasoned reporters come out of her office in tears, with editing and proofreader marks all over their copy. Let me read your first few stories before you turn them in. Janelle's a good person, but she's a terror when she sees bad copy."

Abby liked the furnished apartment at first sight and signed a six-month lease with the manager. By the time they moved her luggage to the apartment, the day was almost over.

"No use going back to the office, Abby. It's Friday, so you'll have the whole weekend to shop for your apartment things. See you Monday at the office. Oh, we start at nine."

"What a help you are, Carol. Thanks so much."

Abby spent the weekend shopping for food, clothes, and incidentals. The apartment was warm and cozy—a real change from the last two months. She put out pictures of family and friends to make it even homier. She had a wonderful, jolly picture of the "Wildcats" taken at Ollie's speakeasy in Chicago, but it remained in her luggage. It made her cry. *Maybe late*r, she thought.

On Sunday afternoon, she wrote letters to family and to Dan in London. She missed her family and Dan and the rest of the Wildcats. In her letter to her family, she worked hard to make her letter sound cheery, saying little about the violent happenings of the past two months. She described her apartment, her office, and what little she had seen of Paris and Berlin. She finished with:

> I met a kind, young German army officer on the train from Paris to Berlin. He has volunteered to show the city to me, so I'll be in a better position to lead a tour when you come to visit. I can't wait to see you again. Make it soon, Mom and Dad, before Christmas. My old classmates and I plan to meet in Switzerland at Christmas for a little skiing. We are now scattered all over Europe and England and Ireland. Please try to schedule your visit over a long weekend so that I can spend a lot of time with you. Write soon.
> 
> Love, Abby.
> 
> And love to my wonderful sisters, my dear sisters, Jane and Alice.
> 
> (They'll get a kick out that, those pillow-fighting sisters.)

\* \* \*

Janelle was ready for Abby on Monday. "Abby, I want you to get your feet wet by shadowing Tom Walton on an assignment. Berlin is already laying plans for the 1936 Olympics, and Tom will be interviewing several Olympic officials. He'll show you his basic technique for interviewing and how to develop the stories and combine them if it is useful to do so. You probably know basic interviewing techniques, but Tom may surprise you. He's good. He'll also show you how to get advances for expenses and how to prepare an expense report. He'll pick you up at your desk soon."

A short, white-haired man came to her desk later. Abby had a good look at him as he approached. *He looks older than he probably is*, she thought. He was round-shouldered and looked very tired. His brown eyes seemed to be the oldest part of his body, half-closed with surrounding frown lines. It was if he had seen too much of the world and hadn't liked what he had seen.

He straightened up somewhat and forced a smile. "Okay, White, off we go! I'm Tom Walton, your faithful leader, and maybe a teacher of sorts. You know German?" Without waiting for an answer, he continued. "Well, you'll get a big dose of it here. Most of the people speak with their heads down, like they're speaking to someone in the gutter. I think they lost their higher voice tones after they got their butts kicked in the last war. They are a proud people, but now their heads are hanging low. The worsening economy doesn't help. They need something to get them energized. Oh, bring a pad and pencil. There's a ground-breaking ceremony at the site of the new track and field Olympic Stadium, Abby. We want to get there in plenty of time to interview as many officials as we can. Tomorrow we will write another story based upon interviews with the workers and sidewalk supervisors. You know what a sidewalk supervisor is?"

"Yes, sir, they are usually retired older men with nothing to do except to kibitz about the building and how slow things are going. My father is a building designer and contractor in America."

"Hey, that's great. Okay, let's use the company car today. First, we have to get some money for gas and food." He walked up to the accounting window. "Miss Tillie hates to give us money, like it's hers. Right, Miss Tillie?"

"Don't trust you, Tom. Miss, watch him with this money and don't believe a word he says."

"Let's get out of here! Abby, you got your press pass? I've got the camera."

The site of the Olympic Stadium was several miles from the *Tribune* office. "How long have you been a foreign correspondent, Mr. Walton?"

"Call me Tom. About fifteen years here in Europe. I was a war correspondent on the front lines during the war in 1917 and 1918. Saw enough blood to last a lifetime. Brave boys ordered to climb out of their trenches to charge German machines guns. Mowed down like wheat being harvested. I've never been the same after witnessing that."

"That must have been awful!"

"That it was, Abby."

They parked near a group of officials dressed in long black dress coats and bowler hats. Another group of about fifteen men in brown shirts, ties, and caps stood nearby. They had nightsticks on belts around their waists and swastika armbands. "Who are those men in brown?" asked Abby.

"Those are Adolf Hitler's body guards, the S.A., short for *Sturmabtelung*, or 'storm troopers.' The big guy with the small, mean eyes of a pig is the head of the 'Brownshirts,' Ernst Roehm, a brute and a killer. Oh, I see Hitler talking to the officials. Let's get closer."

As they neared the group, a short man ran towards them. He had a gun drawn.

"Watch out," yelled Tom as he stepped in front of Abby, just as the man fired two shots. The Brownshirts were on the shooter in an instant, beating the man with their clubs. The officials in the black coats ran in all directions. Hitler seemed unfazed. The official dedication would be another day.

"Bad mistake, punk-rat, trying to hurt our leader!" yelled Roehm. They continued to beat him until he was dead.

Tom was shot in the arm by a wild bullet. "Here, Abby, take the camera and get off a few shots. It's front-page stuff tomorrow."

Hitler walked over to Tom and Abby, as Abby was wrapping his arm with a big head scarf she carried in her purse. Hitler called over to a Brownshirt medic to assist. "A terrible thing. Are either of you hurt badly? That man looked like one of those Communist bastards," said Hitler in German.

"Don't think it hit a bone," said Tom, grimacing with the pain.

Abby wasn't shy. She also spoke in German. "Mr. Hitler, may I take your picture with the background of the stadium site?"

"Of course." He moved for the shot, preening himself for the camera. He was in a dark green Bavarian wool suit. He removed his hat and fussed with his hair. His dark brown hair was combed down over the left side of his forehead, almost touching his eyebrow. *Not a big man, mid 40's,* thought Abby. He sported a small mustache just under his nose, Charlie Chaplin style. Abby took several pictures.

"Americans! I see you have *Chicago Tribune* press passes," said Hitler. He stepped forward to examine their press cards more closely. "Abby White and Thomas Walton. I am sorry you were endangered by that madman." He paused. "If you stay in Berlin, you will be fortunate to witness the great turnaround of Germany in the near future."

Hitler extended his hand on parting. Abby took it and noticed that it was cold and damp. "I admire you, Miss White. You didn't flinch when you saw a man killed."

"I've seen several men killed before, Mr. Hitler."

"Hmm. Interesting, Miss White. Well, goodbye."

He then turned to Roehm and his guards, motioning them to move. "Some of you take that body somewhere and dispose of it. Take his papers; I want to see where he comes from. The rest of you stay with me."

Roehm brought the assassin's papers to Hitler. "He's from Sicily!"

"My friend Mussolini better stop these madmen in Italy. I will have something on him when next we meet," said Hitler with a smile. Abby missed those remarks while leading Tom to the car.

With directions from Tom, Abby drove their car to a local hospital where they cleaned and bandaged Tom's wound. The doctor said, "You were lucky. It will be sore, but should heal fast. Change the bandage every day and watch for infection."

Driving back to the office, Abby ventured, "He's an interesting man, Hitler. Don't know what to make of him yet. I've been out of the loop, so to speak, finishing my senior year in college. What do you think of him?"

"You saw him at his best, Abby. I think he is a candidate for a mental institution. Wait 'til you hear him making a speech to a crowd. He is maniacal, but he can move a crowd. He's come a long way from being a wallpaper hanger and a corporal in the army. The German elite joke about him, but I think he is a dangerous man, a power-hungry demagogue."

They worked together at the office to put together an eyewitness report of a probable attempt on Hitler's life. The caption under the picture of Hitler that Abby had taken read, "Hitler Unharmed at Dedication of Olympic Site." Tom's arm was in a sling, so he dictated the story to Abby who suggested several additions from her observations. "Not bad," said Tom as he reviewed the material. "Add your name to mine on the byline."

Janelle liked the story. "It is front-page stuff with the picture. European papers will buy it also. Good job, Tom. Sorry about your arm."

"Janelle, Abby White really helped with the story, and she kept her cool enough after the shooting to get his picture."

"That's good. Maybe we have real talent this time."

* * *

Abby called Claus von Fritsch, and they arranged a time for the tour on Sunday, her day off.

"I'll bring a picnic basket with some various wines we can try. And I know a great place to picnic," Claus told Abby.

Claus wore a black cashmere wool sweater over a white shirt and gray woolen trousers. He looked like a different person out of his captain's uniform. It was a sunny Berlin day in early spring, but still with a cool breeze. Abby was excited.

They drove leisurely around the city in Claus' two-seat Opel. Claus slowed down to point out government buildings, monuments, and good restaurants. Abby had a city map on her lap and took notes as Claus described places in candid detail. She was fascinated by the huge Reichstag government building, the Brandenburg Gate, and the wide streets and boulevards.

He finally parked at a picnic area in the Tiergarten Park overlooking the Spree River where sightseeing riverboats and smaller boats moved slowly along the shore. It was a welcome break for Abby from the clatter of the *Tribune* office.

Claus talked about Berlin with an air of love and pride as he spread food and wine bottles on a wooden table. "I so miss Berlin when I am in London. London has its beauty, but this is home. I guess that you feel that way about Indiana?"

"You know, Claus, I wanted to see other places, so I enrolled in Northwestern University, which is just north of Chicago in the pretty town of Evanston. Still, I love Indiana with its vast fields of corn, wheat, and soybeans. Your Spree River reminds me of the beautiful Wabash and White rivers that meander their way through my home state.

"Sounds very nice," said Claus.

"The land is much different from European land," said Abby. "I hope you get to visit America someday—you would be surprised at its vastness. Now, enough of geography. Let's get to the feast you brought. How thoughtful! And what a wonderful setting over the river!"

There were enough meats, cheeses, and breads to feed a family. Claus then presented the wine with a connoisseur's flourish. "If you plan to drink wine in Germany, there are basic things you must know. There are thirteen major wine regions in Germany. Most are located along the western rivers of the country. Here are two white wines: Riesling and Bacchus. And these red wines are *Spatburgunde* (Pinot Noir), and we'll uncork each bottle to let them breathe for a while."

Abby knew her wines fairly well, but she was enjoying Claus' performance. "Now we must sip some of each?" she asked.

"Yes. Before our palates are compromised by the food. I'll cork the bottles we don't use and give them to our service personnel at home."

"I like the Pinot Noir and the Baccus, Claus."

"So do I, Abby. Now to the food!" They chatted while they filled their plates.

"Claus, I told you on the phone that I met Adolf Hitler on an assignment this week where somebody tried to shoot him. What do you think of him?"

Claus looked around to see if anyone was within listening distance. "It's too bad he missed. He's a clown, Abby, but a dangerous, political clown. No one in the German Army trusts him. He is grabbing more power every day it seems. Unfortunately, most people are fed up with the current 'do nothing' government and think that he might be the leader they need." Claus paused and then continued, "I suggest you skim through *Mein Kampf*, the book he wrote in prison where he was serving time for treason. He has a warped sense of Aryan superiority and blames the Jewish people and other so-called 'inferiors' for all of Germany's problems."

When Claus finally dropped Abby off at her apartment, the sun was setting in the west. "Abby, before I have to return to London, I would like you to meet my family. They said they would love to meet you. They know a lot of people in Berlin. It may help you in your work."

"That would be very nice, Claus. I would love to meet them. And thanks for the wonderful tour and picnic."

"I'll call you. And stay away from that Hitler person in the meantime. He attracts bullets."

# Chapter Fourteen

***Lyon, France***

Hardly a minute passed after meeting Esther at the train station that her parents, Melvin and Mira Frankel, didn't quiz her about her journey from Chicago to Lyon.

Now they were sitting at their table in their country kitchen, always the venue for conversations and queries in the family. Esther was happy to be home. It was comfortable speaking in her native French after years in America.

"Did you almost get killed?" asked her mother.

"I was safe, Mother."

"Then why are you carrying a handgun?"

"You *did* have to see that while I was unpacking. It was just precautionary."

"Well, whatever, I don't want a loaded gun in our house."

"It's unloaded, Mother, so let's change the subject. How's the jewelry business, Dad?"

"Very good right now, Esther, almost too good." Melvin straightened himself in his kitchen chair. "I think stock market prices are inflated worldwide, not much real assets behind them, so I'm selling off some of my investments and converting into cash and diamonds." He spread his hands on the wooden table. "Enough of that."

He looked at Esther and clapped his hands. "Belated congratulations on a successful college career! I'm glad you have a few days with us before starting with the newspaper."

He winked at Mira. "Now, are you going to tell us what was in those two letters we've been holding for you?"

Esther smiled. "You ol' cat! Your curiosity may be your undoing if you're on your eighth life! Okay, dear Father, the one from England was from Jacob Bernstein, a young man I met on the *Bremen*. He is a Purdue University graduate who was heading to Cambridge to work on an advanced degrees in physics. His letter said he got his position and has a great professor mentoring him. I met his family on the ship. They live in Paris. A nice young man, but I hardly know him, unlike my friends from Northwestern and the people I met in Ireland. Jacob wants to visit me over the December holidays. This could be a problem since I'm committed to joining my college friends in Gstaad for skiing."

"Oh, can you tell us about the letter from Ireland, Esther?" Mira said, scooting forward in her chair. "This is exciting!"

"My, Mother. You need to get out more often, and travel more." She smiled at her mother and went on. "The Ireland letter was from a young man named Sean O'Connor. He is friends with Dan O'Gara, a fellow Northwestern student from Kinsale, Ireland. He really helped us avoid harm from Al Capone's friends." She paused and looked at her parents. "I hope to see Sean in Gstaad."

"Oh, I hope you will see Jacob Bernstein before you go to Gstaad," said Mira.

Esther's work at the newspaper, *The Lyon Press*, was fairly mundane at first. Then she convinced her supervisor to let her interview people on the streets and in shops. She stopped people from all walks of life and found that most people loved to talk about their jobs and life in general. She interviewed celebrities, schoolchildren, clerks, beggars, athletes, housewives, and the like. Her following grew, and the people kept asking for "more Esther." The editors responded, and instead of one story a week, they asked her for two stories each week. They agreed that she captured the basic personality and mood of her interviewees. Some were cheerful, some bitter, but all remarkably interesting. Her editors increased her pay, and the paper printed her picture with a brief biography since readers wrote that they were surprised that such insightful stories were coming from such a young person.

\* \* \*

Cambridge shut down for the holidays early in December since many of the students and faculty were from other countries.

Jacob wrote to Esther and asked if he could visit her in Lyon in December before going home to Berlin. He would stay with an aunt in Lyon.

His letter to Esther showed his anticipation!

> My parents and sister, Ruth, will be glad to get rid of me for a few more days. I do love Lyon, especially the parks near the confluence of the Rhone and Saone rivers. It may be too cold to picnic, but I know of some great restaurants nearby.
> Yours, Jacob

While Esther had mixed feelings about Jacob's visit, her mother was ecstatic at the news. "Of course he can visit us, Esther. Please let him know that he will be welcomed. I will fix him a nice dinner. I hope you like him more after his visit. It would be wonderful for your father to have another Jewish man in the family."

"Mother, stop that. He is just a friend. I now have several new friends. He is just one of them. A nice young man, but that's all."

\* \* \*

Summer slipped quickly into the fall and winter seasons, and soon Jacob appeared at their door. Esther had forgotten how tall and handsome Jacob was. At dinner, her mother and father peppered him with questions about his family in Berlin and his work at Cambridge.

Esther couldn't wait to get Jacob out from under the questioning of her parents. As they left for a long walk, Esther apologized to him for her parent's inquisition.

Jacob laughed. "No more than my mother's questions to you aboard the *Bremen*. They are all so worried about their children meeting the 'right' people. They are not far removed from the past generations when marriages were arranged within the Jewish community. They don't realize, or choose not to realize, that this is a new age of freedom from the old ways. We are young and may make mistakes, but the mistakes will be ours to make, not theirs."

Esther enjoyed and appreciated his candidness and told Jacob she believed the same about Jewish tradition. "I think it's time for our generation to be free thinkers and doers, and not try to please our parents or the synagogue hierarchy. I can still remember a declaration by Patrick Henry during the American Revolution: 'Give me liberty or give me death!' Of course, it's not as bad as that, but you know what I mean."

They strolled down the Cours Lafayette where Jacob found one of the restaurants along the Rhone River that he remembered. It was very near the Pont Lafayette Bridge and had a good view of the busy river from its patio. They ordered a platter of frommage with crackers and a bottle of Merlot from the Avignon region of southern France.

Jacob was well into his second glass of wine when he began talking to Esther about his future, and intimated that it could involve Esther. "I have found science, specifically nuclear physics, to be my field of great interest. This is much to the consternation of my father who wants me to join his Berlin commercial real estate company. I'm sure I'll hear more about that when I train home from Lyon."

"Where do you think you will end up after your graduate work at Cambridge?" asked Esther.

"My masters and doctoral work will take several years. After that I will probably go to America. Several universities there are heavy into nuclear physics. I could teach, write, and join an experimental team. Rumors are that Albert Einstein may move soon to America from Germany because the growing anti-Semitism. His work has been amazing. I would like somehow to be on his staff. I remember, Esther, you were saying that you would like to go back to America someday. Is there a chance that we might have common objectives and be a team?"

Esther chuckled. "Jacob, you make it sound so much like a mathematical equation for achieving happiness. That's sweet, Jacob, but there has to be some romance in your equation. We hardly know each other. Just a couple of days on the *Bremen*, some letter writing, and now your visit. Any relationship takes time. It takes repeated exposure to each other. It *is* possible that we could join together as a team, but that could be some time away. Okay? Like you, I have my objectives. I want to be a good journalist and parlay that into writing novels. Maybe I will succeed and maybe I won't. I *do* want to live in the United States. Time will tell, Jacob."

They took the long way back to the Frankel's house, chatting all the way. A cab came to take Jacob to his aunt's house. Esther gave Jacob a warm hug and kiss. "Please keep up our letter writing, Jacob."

"I will, dear Esther."

As the cab pulled away Esther thought, *What a wonderful dilemma. Sean and now Jacob!*

# Chapter Fifteen

*London*

Patrick and Darcy O'Gara had taken the likeable Sean O'Connor under their wing after Dan left for his post in London. They sponsored him on his return to college in Cork where, with more personal application, Sean excelled in his engineering studies. At school break times, he worked for Patrick's company and earned money for his rendezvous with the Wildcats at Gstaad in Switzerland.

Dan, in London, was still the conduit and planner for the meeting. He made reservations for the long weekend of skiing. "Bring your own favorite beverage, and I will provide the mixes."

His letter to Karl's father's address was returned unopened. Dan wrote another letter to the Atlantic City, New Jersey address. Karl did respond.

> I am still very busy with the "Friends of New Germany" and can't make it to Gstaad. Maybe next year. I'm still with Peter Faben and Hans Strasser, whom you'll remember.
> Best to my Wildcat friends!
> Karl
> P.S. We sank your (their) car in a gravel pit in Pennsylvania.

At the *Times* of London, Dan was assigned to tag along with Robert Shaw, an experienced journalist who routinely handled national news. A staff member told Dan that Shaw had the instinct and ability to sense the importance or lack of importance of a "happening." Dan noticed that if it seemed important, Shaw worked hard to dig deeper to get the true facts, not just what a person or persons wanted him to know.

"Remember, Dan, every one of the people you will meet have their public and private faces. You must get past the public face with penetrating, polite questions. If you can break through to the private person, you will have a valuable source for information, not only for the first story, but for other stories yet to come. Basically, you must gain their trust."

Dan took the usual ribbing for being a rookie, and "an Irishman to boot." But he kept his cool and laughed it off in public. In private, he still hated the British as a class for what they did to his beloved Ireland and his father and uncle. *I just can't let that go, the bloody bastards!*

He worked diligently with Shaw to learn his craft, and eventually was given his own assignments, developing his own style and flair in writing a story. He also wrote weekly to Abby in Berlin. He missed her dearly and told her so.

> You have such a pretty face, sweetheart, but you also have a keen intelligence and graceful bearing that I both love and admire. I can't wait to see you at Christmas. It looks like it will be just the four of us: Esther and Sean and you and me. Karl finally wrote that he is busy with his German group in Atlantic City.
>
> I believe we'll never see him again. We will see.
> Love, Dan

# Chapter Sixteen

*Berlin*

Abby received a letter from her parents late in November. Her father said they must postpone their trip to Berlin because of the financial crisis in the United States. The stock market crashed on October 29, "Black Friday," he explained, and many of his building contracts were cancelled. In addition, the money owed to his company by clients might never be recovered due to the bankruptcies and foreclosures. He added some details:

> It is a terrible situation here, Abby. People are losing their life savings due to bank failures, and are being let go from their companies by the thousands. I must stay here to try to mitigate the damage caused to our firm due to cancellations of building construction. I do hope you understand.
> Love, Dad

Abby did understand. Germany and the rest of the world were caught up in the same financial crash. She wrote back quickly.

> I am so sorry that this economy has so terribly affected the firm. Your place is with the business right now. I will probably get a leave next summer. (Who knows now?) I will come home for a nice visit. I miss you so much, and I pray that things will be back to normal soon.
> Love, Abby

The *Tribune* office in Berlin was notified by cable about "Black Friday" before most Berliners knew about it. Abby heeded the advice of Tom Walton to take cash out from the bank accounts she'd established in Berlin. That saved most of her money in Berlin. Her father was a cosigner on her accounts in the United States, and he moved her money out of questionable banks to safe havens.

Circulation of the *Tribune* was down all over the world. Many people could not afford hard-copy newspapers and relied on their radio for news. Several people were laid off in the *Tribune*'s Berlin office, but not Abby or Tom Walton.

The military and civilian elite were not bothered much by economic conditions in Germany at the start. Parties were still held at the embassies in Berlin, and their social life went on. Before Claus von Fritsch's military leave expired, he introduced Abby to his parents, Otto and Marie von Fritsch. The von Fritsches were delightful people, full of energy and humor.

"Abby, you will go with us to some of the better parties and events held in Berlin," said Otto. "I can tell it won't take long for you to be accepted by the social set. Your German is very good, and I must say you are beautiful. My, you could be the daughter we never had! Can I introduce you as Claus's special friend?"

"Of course, sir. And I am grateful for the opportunity to meet people. Besides being very entertaining, I'm sure, it will broaden my understanding of Berlin and its people. That will be very helpful in my work at the *Tribune*." She paused and smiled. "But please understand, sir, that Claus and I are just good friends now."

\* \* \*

On the train to Gstaad, Abby thought briefly about the gala holiday parties she would miss in Berlin, especially since Claus would have Christmas leave and would have been her escort. *I hope I get back before his leave is over. An interesting man.* But now she was more excited about seeing her old friends again, the Wildcats.

# Chapter Seventeen

*Gstaad, Switzerland*

Abby had the longest way to go, more than 700 miles, having to make two connections to reach Switzerland. Even with the distance and connections, she arrived at the Lausanne hotel before Esther, Dan, and Sean. It was a glorious reunion with lots of hugs, kisses, and laughter in the foyer of the hotel. For the first night, Abby and Esther roomed together again, and Dan and Sean bunked together. They met later in the hotel bar to toast their fallen friends and classmates from the St. Valentine's Day Massacre, Carol Martin and Harold Hubble.

The next day they took a shuttle bus to the chalet village of Gstaad in the Berner Alps and stayed three nights in the Gstaad-Saanenland lodge. On the day of arrival at Gstaad they went to the ski slopes and rented skies and poles. They started at the beginner's runs with Esther. It was great fun, even with Esther screaming, "No, no, I'm going to crash!" Sean skied backwards, arms outstretched; holding Esther's hands to brake her speed and guide her. By mid-afternoon, Esther was able to make turns and brake herself.

"You're a natural-born skier, Esther. Did you take dancing or a lot of gymnastics in school?" asked Abby.

"Took dancing with some ballet. Hated it!"

At après ski in the lodge, they had hot drinks laced with rye whiskey, and replayed each person's fall in the snow with laughter. The sun was setting after dinner when Abby made a declaration to her fellow Wildcats. "Sean, I might stumble in the dark and go into your room by mistake. Do you think you can find another place to lay your head?"

"I think there might be a place for him in our room since you won't be there," said Esther.

When they finally made their way back to the Lausanne train station, they were tired but happy skiers and lovers. Their last glasses of wine, before the trains started taking them away, were sipped solemnly.

"Put your right hand in the middle of the table on mine and say after me, 'We will,' said Dan. "I pledge that this holy foursome will meet here again, same time, next year."

Their three right hands rested on Dan's in the middle of the table, and they all said, "We will."

# Chapter Eighteen

*Berlin*

The city became more unstable with the poor economy as time went on, but the parties continued. Otto and Marie von Fritsch took Claus and Abby to a New Year's Eve party in the Reichstag ballroom the night before Claus had to return to London. The parents moved them from group to group, carrying their champagne glasses as they went. They introduced Abby as a friend of Claus's and a foreign correspondent for the *Tribune*.

William Shirer, a senior foreign correspondent for the *Tribune*, kept a desk in the Berlin office. He was more of an itinerant writer who covered all of Europe and some of the Middle East. He was also at the party and took Abby away from the von Fritsches for a while to introduce her to other people. Abby soon returned to Claus and his family where they had a champagne toast to wish Claus a happy return to London.

\* \* \*

When she first met William Shirer in the *Tribune* office, he'd offered to take her to lunch to get acquainted. He was a serious, bespectacled young man, recently married, who seemed much older than his twenty-eight years. He was taller than most men, but he stooped slightly as if his height might be intimidating to others. His briar pipe hardly ever left his lips, except when he was refilling it or fidgeting with it.

During the long lunch, he gave her his impression of the foreign correspondent's job, and his insight on current events in Germany. He spoke with a reedy voice. "Abby, I must alert you to what's about to happen here in Berlin, and even the whole of Germany. Hitler is about to take over the government because the people now believe that he is the one who will take Germany forward. In spite of Germany's agreement with the Treaty of Versailles, he is secretly laying plans for building an army and a fleet of warships. Come with me to his next outdoor rally of the Nazi party."

* * *

It was three weeks later when William and Abby sat in the press section near the speaker's dais. She was anxious to see if Hitler was the spellbinder that her friends described. A heavy Wagner piece played by a full orchestra set the tone of the rally. An immense Nazi banner covered the back of the stage. Searchlights played back and forth on the banner and the brown-shirted SA (*Sturmabteilung*) troops marching down the center aisle. They were followed by hundreds of ardent followers, mostly men, dressed in dark suits with swastika armbands.

William leaned over, whispering to Abby. "Quite a show, Abby, and it really hasn't started yet. Wait until Hitler speaks. He was coached by an actor named Hammel, who was also a professional speaking coach. After the Brownshirts found out that he was Jewish, though, they shot and killed him. Hitler will start out slow in a low voice as he was coached to do, then will build up to where he looks and sounds like a madman." Abby frowned and moved forward in her seat.

The Fuehrer finally entered the staging area from the left and was flanked by his chief lieutenants, Martin Bormann and Rudolf Hess. The orchestra broke into Wagner's *Rienzi Overture*, one of Hitler's favorites. "Late as always. It's to build up the suspense," said William. The cheers and applause were deafening. Hitler smiled as he passed the press section and then saw Abby. He pointed to her and gave her a personal wave and wide smile. "You must have made quite an impression on him, Abby," William said.

On the dais, Joseph Goebbles, the Nazi propaganda leader, gave an elaborate introduction of "our brave leader" in his shrill voice, then backed away to stand with Bormann and Hess. Hitler started slowly. His voice was so soft, the audience leaned forward to hear.

"How many of you have read my book, *Mein Kampf*, the story of my struggle for the Fatherland?" Everyone who could hear him raised their hands. The others had to ask their neighbors what he'd said, and then they quickly raised their hands also.

Suddenly, he raised his voice along with his right hand. "Some of you appear not sure. You *must* read my book of you want to be a member of the Nazi party. It tells you why our Germany is in so much trouble and what we must do now! Now! Not tomorrow or next year!"

Now his face turned red, and he began his lambasting of Communists, Jews, and non-Aryans. Rocking back and forth on the balls of his feet, his voice roared, and his arms went in rhythm with his exhortations and condemnations. The crowd answered each rant with cheers and applause. The atmosphere gradually but steadily intensified, charged with electricity as the audience was swept up in his speech.

Abby reached for William's hand, and he squeezed hers to reassure her. Abby knew she was in a macabre scene, like nothing she had ever seen before. *This man acts insane, and these people adore him.*

Wrapping up his tirade after an hour, Hitler's sweat was running down his face and onto his brown uniform blouse even though it was a cool evening.

Abby was too engrossed as a spectator to take notes, but she noticed that William wrote keywords on his tablet without taking his eyes off Hitler. *An experienced reporter*, thought Abby.

It was late when the rally was over, and William walked Abby back to her apartment building.

"What do you think, Abby?"

"I'm afraid for Germany, William. Maybe the German people will wake up and somehow get rid of that man."

"Maybe." He paused. "Abby, I will be leaving Berlin for Budapest tomorrow afternoon. In the morning, you and I will write the story on what we saw tonight."

The next morning they sat together at a table in Shirer's office.

"We have to be cautious and objective with this news story. The United States still has a lot of pro-Hitler people. 'The Friends of New Germany' has been selling out arenas in several large cities, besides marching in any parade they can find."

*Peter, Hans, and Karl back in Atlantic City are doing their part for Hitler, and spying to boot*, thought Abby.

"Okay, Abby. Here we go."

He typed rapidly with his pipe in his mouth, stopping occasionally to gather his thoughts. He finished and handed two pages to Abby. Abby's name was below William's on the byline. She marveled at his skills of reporting the rally in a factual, almost neutral tone. He hinted at Hitler's ability to mesmerize the crowd, but noted that the audience was already loyal Nazis and was eager to hear him speak.

"I can't begin to suggest any changes, and I certainly don't deserve my byline with yours," said Abby.

"Oh, yes you do! You were with me. I observed the effect of Hitler's speech on you. You confirmed my feelings, and so you contributed to this story. Besides, they say Hitler reads everything written about him. He will see your name on the article. Maybe you can try for an interview with him while I'm wandering around Europe and the Middle East."

\* \* \*

Abby met old-line German generals and their wives at parties, and their conversation would eventually turn to Hitler. Their derision of Hitler was apparent. They called him the "little corporal," the "bristling martinet," and the "wallpaper hanger," the latter for his employment in Austria after his service in the war in 1918.

Abby also met exiled royalty from Russia, the White Russian opposition who fled after the Bolshevik revolution and after the murder of Czar Nicholas and his entire family in 1919. The titled families took refuge in Lithuania, Germany, Switzerland, the U.S., and other countries, usually where they had relatives.

At a Swiss Embassy party, Abby met a young woman about her age, Princess Lydia Viazensky, a White Russian, who with parents and three siblings barely escaped the purge of the Red Russian Bolsheviks. They had to leave their homes and land to the revolutionaries, carrying what personal possessions they could with them.

Lydia and Abby became good friends, perhaps because both had been chased by people who wanted to kill them. While Abby didn't tell Lydia about her recent terrifying experiences, Lydia seemed to sense that Abby had some underlying anxiety below her outward appearance of confidence. Lydia was a social butterfly and a chatterbox—a refreshing change for Abby. She reminded Abby of a young Hungarian actress, Zsa Zsa Gabor, who had just been crowned Miss Hungary and was in newsreels in movie theaters. Soon Lydia and her friends and relatives invited Abby on their occasional weekend train excursions to Bavaria, Vienna, and other places new to Abby. The exiled Russians loved to hear stories about America. Most of them were tutored in English when they were children, and were fascinated by Abby's accounts of her grandmother Cass' homesteading in Kansas and her harrowing experiences with renegade Indians. In turn, the displaced royalty opened new doors for introductions for Abby that helped her journalistic work at the *Tribune*.

It was a whole new world for Abby. The people she met were different and exciting. The ordeal with the Capone gang and the Wildcats began to fade into the past. Just as she was reflecting on that, she received a letter from Dan in London. "Save your money, Wildcat, the holidays are coming!"

*Yes, I pledged to them that I would go next year, and I will. Will it be the last time?*

\* \* \*

It was a crisp fall day in October when she was walking home through Tiergarten Park and a man approached her. He took off his hat and smiled. "Excuse me, Miss White. I'm Warren Walters from the American Embassy. I have never met you, but I have seen you from afar at celebrations at the Embassy." He showed her his Embassy pass.

Abby remembered seeing him but knew nothing about him, except he was tall and handsome with straight black hair combed back. "All right, Mr. Walters, I do remember you lurking in the halls of the Embassy. How can I help you?"

He laughed heartily. "Didn't know I looked so obvious!" He paused and gave an "aw shucks" facial expression. "Miss White, this is Embassy business. Can we go somewhere where we can talk in private?"

Abby was curious and pointed to the café where she and her friend, Carol, from the office, often had tea. They found a corner booth and ordered tea. It was quiet in the room since dinner patrons hadn't arrived yet.

"I will level with you, Miss White. I'm an intelligence agent in the U.S. Department of State. Washington assigned me to Berlin because of their increasing concern with the instability of the German government. They tell me that President Roosevelt is personally concerned with the rise of Adolf Hitler. His flaming rhetoric and militaristic leanings seems to be catching hold with ordinary German citizens."

"So, Mr. Walters, how does this concern me? Please get to the point." *About thirty-years old, more or less,* Abby thought.

Walters remembered hearing that Abby White didn't tolerate fools or boring talkers. The dossier on Abby White included the almost unbelievable experience of courageous students from Northwestern University evading the Capone organization. Their capture would have meant certain death. The report said Abby White had played a leadership role in the successful escape of the survivors, and, in their defense, was said to have killed at least one of the members of Capone's mob. Walters's agency believed that this was the caliber of person they needed for their work.

"May I call you Abby, Miss White?"

"You said this was Embassy business. Let's leave it 'Mr.' and 'Miss' for now. Please get on with it."

"All right, Miss White, here goes. We believe that you would be an excellent source of information who can help the United States determine if our country should really be concerned with recent events in Germany."

"You want me to be a spy, right?"

"Well, I guess that's what it's all about. I'd rather use the title, 'Agency Specialist.'"

"Sir, I have a great job, and I'm kept very busy. Sorry, Mr. Walters, you'll have to find someone else."

"Miss White, please, can we explore this a bit more? We have observed that you have made innumerable friends and acquaintances in your relatively short time in Germany. You know most of the highest ranked German generals and their wives, the Berlin press corps, expatriates like Princess Viazensky and her friends, and even made an acquaintance with Hitler himself. We have also observed that you are well respected by all parties. Even more, they enjoy your company. There is no one in Berlin who can be of greater help to our country and, for that matter, our friends in England and France."

"It looks like your people have done their background work, but your flag waving doesn't move me," said Abby. "I'm sure your dossier includes my very harrowing experiences with a vicious criminal organization that killed some of my friends. I love my country, but I don't need that risk anymore. Since I have been in Berlin I watched the Brownshirts club a little man to death when he went after Hitler. They would not hesitate to do the same to anyone, man or woman, who crossed their leader. No, I'm afraid you have the wrong person, Mr. Walters."

Abby rose from her chair. "You are an effective recruiter, sir. I'm sure you will find your man or woman. Thanks for the tea, handsome." She walked quickly out the door.

Walters shook his head, made some notes, and finished his tea.

# Chapter Nineteen

*London*

Dan read Abby's letter before the second holiday trip to Gstaad in December:

> I'm looking forward to our reunion in Gstaad with you, Esther, and Sean. I trust you will make the same reservations at the ski lodge with Esther and me sharing a room. However, I do want to make a change in our relationship while there. I'd rather not bunk with you as I did last year. That just happened, and I will take responsibility for that. It was very nice, but I have changed somewhat in how I want to go forward with my life and career.
>
> As I have said before, I think we naturally bonded together during and after that terrifying experience with the Capone mob. Our lives could have ended at any minute. You were my hero and the bravest man I have ever known, and probably will ever know.
>
> I simply need my space now that things are back to a relatively normal life. It's not that I have a sweetheart here in Berlin. I'm very busy trying to get established in my work for the *Tribune*, as I'm sure you are with the *Times*.
>
> Please don't take this as a personal affront. I do care for you, Dan, but I wonder if our love was genuine or just a necessary closure to our terrible misadventure. Maybe things will

change with time. Write soon with our plans for meeting in Lausanne.

    Always your dearest friend, Abby.

Dan wasn't surprised by Abby's letter. Recently, her letters had been newsier and less romantic. Dan wrote back that he understood, and still looked forward to a fun weekend.

\* \* \*

Dan was enjoying his job at the *Times*. It was a challenge for him to meet story deadlines set for him by the editors. After work he would have a beer or two at a local pub frequented by newsmen and foreign correspondents. One evening he happened to sit next to a German correspondent at the bar, and a conversation started almost at once.

"Gerhard Kuntz of the *Dusseldorf Kritiker*. What's yours?"

"Dan O'Gara of the *Times* here in London. Hey, wait a minute. You speak English with hardly any accent, and you look more southern European than German. Are you pulling my leg?"

"Well, I will answer your questions in the order given, my curious friend."

"Now you sound like a German," said Dan.

Gerhard smiled. "My father had me tutored in English at an early age. He later told me that he believed English was necessary to conduct business in Europe, and for that matter, the business world. My grandfather founded the *Kritiker*, and my father was a junior editor before he went into the military in 1916. I think he was grooming me for the newspaper world, even when I was six years old.

"Now, to your straight-forward observation of my blood line. My mother was an Italian. Father met her while on holiday in Naples. She was a tour guide and a very pretty one at that. There was a whirlwind courtship, and they were married in Düsseldorf. I was born about six months later. Then something terrible happened in their relationship, and she deserted us to return to Italy. Father would never tell me what happened. He did keep a few pictures of her hidden in his desk at home, which, of course, I found in due time. Later I was told that she was killed in an auto accident outside of Rome. Gretchen, my nanny, was really my mother as far as I was concerned. My grandparents looked after me when Father left for military service. More than the short reply you expected, Dan O'Gara? That's what a couple of pints do to me."

"Thank you, Gerhard. A man with a very interesting background. A good start of an autobiography."

They soon learned that they had a common hatred of the British. Dan told him about his father being shot and now disabled, and his uncle getting killed in the Uprising.

Gerhard said that his father had served as an officer in the German army and was killed in the Battle of the Somme in 1917. "I was only thirteen at the time, and he was my hero. I still miss him. His army comrade told us that he had his hands up in surrender when a British bastard shot him dead. Dan, now that I know what the British did to your family, how do you work at the *Times* and stay sober?"

Dan laughed. "Because this is a great opportunity to learn the business side of writing. I've submerged my anger for the time being."

That seemed to satisfy Gerhard, but he brought it up again at a luncheon event the *Times* held for foreign correspondents. Dan was part of the host team. At the end of the event, Gerhard pulled Dan aside.

"Look, Dan, I know a way you can get back at the Brits without jeopardizing your job. The Germans are building their intelligence network, and they need a smart agent in London who gets around easily. As a German, I can only go so far without arousing suspicion."

"I don't understand. Why do they want to know what's happening in England? We're at peace. The Great War was over almost fourteen years ago."

"Good question, Dan. Every country wants to protect itself. The more it knows about other countries, the more secure it feels. We're talking about military intentions, offensive weapon arsenals, and defenses in place. I bet the Brits had undercover agents providing information in Ireland during your fight for freedom, and probably still have them there!"

"Well, yes, I'll grant you that. Dad talked about British agents posing as Irishmen." He looked Gerhard in the eyes and shook his hand. "I'll think about this. Here's my card. Call me after the holidays. I'll be out of town 'til then. Skiing in Switzerland."

# Chapter Twenty

***Gstaad, Switzerland***

It was a different kind of reunion when they met again at the Lausanne hotel, more serious and reflective and less collegiate. They had matured quickly. Dan led the Wildcats in their toast to their classmates who were killed that day on Clark Street in Chicago. But now there were no tears, and they didn't sing the Northwestern fight song, "*Go U North*." That terrible day seemed more remote as Esther, Abby, and Dan were now deeply immersed in their fledgling careers. Sean O'Connor was now an inducted, honorary member of the Wildcats for his heroic actions in Ireland. He had recently finished his degree in chemical engineering and was working as the technical manager at Patrick O'Gara's brewery plants. He and Esther had been corresponding weekly, and their relationship had become even stronger.

The group stayed at the same Gstaad skiing lodge, The Saanenland. Abby told Esther that she had decided not to sleep with Dan and the reasons why. She suggested that Esther get her own room if she wanted to be with Sean.

Esther told Sean, "My dear, loving letter writer. Would you join me in my private room?"

Sean nodded and smiled. "Sorry, Dan. Hate to leave you!"

The skiing conditions were near perfect. Fresh snow had fallen during the night, and the massive pine trees on the ski slopes were heavy with snow that sparkled in the sunlight. It was a holiday that was different from a year ago, "but still wonderful," Abby said to Esther. When they parted in Lausanne, there were no pledges to return for a reunion. They were no longer a group of college kids—they were now on their own in a tumultuous world.

# Chapter Twenty-one

*London—1932*

It was a harsh, bone-breaking winter in London that year. Dan pulled up the collar on his overcoat as he walked from the *Times* to meet Gerhard Kuntz at Jimmy's—a new hang-out for newspaper men.

"How was the skiing, Dan?"

"New snow. Great powder. Couldn't want for better trails."

Dan was still down from Abby's gentle rebuff at Gstaad. A shot of whiskey before his beer didn't help his dark mood.

"Well, I spent Christmas with my grandparents in Dresden," said Gerhard. "I did manage to get away with my fiancé. We set the date for our wedding. August something. Guess I'd better show up."

Dan chuckled but made no response. *Where did I go wrong with Abby? Okay, stop it, it's over! Find yourself a girl here in London.*

"Hey, Dan. Did you get a chance to think about serving the cause?"

"Yes, I did. Will I need a trench coat and magnifying glass?"

Gerhard slapped Dan on the back. "Good decision, pal!"

He lowered his voice. "Headquarters said if it was a 'go' with you, I should ask you to try to get assigned to the political/military desk at the *Times*. That would give you better exposure to the information that is important to us. Even the most mundane 'off-the-record' or 'I-shouldn't-tell-you-this' can carry valuable intelligence data. Our office in Germany can piece together what you provide with information from other agents. They call it the 'jigsaw puzzle method.'"

He looked directly at Dan, who still seemed somewhat unresponsive. "Are you sure you want to help, Dan?"

Dan thought of his father and uncle. "Yes, I'm sure."

"All right. Can you meet me this weekend? I need to go into more detail with you. It's too bloody cold to sit outside, and it's too noisy here. There is a quiet restaurant called Shakespeare across the street from the entrance to the Tower of London Exhibition Hall. Meet you there at two o'clock on Saturday. Okay?"

* * *

The sleet-laden wind was whipping capriciously around the streets of London as Dan reached Shakespeare's Pub and Grill. Gerhard was sipping on hot tea in a booth in the rear, smoking a cigarette. Most of the noon diners had left.

Dan ordered tea and scones. They waited until the server left to begin talking.

"Dan, you need to sign this contract with our intelligence bureau before we begin. This confirms your allegiance to Germany and the Nazi party, and puts you on our payroll."

Dan read the paper, signed it, and pushed it back to Gerhard.

"You will be paid handsomely and given special rewards for superior information, and for carrying out special missions. I might add that we had done extensive background checks on you, as you might imagine. We realize that your family is well-off and you have a decent salary with the *Times*. You probably don't need the money as much as some. I suspect your satisfaction will come with giving it back to the Brits for trampling Ireland."

Dan squirmed on his seat and smiled.

"We also know about your skirmishes with Capone's mob. You did some amazing things to protect your friends. In American terms, you are 'one tough guy.' That's what we need—resourcefulness, skills, and a cool approach to possible mayhem.

"Your code name will be 'Lightning.' That's how you will sign any messages to me. No real names. Mine is 'Fox Den.' Here is the address to drop your messages to us and pick up messages from us. Here is your key. There are no other mailboxes or residents at that address, but other agents may be using that drop box. We own the building through a surrogate. Memorize the address and burn the paper. I will be checking the box every day. We will meet like this every two months or so. I will let you know the time and place. No more meeting after work for a pint."

Gerhard went into detail regarding covert ways to get intelligence data, then passed him a large padded envelope containing a Sida miniature photo camera with instructions, several rolls of film, and a small Sauer Model 2930 handgun with a box of ammunition. "You may never need the gun if you execute your missions with skill. It's just for insurance."

"What if they catch me?" asked Dan.

"You will be arrested, questioned, and probably be deported to Ireland. Your job at the *Times* will be lost, but we will find you another spot in a country friendly with us. Are you still with me? It's not too late to turn back."

"I'm okay, Gerhard."

It was late afternoon when they left Shakespeare's. The sleet had changed to snow. Dan wrapped his wool scarf around his face and pulled his hat down. He trudged to his apartment in the deepening snow. *What have I gotten myself into?* He stopped and looked up. The sky was iron-gray and cold, like his world. And he seemed to be getting lost in its grayness.

# Chapter Twenty-two

*Nice, France*

Esther sat on the patio of a coffee shop on the Promenade des Anglais, enjoying the warm sun and her view of the Mediterranean Sea. The surf was quiet and just a bit frothy. The pale green seawater changed rapidly to a teal blue as the sea deepened. She relaxed and reread her letter to Sean, making sure it was the best she could do before mailing:

> Your letters were forwarded to me from Lyon. I'm sorry I haven't written before this, but my life has been in a bit of turmoil lately. My sister, Silvia, saved your letters from destruction, and mailed them to me after I sent her my new address.
> 
> It wasn't long after our wonderful time in Gstaad that I discovered I was pregnant. My dear parents weren't so dear then. They are Jews of the most orthodox kind. They said they were "horrified"—probably not much different from the reaction of Irish Christian parents, except mine told me I would have to move out of Lyon. "Disappear in shame" was the term my mother used. To be impregnated by a "goy," a gentile, was apparently the worse kind of evil in their minds. They are not bad people, just firmly immersed in strict ethics, which are passed down by generations.
> 
> As my mother gathered my things together, I went to my newspaper office and talked with my editor. He said he had a good friend, Joseph Foch, who was the editor-in-chief at the

*Nice Phare*. With my permission, he called him immediately. Mr. Foch was apparently familiar with my work in Lyon and said he would be pleased to take me, with child and all! He and his wife met my train and helped me find a suitable apartment not far from the *Phare's* office. They are very caring people and seem to have adopted me.

I want to have this baby, Sean. If it is a boy, I know he'll be as strong and as handsome and kind as his father. If it's a girl, I will love and protect her also.

Sean, you should not let this change your life one bit. Remember, I invited you to *my* room at Gstaad. I will be just fine. As I left, my father slipped me sufficient funds to last. Take care of yourself, Sean, and don't drink too much of Mr. O'Gara's beer.

As ever, Esther

# Chapter Twenty-three

*Ireland—Sean*

Sean told Patrick and Darcy O'Gara at their cottage that he was leaving Ireland for Nice to be with Esther. "I will marry her if she will have me."

With Dan in London, Sean's leaving would leave a vacuum in their lives. Patrick tried to make light of it as he began to tear up. "Well, it's about time you went out on your own. It took Esther to get you moving from under your security blanket here." His tears started. "Oh, Sean, we will miss you, dear lad. It's a good thing your parents have more sons. They won't miss you as much as we will. I'll be sad to see the back of you when you leave."

"Patrick, now we have good reason for a trip to the French Riviera!" said Darcy.

Darcy, Cormac, and Sally shed their tears when Patrick brought Sean by the cottage for a last goodbye. A driver and Patrick drove Sean to the port of Wexford to catch the same ferry, the *SS Waterford*, which Abby and Esther had taken on rough seas to France. After reaching Le Havre, Sean trained to Paris, and then caught an express train down through the south of France to Nice.

Sean reviewed his French books on the train. He found that *Nice Phare*, Esther's newspaper, meant "Nice Lighthouse" in French. He had taken elective French classes, both written and conversational, along with his required engineering curricula. He wanted to surprise Esther, but now, he mused, his new ability in French might also help him get work in Nice.

## Chapter Twenty-four

*Nice—A Marriage*

Sean had written Esther that he was coming to Nice to stay. His letter arrived two days before Sean.

*Oh, my, I truly hope it's not because he wants to do the "right thing,"* thought Esther.

Esther's fears were unfounded. Sean jumped from the train at the Nice train station and ran the length of the platform to hug and kiss Esther. "*Je t'aime beaucoup,*" he said. (I love you very much.) "No, I mean, *je t'aime a la folie!*" (I love you madly!)

They were married the following weekend with John and Maria Foch as their witnesses. The Fochs were in their fifties and had no children of their own. They told Esther and Sean that they were "destined" to help them and their unborn child.

It didn't take long for Sean to find work. The French government was starting to rebuild their navy, and Nice had a large shipbuilder that needed engineers.

Esther restarted her personal interviews on the street in Nice for the *Nice Phare* until she needed a maternity leave. The newspaper made a short printed announcement of her temporary leave, but the newspaper's office still received many telephone calls asking what happened to the "Esther's Friends" column, so they had to print her leave announcement several times.

Daniel O'Connor, a healthy eight-pounder with curly locks of red hair, was born on a beautiful day in September. Sean and Esther agreed to name him after Dan O'Gara, their good friend and comrade against the Capone gang.

They loved Nice and made new friends with couples who had small children like Daniel. But soon, as world events unfolded, their idyllic lives would change forever.

## Chapter Twenty-five

*Berlin—Warren Walters, 1933*

It had been months since Warren Walters of the American Embassy met Abby. She liked the man, but she wasn't going to call him. She had been very busy at the *Tribune*, and besides, she was seeing more of Claus von Fritsch who was making more trips from London to Berlin on military business.

"Warren Walters here, Miss White. Remember me?" he telephoned.

"Let me think. Wait, you're the fellow Yankee who disappeared after a tea date some years ago."

"Hey, it hasn't been that long." He paused. "Well, all right, it's high time we meet again. How about tea after you get off work, say about six o'clock?"

"At that time of day, I'd rather have a glass of Merlot. There's a pub I like called Mozart's. Know it?"

"See you there at six, Miss White."

They sat in a dark corner of a cavern-like room with old tapestries on the walls and ordered wine. A gray-haired pianist in tails played a piece from Mozart's *Don Giovanni* softly in the background. Abby loved this place. This was *her* place to wind down after the daily bustle at the *Tribune*. She looked intently at Warren. *Thin but athletic, a hard and handsome face, as if carved out of marble.*

"Thank you for meeting with me once again, Miss White."

"All right, call me Abby. Is Warren your real name, you cloak-and-dagger person?"

He smiled. "Yes, Warren Walters. Warren to you."

"Do they call you War for short? That *is* an aggressive name."

Abby leaned across the table. "I'm giving you a hard time, Warren, because I'm testing your verve and patience all at one time."

"Why?"

"Because I would like to know you better, and I have the innate feeling that I will *need* to know you better and develop a trust in you. These are times when we all need trustworthy friends. Meeting once a year won't do it."

"Well, I can tell you that I'm a Midwesterner like you. Born in St. Louis and went to Cornell. My father served four years as the mayor of St. Louis. I did graduate work in political science at Georgetown, which led me to work in the State Department."

He smoothed his hair with one hand and frowned. "Never married—too busy I guess. I consider this embassy work to be a stepping stone for me. I'm looking for the big moment to break away from the rank-and-file government nerds and be a well-known international figure. I want my parents to be proud of me—especially my mother. Time for a little story, Abby. When I was about five playing in the next room, I heard my mother telling a visiting female friend, 'Warren is such a dolt, nothing like his older brother. I can't wait till he reaches the age of reason, then I'll put him up for adoption.' The visitor chuckled. I still remember that day. After that I was always trying to please her so she wouldn't send me away." He paused. "My mother had a year at Vassar and never got over it. Even with strangers she meets for the first time, it's 'that reminds me of my time at Vassar…' I don't like her attempt at elitism, but at the same time I unconsciously try to emulate her."

"Warren, why are you telling me this? I hardly know you."

"I don't know. You seem like a good listener. I really have no one at the Embassy to whom I can tell personal things."

She changed the subject. "Do you have your 'Special Agent' yet?"

"No, Abby, I'm still holding out for the best prospect—you."

"I am now somewhat interested, Warren, but I still need more information about you personally, and more about your work background and training. You have covert people who dug up all the facts on me. I don't have that luxury. If I am going to trust my life with your organization, I must know more—period!"

"I understand. The big boys said they could give you a top-secret clearance if you joined us. I'll have to get their approval again. You'll then have to sign a loyalty, nondisclosure contract. It's done with everyone, including me and the big boys. There's always somebody 'bigger' in the intelligence service. After signing, I can tell you a lot more."

"Well, tell me in general, what would American Intelligence want me to do?"

"To start, just listen, do some eavesdropping on conversations. As we talked about before, you are privy to some of the top military and political people in Berlin at the parties for the elite. You are now well-respected as a journalist and are somewhat of a celebrity in your own right. You are good friends with the von Fritsch's, and that's pretty special. People might talk 'off the record' or 'don't quote me on this.' That could be important information.

"For example, a ranked general officer might remark that he is leaving for field exercises in the Stuttgart area. Since the German military is still under restrictions, according to the Treaty of Versailles, this would be good intelligence data. We can piece together what we learn from other sources to get the whole picture."

"How would I get the information to you?" asked Abby.

"We have a series of mail drop stations. Each agent is given specific instructions. That's enough for now, Abby. The next time we meet, I will bring a contract to sign and some tools of the trade. Do you still carry that Beretta?"

"How did you know that? Yes, I always carry it in my purse. It's fully loaded with hollow-point slugs. There may be Mafia friends of Capone who are still inclined to try something, even though Capone is in prison for tax evasion. Will that be a problem?"

"No, Abby. It will save us giving you a weapon for protection."

He paused. "Thank you for meeting with me again, Abby. I *did* call your office last winter during the holidays, and they said you were away on a short leave. Did you have a pleasant time?"

"Oh, yes. College alumni friends now living on the continent and in Britain had a skiing reunion at Gstaad in Switzerland. Are you familiar with Gstaad?"

"Ha! Hold onto your seat for my little story about Gstaad. You said you wanted to know more about me personally. Here's more. Skied there but once. Just once! I was by myself on a business trip to Lausanne, and decided to take a break and go skiing. I got lost high up on the mountains. Didn't see the way down. Trail markings seemed nonexistent. It was snowing harder, turning into a white-out and starting to get dark. The slopes were turning icy. I needed a miracle. Then an older couple skied up to me from nowhere and asked if I needed help. I swallowed my pride. Yes! They led me down to safety. They were from Bern and skied Gstaad often. At the base of the mountain, we had a couple of beers and a long conversation. We still exchange letters. I visited their chalet once. Lovely people, the Bexels. I always thought their place would make a good 'safe house' if I ever need it in my intelligence work. Switzerland will always be neutral since many individuals, corporations, and countries stash their money there for safety, even the Nazis…"

"Warren, before we part, an important question: If I become an agent, what would the Germans do if they would catch me?"

"You are an American citizen and would take immediate refuge in our Embassy. We have our sources within German police and military offices to warn us that one of our Americans is in trouble. By international law, a country's embassy buildings and grounds are considered sacrosanct. The Embassy here in Berlin is as American as the White House! We are not at war with Germany, but they would probably say you are 'a persona non grata' and would ask that you be expelled. You wouldn't be effective at the *Tribune* or as an agent, so you would probably go home to the U.S. or wherever you choose."

He touched Abby's hand. "Abby, we will help you be a good agent and be safe. Not to worry."

"All right, Warren, let's go forward. By the way, I know some German aliens in America who were gathering intelligence on our military installations. Ran into them on our escape from the mob. So I want to even the score."

"Now *that* would be interesting for Washington to know," said Warren. "We can report this after you sign on. Okay? I'll call you when we have the agreement ready."

That night in her apartment, Abby took a break from writing letters and walked to her window overlooking downtown Berlin. *You wanted adventures like Grandmother Cass had. It looks like you're going to get more of them.*

# Chapter Twenty-six

*Atlantic City*

Karl Kruger, Peter Farber, and Hans Strasser sat on the deck of their Atlantic City, New Jersey, beach house ruminating about the coded message they'd just received from Germany:

Achtung Atlantic City-
 Close operations and return to Berlin as soon as possible. Report to 122 Friedrichstrasse for reassignment. Carry all relevant secret material to Germany and burn the rest. Wipe off all fingerprints on your weapons and bury them carefully in a remote place. Acknowledge receipt.
 Hans Oster
 Abwehr Chief

Karl wasn't surprised. A U.S. Congress investigation concluded that The Friends of New Germany organization represented a branch of Hitler's Nazi party in America.

"I'll be glad to be back home again," said Peter. "Germany is returning to greatness with Hitler as our leader. We'll be more a part of it now." The three agents spent the evening mulling over Hitler's rise to power.

Hitler had been elected Reich Chancellor of Germany by a desperate populace who believed that Hitler was a preferable alternative to continuing with a feeble government doing little in the steep financial depression.

After a fire in the Reichstag building, allegedly set by Communists according to the Nazis, Hitler quickly turned the nation's fragile democracy into a one-party dictatorship. The Nazis then controlled all aspects of German life and promoted the myth of "Aryan" racial superiority and aggressive anti-Semitism. In addition, Hitler considered the Brownshirt SA as a competitor and had its leaders killed, including Ernst Roehm. The most heinous regime in modern history had begun—Hitler's Third Reich.

# Chapter Twenty-seven

*London—1934*

Gerhard Kuntz thought about his last meeting with Dan O'Gara. *Will he be a good agent for us? We'll know soon enough.*

An SS instructor in Germany once told him that certain persons have a natural predilection to live in that curious world of espionage and deceit. Those persons make good spies. Gerhard himself liked to walk the exciting tightrope in serving his Fatherland of Germany as a spy in England.

Dan's performance at the *Times* of London put him in good standing with his editors, and he was able to parlay that into a move to the political/military desk at the newspaper—exactly where Gerhard wanted him to be.

His press credentials and security clearance allowed him to attend briefings at the Prime Minister's headquarters and to gain access to certain military projects. His past history showed no evidence of any subversive activity. In fact, his recent brave fight against criminals was noted as a plus. He had an open license for spying.

On a drive south of London to cover a story, he noticed workmen erecting a metal platform behind a chain-link fence. There was an armed guard standing watch at the gate. He stopped his car and wandered over to the guard who told him to get in his car and move on. Dan showed him his press card and security clearance pass, and then chatted up the guard who was glad for someone to talk with during his boring duty. It wasn't long before Dan had the guard laughing at his jokes.

"So, what's going on here?" asked Dan.

"Oh, some new special equipment. I think they call it radar. Uses radio waves to detect things flying in the air, they say." said the guard.

After a few more jokes, Dan continued on his way. A message to Gerhard was left in the mail drop box that night.

The following morning, he received an urgent message from his mother, Darcy, telling him that his father was very ill. "Please come home as soon as possible."

# Chapter Twenty-eight

*Ireland—Patrick*

Dan was soon at the bedside of his father, whose old injuries from the fight for Ireland's independence had taken their toll.

"Dan," Patrick whispered. "I'm glad you were so close in London instead of America. Don't think I'm going to make it."

Dan waited for his mother to leave the room, and then told his father of his work for the Germans. "I'm doing it to get revenge for what the Brits did to you, Uncle John, and Ireland."

"Oh, son, you're playing a dangerous game, you are. What happened to me and John is old history. Besides, John and I shot our share of Brits in return, you bet. Don't ruin your life over what happened to us. Please! I need you to watch over your mother. She's a strong woman, but she will need your help. I'm sorry to have to ask things of you, Dan. You're the only one she will have. I wish we could have had more children…now let's pray together. I hope I will see you someday after."

Patrick died the next day. There was a typical Irish wake with the open casket in the living room and an Irish flag draped over the end of the casket. A celebration of Patrick's life went on with many anecdotes told about Patrick. Shamrock Beer from Patrick's brewery, and laughter, were in abundance.

Darcy sat with Dan on the veranda of their home on the evening after Patrick's burial. She finally took time to cry, and cry she did, resting her head on Dan's shoulder. Then she reminisced about her life with Patrick, telling Dan stories that he had never heard before—like when they had first met. She said she was with another young man at a church dance when Patrick walked between them and introduced himself, with barely a nod to the other fellow. She told her mother about this "brash, loudmouth who drove off her date." Dan laughed, and then he cried with her.

"Mother, I'm coming home after I tie things up in London."

"Dan, no. I'll be just fine, you hear? You have a good career going for you in London. You have your life to live, just as we have had ours. I still have Cormac and Sally, and a very good manager at the brewery. Don't you worry about me."

He spent a few more days in Kinsale helping Darcy wrap up matters with their lawyer. Before he left he wrote letters to Sean and Esther in Nice, and to Abby in Berlin.

# Chapter Twenty-nine

*London*

Soon after Dan returned to his apartment in London, there were letters of sympathy. Sean was beside himself. Patrick was like another father to Sean—and to Abby and Esther he was the wonderful man who'd protected them from Capone's goons.

Dan settled back into his job at the *Times*, still deliberating on what he should do. His mother, Darcy, was very adamant about Dan continuing his career in London. He made his mind up after picking up a terse note from Gerhard Kuntz:

> Lightning. Where have you been? I expected you back from Ireland a week ago. Bring your latest observations to our regular place on Saturday, the 7th, at 0900. Also, bring your bag for a short overnight trip. Fox Den

Dan dropped a note confirming the meeting, and told him of his father's death.

He arrived at Shakespeare's before Gerhard and ordered tea. Gerhard came through the door with the usual burning cigarette dangling from his lips. He smoked German cigarettes, which gave off a trail of foul smoke.

"Well, Dan, why have you been gone so long? You have a responsibility to our organization that is higher than your responsibility to the *Times* or your family. Did you bring everything I asked?"

"Yes. But Gerhard, I must resign from your organization and my *Times* position and return to help my mother now that my dad has died. I'm all she has now. I will help run our family business."

Gerhard smiled—actually, it was more like a smirk. "Sorry, Dan. You will keep your job at the *Times* and continue to serve as our agent. Germany is very anxious to hear details about the radar site you found in England. It is of major importance to Hitler and Hermann Goering, his deputy in charge our air force plans."

Dan rose from the table. "Goodbye, Gerhard."

"Stop there, Dan. I have a gun trained on you under the table. I was prepared for your 'poor mama' proposed exit. It won't work. You have signed a contract with us."

Gerhard stood up. "There is a car waiting for us outside. Walk quietly to the door ahead of me. My Luger will be in my coat pocket trained on you, so don't even think of running." At the curb, he motioned to the driver. "Get out and frisk him and then go through his bag. He may have a gun." There was no one on the sidewalk near them to take notice.

He had Dan move to the front passenger side door. "Get in. I'll be right behind you with my gun to your neck."

"No, gun, sir," said the driver after frisking Dan and checking his suitcase.

Gerhard laughed. "What kind of an agent are you? Forgetting you weapon!"

He told the driver. "Keep your gun on him while I make a phone call."

Finally, the sedan moved slowly away from the curb and then weaved into traffic. Gerhard spoke some orders in German to the driver.

"Where are we going?" asked Dan.

Neither the driver nor Gerhard answered.

Dan didn't know the English roads that well, but he determined that they were headed northeast after passing through Colchester. They bypassed the port city of Harwich and finally reach the small harbor town of Bawdeey and drove slowly to a small marina. An ocean-going speedboat was tied up to a dock with a small crew standing by. No one at the marina paid much attention to the boat or the two passengers now going aboard.

Gerhard spoke in German to the captain and the two crew members, telling them that Dan was a reluctant passenger. "He is not to escape. Shoot him only if necessary."

"Okay, Gerhard, cut the crap. Where are we going, and when are you going to let me go?" said Dan.

"Sorry, Dan, you don't need to know the answer to either question."

The speedboat sped northeast through the upper English Channel into the North Sea.

# Chapter Thirty

*Wilhelmshaven, Germany*

It was after midnight when the bow of the boat bounced through wave crests as it slowed to enter a port. A large sign on the dock was lighted in the darkness and read *"Willkommen zu Wilhelmshaven."*

*Damn. I'm in Germany!* thought Dan.

They were greeted at the dock by an officer and three soldiers, all wearing black uniforms with swastika bands on their left arms.

"Ah, the new SS uniforms for Hitler's elite storm troopers," said Gerhard.

"What does SS mean," asked Dan.

"*Schutzstaffel,*" said Gerhard. "Protection Squad."

Gerhard repeated the words that he had used with the boat crew, and the SS troopers immediately surrounded Dan.

Their cars stopped at a government building that had been darkened by soot and age from its original limestone grandeur. There were bars on the windows.

Dan was ushered into a room that was bare except for a table and four chairs. A single window was blackened from the inside, and there was a large mirror on one wall.

He was left alone for an uncomfortable half-hour. Finally, Gerhard came through the door followed by a short, bald man about fifty, wearing a plain black suit with a white shirt and a black tie. His pasty-white, oval face was nearly covered with thick, round glasses.

"Dan, meet Major Albert Hofer, of the SD unit of the SS-Gestapo. The SD is the intelligence section of the Gestapo."

Hofer smiled and sat opposite Dan and put a portfolio on the table. Gerhard took the chair to Hofer's left.

"Mr. O'Gara. How do you do?" He spoke in broken English. "I want to ask you some questions about your work for us. First, do you need any water or food?"

"No, thank you. What is this all about?"

"Well, according to your report to Gerhard, you obtained some good, but limited, information for us on your country road travels, but now you want to resign. This presents a dilemma for us as you can understand, I trust."

"As I told Gerhard, my father died unexpectedly. Since I am an only child, I need to go home and to help my mother and run the family business."

Hofer rose from his chair and paced around the room. "A noble desire, young man, but not in keeping with the agreement you recently signed with us. We expect better from you."

"I didn't expect my father to die either. Things have changed."

"All right," said Hofer. "Why didn't you take pictures of this so-called radar installation?"

"Because there was a guard there, and I didn't want to arouse his suspicions."

Hofer compressed his lips. "Hmm. All right. Here's some paper and a pencil. Please sketch a picture of what you saw."

"There wasn't much to what I saw. They had apparently just started construction."

Dan talked as he sketched. "There was a concrete pad about forty meters by twenty meters with steel stanchions about ten meters high rising on the pad's four corners. There were cross-bar reinforcement rods in the middle, like this. I didn't know what it was, but the guard mentioned radar after I showed him my security clearance."

Hofer smiled and held his hands out, palms up. "Well, that doesn't tell us much, does it? By now, there has to be a much larger structure. We need you to go back and take pictures. We also need to know the locations of other such installations, if any, the British pigs may be erecting."

"Sir, I told you that I must resign and go back to Ireland to help my mother."

"Mr. O'Gara. Dan. I will put it to you plainly. If you don't carry out your assignments, there will be no mother to help. Understand?" Hofer pounded on the table. "This is of the upmost importance to the Fatherland and to our Fuehrer!"

Dan started to sweat. "Are you telling me you would harm my mother? My God, what kind of people are you?"

"We are patriots, like you pledged to be."

"Why not use one of your other agents?" Dan said.

"We have an investment in you. You have a key position in London. You have a press pass. You have a security clearance. You have signed our contract. And there is more at stake here than one or two people's lives," Hofer said.

Hofer walked to the door and Gerhard followed. "When you have made up your mind, tell the guard at the door that you want to see us."

Dan sat in the room thinking. *I've seen what gangsters can do, and these people are gangsters. I was so wrong.* He explored his options—there were few. *I'll negotiate this.* He called to the guard.

When Hofer and Gerhard returned to the room, Dan stood up. "Okay, I will take pictures and try to find out about other locations. The latter may be difficult, but I may be able to use my press card and security clearance pass to snoop around, as if I'm writing a story. I may have to pay off people to get this information. Are you prepared to provide money for this?"

Hofer smiled broadly. "That's better, Dan. Yes, we can funnel the money through Gerhard, who will remain your handler," said Hofer.

Dan looked at both of them. "Now, after I do these assignments, I want out of that contract, and I want it in writing."

It was now Hofer's time to pace again. "We'll see about that when the time comes. Right now, you are in no position to make demands of us. Take him back to London in the morning, Gerhard, so he can go to work. I don't think there's any need to guard him now."

Hofer extended his hand to Dan. Dan wouldn't shake it. Hofer turned on his heels and opened the door. He looked over his shoulder and grinned. "Say hello to Darcy O'Gara in Kinsale for us."

## Chapter Thirty-one

**Berlin—Abby's Contract**

"Hello, Abby. This is Warren. Can you meet me at Mozart's after work tomorrow?"

It was late in the evening. Abby was in her nightgown reading by the small fireplace in her apartment. "Let's see. Okay, at six o'clock? Are you buying? I'll be hungry this time."

"I'll pick up the check, you poor waif. See you then."

Germans, like most Europeans, tended to eat later in the evening, so Mozart's was still quiet as Abby and Warren sipped on their glasses of cabernet. The pianist was playing an obscure, haunting sonata by Franz Liszt, which covered their conversation. Warren passed a paper across the table to Abby along with a pen. "This is the contract, Abby. Please read it carefully. It's mostly about your acting as an agent for, and your allegiance to, the United States."

"Who drew this up, Warren?"

"It comes from the Intelligence branch in Washington, D. C. It's a standard form that we all must sign."

Warren studied Abby as she read the agreement by candlelight. *What an elegant lady—so beautiful, bright, and self-assured*, he thought.

"I see nothing wrong with me signing this, Warren. Let's get on with it." She signed and then passed the paper back to him. "Do you have a carbon copy or another blank form for my records?"

"Abby, I wouldn't recommend that you keep a copy of this. It could be incriminating if someone would find it on your person or in your apartment.

We will keep a copy of this on microfilm at the Embassy in a secured place. You can review it there if necessary. The original will be sent by diplomatic pouch to our Washington office."

"All right. What's next? I'm getting hungry."

Warren shook his head and chuckled. "Here's a package for you. There's no weapon since you said that you still carried your Beretta. It's a Zeiss Ikon camera and a user's manual, Abby. It has multiple lenses so that you can take pictures of documents or battleships. We've included several rolls of film."

"Who is 'we'? Abby asked. "Whom should I contact if you're not available?"

"Getting to that. You are to go to the American Embassy in an emergency. Take your press pass and other personal identification with you. Go to the desk and ask for 'Ben Franklin.' The Marine guards will let you in without questions. There will be an agent there in quick order. In an emergency, don't try calling on the telephone from your apartment—your line may be tapped—just get to the Embassy."

Abby put the camera package in her purse. "Can we order now, Warren? I'm famished."

Over dinner, Warren continued. "Your code name will be High Mountains. Mine is Dark Cave. We'll use these names to sign messages to each other. If it is urgent that I see you, include 'there is snow in the mountains' in your message. Use block letters in your messages. Personal handwriting is like leaving fingerprints. That's also why it is best to use gloves when sending messages."

Warren looked around slowly at the tables nearby. More patrons were being seated. Warren slid a small envelope across the table and lowered his voice. "Here is a note with an address on it and two keys. There is a small apartment building at that address, which our agency controls. It's not far from your apartment. The larger key opens the outer door to the building, and the smaller key is for the message drop box located on the wall to the left as you enter. Now, please memorize the address and pass the paper back to me. I'll burn it."

During dessert and coffee, Warren asked Abby to repeat what he had told her. She did.

"Excellent, Abby."

"When will we meet again?" Abby asked.

"Not as often as I would like. It may be sometime. We must be careful. They are not nice people, the Gestapo. There seems to be a lot of recent activity by Hitler's crew, so just listen for now—maybe there will be more loose talk at the parties you attend. Take no chances, Abby," Warren said as they left Mozart's.

"The same for you, handsome," Abby said. Then they chanced a hug and a kiss in the darkness.

"Not a good start, Abby. My fault."

\* \* \*

As the years rolled on, Abby was feeling some guilt about not going back to Indiana for a visit, but letters from home reassured her that all was well with the family, and that her father's business had stabilized despite the continuing financial depression. She believed she had enough to do with keeping her job at the *Tribune* while others were losing theirs. With the decrease in the bureau's staff, Abby had a greater load. Her assignments were interesting—she was sent to interview Mussolini, De Gaul, and the fascist dictator of Spain, Franco. She couldn't leave for the U.S. anyway, especially with this new, exciting role with U.S. Intelligence.

In Germany, Hitler's rise to dictatorship was welcomed by the German people as they grasped at political straws. The Nazi Party was seen as their best way out of the Depression. The people looked the other way when Nazi students at Berlin University burned Jewish and leftist books in front of their school buildings. The average person began to accept Hitler's blaming the Jews for all their troubles. No one questioned Hitler when Jews were banned from positions in the Nazi-run city and state government offices.

Abby joined Claus von Fritsch and his parents at parties as usual. Abby sensed that the parties among the elite seemed to serve as a catharsis for all the upheaval in Berlin. Her friend, Princess Lydia Viazensky, the Russian expatriate, still the party animal, loved to tell Abby the latest rumors about the Nazi government. She had no idea that Abby was now a spy.

"Abby, the Nazi military is getting it together again despite the restrictions of the Treaty of Versailles. A young captain confided to me in a whisper that they are secretly building submarines—U-boats, they are called—at hidden locations and are sending future crew members to other countries for training. Not only that, they are training pilots by using gliding clubs."

The next day Abby left her first message in Warren's drop box, which detailed Lydia's observations. "Needs confirmations," Abby added.

The unexpected happened at the *Tribune* office one day when a letter addressed to "Miss Abby White" was received. The return address was The Ministry of Propaganda. Abby opened the letter with trepidation. *Have they found me out already?* Not so. The Nazi Propaganda Office had invited Abby to a special press briefing for a few selected international journalists.

Joseph Goebbels, Hitler's propaganda chief, had advised Hitler that he needed to "create a friendlier, more gentle and peaceful image" to the world so they could buy time to rebuild their military machine. Hitler finally agreed that it might be useful. He remembered Abby White and had told Goebbels to invite her. The weekend press conference would be held in Berchtesgaden, high in the Bavarian Alps, where Hitler kept a home. Abby's Berlin bureau chief, James Hoffman, was delighted with Abby's opportunity. It would certainly bring prestige to the Berlin *Tribune* bureau and help cement their position with the editors and publishers back in Chicago who were trying to cut costs due to the Depression.

"Go, Abby," Hoffman, said. "But watch out for Goebbels. He has a sarcastic, razor-sharp wit—a clever, diabolical man who preys on women."

# Chapter Thirty-two

*Berchtesgaden, Germany*

Abby read about her destination on her train ride. Berchtesgaden was a small and colorful Bavarian town, surrounded by Watzmann Mountains at 8,900 feet and the Mountains of Steinererne Meer, all which measured more than 6,000 feet. The conference hotel, Berchtesgaden Hof Hotel, was frequented by famous visitors over the years, such as General Erwin Rommel of the German Army and Heinrich Himmler, Hitler's chief deputy, and the English leaders, Neville Chamberlin and David Lloyd George.

It was also the place where Hitler kept his girlfriend, Eva Braun. For appearance purposes, she was not allowed to stay in Hitler's mountain villa, the Berghof. Now Hitler told her to go home and visit before conference visitors arrived at the hotel.

The selected correspondents were from England, France, the United States, Italy, Sweden, and Switzerland. Abby was the only female in the group. They all were searched by the Gestapo when they entered the Berchtesgaden Hof Hotel. Abby had her Beretta strapped to the inside of her thigh, in a soft leather holster. It was a small, lightweight gun, so it was comfortable, and it was comforting to have it so close to her. A guard started to pat around her legs, but the ranking Gestapo officer said, "Nein!"

The journalists were served an excellent dinner with a very good Bavarian wine provided. Abby was surprised since she had heard that Hitler did not favor liquor, very rarely drank wine or beer, and never smoked. Hitler did not appear at the dinner. Goebbels suggested an early retirement to prepare for the morning conference.

Goebbels had choreographed the setting for the press conference held on the large, inlaid stone veranda at the rear of the hotel. When the correspondents arrived after breakfast, Hitler was seated in the warm sun with his German shepherd at his feet and one of Goebbels' little daughters on his lap. Abby noted that he was wearing the same forest green Bavarian suit that he'd worn at the Olympic site months earlier. Goebbels said pictures were permitted, and flashbulbs started popping. *How can this peaceful-looking man with a little girl on his lap be thought of as such an evil man? What staging!*

Goebbels introduced the correspondents one by one. Hitler did not rise from his chair as the correspondents were paraded before him, but when Abby approached in her turn, Hitler set the child on the floor, rose to his feet, and extended his hand. "Ah, no need to introduce Miss White, Joseph. We met under unique circumstances some time ago. Welcome, Miss White."

The briefing was opened with Goebbels reading a well-prepared list of all the accomplishments of Hitler and the Nazi Party since taking office. He had to pause frequently to let the interpreters translate his German into English and French. Goebbels had a high-pitched voice. To Abby it sounded like a soprano's off-pitch shrill. Thomas at the bureau said he acted like a "sissy," but he was anything but. His several children belied his effeminate manners and gestures. With an adoring smile, he asked his Fuehrer to say a few introductory remarks.

Unlike his ranting and raving at the Nazi rally that Abby and William Shirer had attended, Hitler sat back down in his chair and spoke softly, all the while petting his dog.

"As you can see, I am not the ogre that some of the misguided people of the international press have portrayed me. I love my gardens at my home, little children, and my dog, Blonda." He paused. "We only want what is right for our Fatherland, no more, no less. We only want a Germany that the German people can be proud of once again."

Goebbels smile widened even more and he led a small applause for his Fuehrer.

There was a break in the briefing and Hitler and Goebbels left the veranda. Coffee, tea and sweet rolls were served to the correspondents. Abby chatted with the other foreign correspondents in German and English. She knew enough French to get the gist of what the Frenchmen were saying. They gushed with enthusiasm for the Fuehrer. This was a surprise to Abby; he could charm even the most experienced newsmen.

Before starting the next session, Goebbels announced the schedule for the rest of the news conference. "After this session, there will be open-top cars in front of the hotel for the group. You will be taken for a motor tour of the lovely Berchtesgaden area. We will pass by the country house of the Fuehrer, the Berghof. All his flower gardens are in full bloom. Upon your return, an early dinner will be served at seven o'clock. Your cars will leave at nine sharp in the morning for the train to Berlin."

"Now we will start the question-and-answer session. I will act as the moderator. Our interpreters are here to help."

All the correspondents spoke in their native tongues, which were translated into German for Goebbles and Hitler. The male correspondents were first with Goebbles. Each one had an easy question for Hitler, such as "How old is your dog?" and "Do you hike in those mountains up there?" and "How often can you vacation here?" Abby thought they talked just to hear their own voices.

When at last Abby was recognized by Goebbels, she rose from her chair and spoke in German directly to Hitler. "Herr Hitler, can I ask a serious question about your policies, or is this briefing restricted to what we have heard—nothing controversial?"

Goebbels smile faded, and he looked at Hitler who now carried a frown. Hitler nodded to Goebbles to proceed. "Miss White, please ask questions that will not offend your host, our Fuehrer. What is your question?"

"Herr Hitler, the world had observed your animosity toward the German Jewish population. It seems to become worse as time progresses. Can you please comment on this, sir?"

Hitler stood, his face reddening. "If you had read *Mein Kampf*, Miss White, it states my belief in no uncertain terms that Germany needs to recognize and strengthen our Aryan heritage. We must attempt to rid Germany of troublemakers who we find not to be of the pure German race. It is necessary that this action happens if our Fatherland is to again be a major nation on the world scene."

"But, sir, these people are an important part of the German citizenry, its economy, and its financial position."

"All obtained through trickery and deceit, Miss White. The Jewish problem will take care of itself. Right now, I'm also concerned with living space, '*lebensraum*,' for our true German citizens."

He again nodded to Goebbels who announced the end of the session. There was guarded applause for Hitler as some of the correspondents looked at Abby with admiration and others with distain.

Abby thought she might be asked to leave the conference, but instead she was invited on the tour of Berchtesgaden and its environs. The cars stopped at the foothills of the surrounding mountains, a small portion of the Bavarian Alps, and let the visitors stretch their legs at the various trailheads. The gentian flowers of the mountain meadows, including the beautiful Blue Monkshood, were unique and in abundance.

Before returning to the hotel, the cars stopped at the Berghof, Hitler's house. The visitors were led around and through several separate gardens, all offset by manicured lawns and shrubs. Hitler was not to be seen.

It was interesting to Abby that none of the other correspondents chose to walk with her on the tour. It was not that she was a woman—she had talked with most of them during session breaks. She surmised that her challenging question to Hitler made them leery of any presumed connections to Abby. Hitler and his consortium of fanatic followers were enough to intimidate the bravest of men.

At the final dinner that night Abby was seated next to a correspondent from the Paris *L'Illustratron* newspaper. After his third glass of wine, his tongue loosened and he chanced a whisper to Abby. "You were impertinent to ask that question about the Nazi policy on Jews, Miss White," he said. "I admire you, but I hope you haven't made any enemies as a result."

"Monsieur, I thank you for your concern, but I wanted to hear his clarification and confirmation of this discriminatory, unbelievable policy. Writing a book full of hate, years ago, while in prison under duress is one thing. Continuing today to make it a reality is another. His thinking is irrational and shocking."

The Frenchman sat opened-mouthed and said no more.

The dinner was over, and Abby was going to her room when an SS officer stepped in her path and smiled. "Miss White, excuse me, but the Fuehrer would like a word with you. Please follow me." He led her to a small, dimly-lighted alcove off the hotel's library and then excused himself.

Hitler rose and greeted her. "Please sit down, Miss White." He sat opposite to her and then started drumming his fingers on the arm of his chair. "Miss White, I must say that I am amazed by your audacity." He raised his fist in the air. "I like women with spunk like you have! A pretty, intelligent woman like you should be on the arm of a powerful man, not writing newspaper stories. Your bearing is regal. You are a blonde Aryan, and you speak German very well. I couldn't ask for a better companion!"

He was tapping his feet now and wiped off beads of perspiration from his forehead.

"What I am proposing to you, Abby White, is that you visit me at another of my retreats, the place I use in Dresden. You will be living in luxury with a houseful of servants. The chalet is really a small mansion on a beautiful lake outside of the city and is very private and secure. Berchtesgaden has become a tourist attraction with very little privacy. My people have counted up to four thousand people a day. My Dresden place is known to only my closest aides. How does that sound?"

"Intriguing, Herr Hitler. But what about your girlfriend, Eva Braun? I don't think she would approve of that."

"How did you know about Miss Braun?"

"Sir, your secret is not so secret. I think your followers are pleased with it and do talk about your romance. It shows them you are a regular man like them and not of the other sort."

"Interesting observation." He paused. "Oh, Miss Braun is a simple country girl—a nice person, but not as dynamic and knowledgeable as you. Now back to my question about my Dresden place?"

"I will take a weekend to travel there. It sounds marvelous. But please understand that I will not be your mistress or paramour. You are a very driven man. I would like to know you better, but not that way. Let Miss Braun handle that."

"All right, Miss Abby White, I do find it interesting to talk with you. I have too many 'Yes Men.' I need someone outside of my organization to challenge my ideas or my actions. And I need to explain my actions better to you. We will call it my intellectual weekend." He smiled broadly. "You have my word that I will not pursue anything physical with you—unless you decide differently, of course."

Before parting, they set a date for the Dresden weekend. "I will send details to your office by special courier. Let's call it another, more one-on-one official press briefing. Your editor should let you go, don't you think?"

Hitler rose and offered his hand, which Abby took. *Still cold and clammy*, Abby observed.

# Chapter Thirty-three

*Ireland—The Visitors*

Sean and Esther finally got time off from their work in Nice to visit his family. Young Dan O'Connor was in tow and was the delight of the O'Connors who had no other grandchildren yet.

They went on for a short stay with Darcy O'Gara at the O'Gara retreat overlooking Tralee Bay. Darcy, Cormac, and Sally opened the house to them. It was a 'welcome home' for all of them. Darcy was especially pleased that they'd named their son after her Dan.

On the second day there, the bell rang at the cottage's front door. Cormac heard it and then remembered that he had forgotten to latch the outer gate after the O'Connors' arrival. He opened the door to see two men in black leather coats smiling at him.

"Good morning. What can I do for you?" asked Cormac.

"We have come to meet one Darcy O'Gara. We are members of Britain's Intelligence Services and need to verify Daniel O'Gara's claim to be Irish with a mother named Darcy O'Gara."

Darcy came to the door with Sean at her side. "I'm Darcy O'Gara, and Dan O'Gara is my son. Why do you need to verify this?" Darcy stood with her arms crossed and a strong, almost defiant stance.

"Your son recently applied for a security clearance for his newspaper work. We needed to verify his Irish background, and we will check for any records with the police," said one man. He spoke in a guttural tone.

"How did you find me here? This is not my legal residence."

The other agent laughed. "We are intelligence agents. It is our job to find people. We know you live most of the time in Kinsale." He looked at Sean. "Is this another son?"

"This is our good friend." Now she eyed them closely.

"May I see your credentials?" Darcy asked.

"Not necessary, Mrs. O'Gara. We now have the information we needed and will be on our way. Thank you." They went back to their car and drove down the driveway and out the open gate.

"Sean, that was strange. Dan told me over a month ago that he had received a security clearance in England. Those men are a little late," said Darcy.

"Did you notice their accents? Both sounded German," said Sean.

"I'll cable Dan at the *Times* about this," Darcy said.

# Chapter Thirty-four

*London—MI6*

Dan was alarmed when he received his mother's cable. *Hofer and Kuntz are letting me know that they can easily reach my mother. They are using my mother as a hostage to make me perform.* He sent a reply to her assuring her that all was fine and that the security people were just slow in their check-ups.

Dan now felt violated, and his Irish temper took another direction. On his lunch hour he took a long walk, ducking through alleyways, reversing courses, always looking over his shoulder for possible followers. He ended his walk at the headquarters of MI6, Britain's foreign intelligence service. He soon sat with two agents in an interrogation room, which, ironically, was very similar to the SS room at Wilhelmshaven—no windows and a one-way mirror on a wall. The pair listened intently, never interrupting until Dan finished. They asked many questions, taking notes as they cross-examined Dan. Finally, one of the agents pressed a concealed button under the table, and soon another man entered the room. The agents' demeanor told Dan that the new man was their superior. They addressed him as 'Mr. Jones.' Jones was a nondescript man about sixty who reminded Dan of a bespectacled accountant he'd met at the *Tribune* back in Chicago. That's where the similarity stopped. Dan was asked to repeat his whole story. All three men then questioned him at length, and then they left Dan alone.

They sat down in Jones' office. "Maybe a good recruit for our S.O.E. section," said one of the junior agents.

"Too late for that," said Jones. "He might make a good double agent now. Let's go talk to him some more."

Jones walked around the table. "Now, why the bloody hell are you here? What do you want from us?"

"I would like protection for my mother and help in getting out of the soup I'm in," Dan said.

Jones chuckled. "So you gave away our secret information to the Nazis, and now you have the goddamn nerve to ask our protection for your Irish mother *and* rescue your ass. Some cheeky nerve, don't you think?"

"Sir, I made a terrible mistake, I admit. As I said, I had the dumb notion of avenging my father's wounds and my uncle's death."

"I hear you, young man. First, let me agree with you that it was a stupid, goddamn 'dumb notion' you had. Now this innocent woman, your mother, is in jeopardy. Secondly, we have no jurisdiction to protect your mother in Ireland. We are 'persona non grata' in Ireland as you might concede. We have no mutual cooperation on anything at present. I suggest that you have your mother disappear without a trace for the time being.

"As for your personal dilemma, we will give you the opportunity to make some amends for what you have done to our government. You can continue spying for the Nazis, but as a double agent. That means you must be willing to provide your Nazi contacts with misinformation, while at the same time provide us with information about their spy networks and information needs. Will you do this?"

"What are my options?" Dan asked.

Jones continued walking around the table. *Like the SS man, Hofer,* thought Dan. "Still trying to bargain, Mr. O'Gara? You have no other options as I see it. We will expose you. The Nazis will likely kill you since you are no more use to them and you know too much about their business. If you could manage to escape to Ireland, they will still find you, I'll wager. The United States will most probably revoke your visitor's visa since they are now in the process of deporting known German agents. Why would they let you, now a known spy, back into their country? Of course, your fledgling career with the *Times* would end."

"All right, I will be your double agent. I don't like the other options."

"I must warn you, if we discover that you've turned on us and have gone back to the Nazis for whatever reason, we will have to eliminate you as quickly as possible, even if you're on German soil. You already know too much about us."

That caught Dan's attention, and his face turned white.

"Now you look shocked, Mr. O'Gara! Clandestine, covert activities are nothing new in the annals of history. We have spies everywhere, and they have spies everywhere. We think we are smarter than they are, and they think they are the smart ones. We kill each other. Our Winston Churchill talked about this recently, and I will paraphrase: 'In the growing possibility of another war, truth is so precious that she always will be attended by a body of lies.' There you have it, young man; you will now be living a life of lies."

Jones continued. "Incidentally, we've had our eyes on Gerhard Kuntz for some time, and now we know that he's in the recruiting business, thanks to you. Albert Hofer of the SD-Gestapo and the Wilhelmshaven site are new to us—all good information."

Jones finally sat down and looked at his calendar book. "This is Thursday. We will have an agreement for you to sign on Saturday. Meet us at this address at ten in the morning." He put a small piece of paper with the address in front of Dan. "Got it?" Dan nodded, and Jones pulled the paper back. "Do not be followed. Bring that camera and the film they gave you. In four or five days we will have some things you can drop to Gerhard Kuntz. That will take some pressure off you and get the ball rolling. Any questions?" Dan shook his head.

"Wait a minute," Jones said. "Do you know how to shake someone off your tail?"

Dan shook his head again.

"I keep forgetting that you're a bloody amateur. Scout several buildings in your area for entrances and exits. If you sense you're being followed, go through an entrance to an office building, take the elevator to an upper floor, wait a minute or so, and then take stairs to the ground floor. Leave by an exit to a street different, of course, from where you entered. Don't use the same building twice. And I don't want you coming here again. Before you leave, my men will assign a mail drop box for you, along with a code name. Good luck until we meet again."

One of the men he first met gave him instructions on drop box messaging and his code name. He lowered his voice and looked Dan squarely in the eyes. "Listen, O'Gara. No matter what Jones says, you can always disappear. One of our double agents told me that he had witnessed SS interrogation methods. He said they first try to break people down by isolation, embarrassment, intimidation, and humiliation. They strip the person and even make men dress in women's clothes. If that doesn't work, the thumb screws and beatings commence. Women are handled about the same way, except that if they won't talk, they are brutalized and raped. They don't waste any more time after that. It's execution with a pistol shot to the back of the head for both men and women. I'm telling you this, O'Gara, off the record."

Thoughts raced through his mind as he walked the long way back to the *Times* office. *Boy, I get in one mess after another! It's my own fault—and it's not too…. Man, I'd better do this thing right. Mom would suffer too. She'll never agree to "disappear without a trace." That is her Ireland, and she will not be moved anywhere else. But she does know how to shoot straight, thanks to Dad. God bless them both. And God bless me.*

\* \* \*

Dan signed the agreement on Saturday. Ironically, it was very similar to the Nazi contract. He handed over the German Sida camera and film to Jones. "What will you do with that?" Dan asked.

"We are having some dummy installations being constructed at various locations other than the true planned sites," said Jones. Obviously, we must take pictures with the camera the Nazis gave you. Does Kuntz want prints or film?"

"Film," said Dan. "One roll at a time if that's all I have taken. He wanted a picture number tied to the latitude and longitude where it was taken. I had no detailed maps with latitude and longitude. When I told him I couldn't do that, he said to record the distance in kilometers and the direction from the nearest crossroad. Like 'Picture number one- Two kilos northeast of Baily and Grosser Roads.' Of course, they want to see many shots of the business end of the radar unit as soon a possible. Technical details must follow. Have to give them some timetable on all of that, I suspect," said Dan.

"One thing at a time, young man. We'll send the first pictures they asked for and then wait to see what they want next. Time is on our side," said Jones. "The support tower will be similar to what you sketched for them. We are working on a dummy radar antenna array that should fool them."

Gerhard Kuntz sent the first film and data to Hofer at the SS headquarters with a note.

"I think the Darcy threat did the trick," he wrote.

"Of course it did. I know a momma's boy when I see him," replied Hofer.

# Chapter Thirty-five

*Nice—1938*

As time progressed, Esther developed a widespread following for her "Esther's Friends" column. Most of the newspapers in France carried her now-syndicated columns, along with several French language newspapers in Switzerland. Her salary had been increased several times over the years. The *Nice Phare* publishers and editors knew they had a gifted writer who could turn the most innocuous and out-of-luck person into someone of interest with whom the reader could find empathy—someone with their same failures, fears, successes, setbacks, and hopes. Somehow it helped people cope with the bitter worldwide Depression and the winds of another war.

After dinner one evening she sat with Sean to go over letters she had recently received. Dan O'Gara, one-time leader and still letter coordinator for the Wildcats, wrote from London that Karl, Peter, and Hans, the Atlantic City trio, were now back in Germany. Karl Kruger and Hans Strasser had been assigned to SS police units in Berlin, and Peter Farber was sent to a military post. Esther read the letters out loud.

"I'm sorry, Esther," said Sean. "Tell me about the Atlantic City guys again. I never got to meet them."

Esther apologized. "I keep forgetting that, Sean." She told him that Peter and Hans were friends of one of the Wildcats, Karl, who was also a fellow student and a native German. "They took us in when we were trying to escape from Capone's killers." She said Abby White was sure that all three, including Karl Kruger, were German spies.

Jacob Bernstein had written to Esther and Sean from the United States. His new address was a surprise. Jacob said that after he completed his doctoral studies in nuclear physics at Cambridge, he was offered a position on a project team at the Institute for Advanced Studies at Princeton, New Jersey, which he quickly accepted. The Institute was the home of Albert Einstein, who, on a visit to the United States to lecture in 1933, decided to stay permanently. Jacob believed that Einstein sensed the growing anti-Semitism in Germany and decided not to return. Several top German scientists then fled Germany to join him. "I am in the midst of brilliant men," Jacob wrote. "I am very fortunate."

Jacob had continued to exchange letters with Esther even after she and Sean had married and had their son, Daniel. He was a philosophical man, collegial, and one who accepted life events with ease. He reasoned that if he couldn't have Esther as his wife, he could still have Esther and Sean as his good friends, even though he had never met Sean. He reminisced in his letter about their brief time on the *Brennan* and how he missed the Wildcats when they got off at Galway. Jacob closed his letter by expressing his concern for his family in Berlin:

> Esther, you'll remember my father, Leonard. He writes that they don't feel safe in their native city of Berlin anymore. But he vows that the Nazi hoodlums will not drive him, my mother, or my sister from their home. Father said that Ruth was discharged without cause from her longtime position in Berlin city government, along with other Jewish workers. I cabled my father to get the family out of Germany. He responded with "I am a Berliner since birth, and I will not leave. Things will get better."
>
> Maybe Hitler will stop this when he feels more secure, but I can't help being worried. Esther, my dear friend, please pray for them as I am doing.
>
> Jacob

"They are such nice people, Sean; I hope they will be safe. The Nazis sound terrible. Now I'm worried about Abby in Berlin."

In the gray time between night and dawn, Esther lay awake. She remembered how caring and protective Abby had been for her. *She kept me from panicking and actually threw her body over mine when the bullets were flying in Michigan and Ireland. Please protect her, dear God.*

## Chapter Thirty-six

*Berlin*

The sun had started to tilt downward as Abby walked briskly from the *Tribune* office to Warren's drop box. The wind was coming from the north and brought a chilly hint of autumn. Abby had to talk to Warren about the next meeting with Hitler. Besides, she missed him. She liked Claus von Fritsch—he was dashing and good company. He would make a good husband. But Warren was something special—very appealing.

DARK CAVE
THERE IS SNOW IN THE MOUNTAINS
HIGH MOUNTAIN

She dropped the note in the box and hurried home to await his call. She was just finishing a light dinner when the telephone rang.

"Hello, High Mountain, Dark Cave here. How are you, and what's up?"

"I need to meet with you. I really need your advice on a special meeting I have arranged with a key person. The meeting is two weeks away. Can you meet me somewhere out of town on Saturday? I'll bring some things to stay over. I really need a break from Berlin too."

Warren responded, "Yes, of course. I'll set things up and leave instructions for you. Be careful, High Mountain."

The next day the *Tribune*'s bureau chief, James Hoffman, went to Abby's desk with an envelope in his hand.

"Can you come to my office, Abby?"

Abby followed him and Hoffman closed his door. "This came by special courier from Nazi headquarters." The envelope was secured with a wax seal embossed with a swastika. "It's addressed to you. May I ask what's going on, Abby?"

Earlier, Abby had reported details of the meeting at Berchtesgaden to Hoffman and had written a summary of the press briefing that was carried by the *Tribune* news services. Her article was mostly discreet, tongue-in-cheek descriptions of the benevolent, dog-loving dictator at his mountain retreat. Hoffman agreed that there was nothing new to report from his political stance except to reaffirm his stance on the Jewish "question." Abby had not told him about the invitation to Dresden.

"May I open this, please?" said Abby.

"Of course." Hoffman was intrigued.

She broke the seal and read, out loud, a handwritten note from Hitler inviting her to a personal briefing at his Dresden house in two weeks. Enclosed were train tickets and a railway schedule with times circled. A driver would meet the train.

"Incredible!" exclaimed Hoffman. "How did you do that?"

"He had me pulled aside before leaving. He told me he admired my directness, etcetera. and I sensed he was coming on to me. I mentioned his mistress, Eva Braun, but that didn't deter him. I told him in no uncertain terms that I would not be his girlfriend, but he still offered a professional one-on-one meeting at Dresden. There may be a good story there, so I agreed to the visit. Don't worry, I won't be compromised, and I know he understands that."

Hoffman shook his head and was silent for a long minute. "I don't know, Abby, that man is weird. I understand that he has had only a few personal female partners—Eva Braun, and, before her, a half-niece named Geli Raubal who kept house for him. He was said to have loved her dearly. She committed suicide in 1931 in Hitler's apartment while he was away. Maybe there were others, but generally he's been a loner. He really is a strange person. A friend theorized that he wanted to be thought of as the "available bachelor" for the German women. I think it's too dangerous for you."

"Sir, I truly believe I can handle this visit and get a better understanding of what this man has in mind for Germany. He is smart and careful in his own way and would not risk doing harm to a foreign correspondent from a U.S. newspaper. He's now trying to put on a better face to the world as evident from the inane press briefing at Berchtesgaden. Sir, if I disappear, you will have a copy of this letter in your office safe concerning my last whereabouts."

Hoffman shook his head and sighed. "Okay, Abby, you've convinced me. Besides, I don't know how I could stop you. It's on your own time on a weekend."

\* \* \*

Warren Walters was facing a moment of decision. He was seriously attracted to Abby White, and he could sense her interest in him. If they became good friends and maybe lovers, it could well compromise his responsibility in shepherding a subordinate agent in the very dangerous business of spying.

He mulled over this dilemma in his office at the U.S. Embassy as he planned the rendezvous with Abby outside of Berlin. There was a little village on the train route north from Berlin toward the Baltic Sea that was frequented by honeymooners. He had read about it in the travel section of a newspaper some months ago and, for some reason, kept the article. *We are in pretending roles anyway—why not pretend we are honeymooners?* Warren prepared an envelope for the drop box. It contained instructions for Abby and a marked train schedule. He told Abby that she would take the same train as he would, but they must not be seen together at the Berlin station. They would board different railway cars and get off the train at Furtinburg, about sixty kilometers north of Berlin. After the train moved on, they would join together and make their way to the Hotel Marie on Lake Silver. *Is this a great plan, or a terrible idea?* Warren wondered.

# Chapter Thirty-seven

*Furtinburg, Germany*

The lobby was quiet. Warren had guessed right—there were few honeymooners in the fall months. The desk clerk was a skinny old man with a dour expression. He peered over his glasses and saw Abby looking at brochures on a lobby table, then looked quizzically at Warren when he said he had reserved two rooms. Warren felt he needed to explain. "We're not yet married, and we're visiting your hotel to see if it would be suitable for our wedding or honeymoon."

The old man smiled and nodded. "Tell you what, young man, since you're thinking about our place for a wedding, I'll give you both rooms for the price of one." He fetched the keys, mumbling something about "More control than Margaret and I had…"

He turned and handed the keys to Warren. "Since you're not on a honeymoon yet, maybe you'd like something to do outside this afternoon. We have a very nice hiking trail that's used often by the hiking clubs in our area."

Abby had joined Warren at the desk. "That sounds like fun," she said. "It's such a fine day for hiking."

The clerk shuffled to a closet near the desk and fished out several hiking sticks of varnished hickory with leather hand straps and pointed metal tips. Warren, at six feet three inches, took the tallest stick in the hotel's inventory.

They had lunch on the hotel's patio that overlooked Lake Silver. There they saw about a dozen other hotel guests. Most were older people dressed for hiking in lederhosen and calf-length stockings. The trees were turning early in the Northwestern region of Germany, and the radiant colors of red, gold, and brown leafed trees were reflected in the mirror-like surface of the lake. Abby told Warren, "This is such a wonderful break from Berlin."

They were well into the woods surrounding the lake when Warren stopped, leaned on his walking stick and smiled at Abby. "Remember when you called me 'mysterious,' Abby? Well, it's your turn to take that moniker. Tell me about this special meeting you've arranged."

"All right. Hold onto your hat, handsome." Abby first told him details of the press meeting at Berchtesgaden. She had a small pocket notebook filled with notes on the press briefing and her personal meeting with Hitler later. She referred to it as they walked.

"I'm wondering about his Dresden house. Have you heard anything about that place? I've cleared the trip with my manager at the *Tribune*. What do you think, Warren? Should I go?"

"Right now, I'm at a loss for words, Abby. It's almost unbelievable. It's not that I'm surprised that he's attracted to you, it's just that he's *that much* attracted to you. No offense intended, my sweet friend. Give me time to think…I've never heard of his Dresden place. Let's keep walking."

Occasionally they would meet other hikers on the trail, coming the other way, including some older couples. Hiking was a national pastime in Germany. It was especially popular in the financial depression—an activity that was free. Everyone they passed waved or nodded a greeting with a smile. Abby started ruminating. *They are ordinary, good people, not like the Nazis, but yet they've voted the Nazis in power. Why?* She told Warren her thoughts, and he agreed. "We may be witnesses to an historic tragedy."

The hiking path had an optional trail that veered away from the lake, and then went up a hill into thick woods. Warren pointed his hiking stick toward the hill. "Onward and upward!" he said.

The path was dappled with sunbeams finding their way through the leaves of magnificent red oak trees. Warren shifted his hands with his hiking stick so that he could hold Abby's hand as they climbed the rise.

"This is a lovely spot for a holiday, Warren. Look, I've been accidentally collecting fallen leaves on the sharp tip of my hiking stick. I'm going to save some for my Germany album."

They walked on through the woods, not speaking for a time, lost in thought. *Something that happens quickly when hiking*, Abby mused.

After some time, Warren spoke up. "I've been thinking, Abby. Of course I have mixed feelings about your visit to Dresden. As your friend, I'm concerned about your personal safety. And as your handling agent, you are my responsibility. From all accounts, that man is a neurotic demagogue with a short temper. His mood swings are legendary."

He stopped and turned to her. He took off his cap and scratched his head. "At the same time, there may be an abundance of intelligence information that can be harvested from your one-on-one visit with the man over a weekend. It sounds like he respects you and wants to get your reaction to his plans and policies."

"I think you're right, Warren. It should be very interesting."

"You have an excellent memory, so I wouldn't risk taking any notes while you're there. Wait until you're back in Berlin. And you'll be under increased scrutiny from his guards. I wouldn't take any weapons with you."

"Even my precious Beretta?"

"Especially your Beretta," Warren shook his head and laughed. "You got me on that one, Abby." Then he turned serious. "Remember how I told you that a pen, pencil, or any sharp object jammed with force into the eye socket can kill a man?" Abby nodded. "That'll be your weapon in a life-or-death situation."

He reached out and held Abby's free hand. "Obviously, what I'm saying is—go for it! Otherwise, we may be missing a great opportunity for an intelligence coup. Hitler has already reincorporated the Saar and Rhineland territories into the German Third Reich. We wonder what's next."

They finished the long hike late in the afternoon and congratulated each other for their successful efforts.

"I want to freshen up before dinner, Warren. Let's meet at the bar in the dining room at six," Abby said.

After Abby's revelation of her Dresden meeting, Warren's responsibility as a lead agent resurfaced. He was now very content with separate rooms. He waited at the bar for Abby, enjoying his favorite drink, Boodles English gin on the rocks. Abby joined him and tried a local wine that was recommended by the bartender. She sipped it and smiled an okay to the bartender.

They carried their drinks into the dining room where people had already been seated.

"What a lovely room," Abby said. "Good ambiance. I like it when they have table candles and turn the lights down."

Abby had lamb chops and Warren a large beef filet. They talked about their childhood years over dinner and continued recalling special times as they retired to the hotel's library with glasses of brandy. The evening hotel manager had a fire made in the large stone fireplace since the outside temperature had fallen. The sofa, which faced the fireplace, had soft throw pillows. The fire warmed them, and the brandy added to their comfort.

"Just think, Warren, we were far apart when you were studying at Cornell while I was in high school in Indianapolis. Who would have believed back then that we would someday be sitting in this dreamy room in beautiful Northern Germany? Let's not waste a moment of it." Abby snuggled up to Warren. "Hey, Stretch, put that long arm around me. Someone didn't close a door someplace, and I'm getting chilled."

The fire was hissing, asking for more wood, but they were too busy hugging and kissing. This went on for a while, and then Abby resolved the issue. "Warren, the train ride and the long hike was a lot for this city girl. I think I'm ready for bed."

"Well, I'm sleepy too. Wood fires always do that to me."

They kissed in front of Abby's door. Then they kissed some more.

"Tall man, my neck's getting stiff trying to kiss upstairs to your altitude. So good night, I guess."

She closed her door. Warren waited, and then knocked softly on her door. Abby opened her door a crack, peeked out, and smiled. "What is it, sir?"

"I'm only human," Warren said.

"So am I. Please come in."

\* \* \*

The next morning, they took a taxi to the train station and risked a parting kiss along the way. "Wait two weeks after Dresden before dropping off your report, Abby. We will be anxious to read it. I know I sound like a worrier, but you've got to be careful. If you feel you are in danger in Dresden, grab a train back to Berlin and get to the Embassy. Even if all goes well there, you will be still be under increased surveillance when you return to Berlin. Remember how I told you to determine if you're being followed, and how to lose a tail?"

Abby kissed him on the cheek. "Yes, sir."

"You must execute those procedures to the letter, my love. Take no unnecessary risks. Don't try to contact me directly. Your telephone and room may be bugged."

They separated at the station and took different railway cars back to Berlin. Abby had trouble reading her book on the train. Her mind wandered thinking about the interesting trip she'd just taken. Then she nodded off. The man watching her stayed awake.

# Chapter Thirty-eight

***Berlin—Lydia***

Before leaving for Dresden, Abby attended a dinner party at the British Embassy. Princess Lydia Viazensky was there, always ready with fresh news and gossip.

"My military friends told me not to repeat these things, and you can guess why," she whispered to Abby during the cocktail hour. "The Nazis have underground manufacturing going on. They're making handguns, machine guns, and ammunition. Even the Mauser Company was ordered to produce their automatic pistols by the thousands."

She squeezed Abby's hand and lowered her voice even more. "Abby, they even have tailoring companies secretly producing army and navy uniforms. It seems to me they're getting ready to go to war."

Just then a tall man in a dark suit approached them, glass in hand. His black hair was sprinkled with gray. "Hello, Lydia. Excuse me for interrupting, but I think I know this young lady." He nodded toward Abby, who took a hard look at the man.

"Captain Dieter of the *Bremen*! What a surprise! What are you doing in Berlin? Where's your ship?"

"It's not my ship anymore. Grand Admiral Raeder has commandeered me for the German Navy and given me the rank of *Vizeadmiral*. I don't have a command yet. Everything is in the planning and building phases. Ha, even my new uniform is not ready. In fact, my office is in the basement of the Berlin Natural History Museum, about as far away from the ocean as one can get."

"It's so good to see you again, Captain, after such a long time. It's a wonder you recognized me," said Abby.

"I never forget a pretty lady—and an American who speaks fluent German. Abby White, isn't it? A beautiful name for a lovely lady!"

"Always the charmer, Franz!" said Lydia.

"Lydia, I was with college friends on the *Bremen* heading for a vacation in Ireland after graduation," said Abby.

"What are you doing now, Abby?" asked Franz.

"I landed a job here in Berlin as a foreign correspondent for the *Chicago Tribune*."

Franz took one step back and spilled his drink. "Oh! What I told you about my new career is confidential. I could be in serious trouble if you write about this, Abby."

Abby shook her head. "I shan't, sir. I have too many other things to write about at present. But you've got to promise me an interview when it's not such a government secret."

Lydia was always forthright. "Franz, what do you think of the Nazis?"

Dieter looked around the room. "I'm not a political person, Lydia. I'm just a sailor doing his duty for his government."

"Well, Franz, I must say you will look splendid in your new uniform—if it ever arrives!" said Lydia. "You must wear it to our parties when you are permitted."

Dieter laughed, straightened up, and saluted the ladies. "It is my pleasure to see both of you again. I hope it is often that we will cross paths." He turned and rejoined his companions across the room.

"My, Abby, isn't it wonderful to be among these dashing men?"

Abby smiled and nodded. "It's exciting and a little scary with all of this talk of war." *Between Lydia and Franz Dieter, I've got a lot of stuff for Warren. And I was told to stay away from the drop box until two weeks after my meeting with Hitler.*

## Chapter Thirty-nine

*Dresden—Hitler*

As Hitler had promised, there was a driver waiting for Abby at the train station in Dresden, an old German city on the Elbe River near the Czech border. The driver wore an SS uniform complete with double lighting bolts on his collars. Ramrod straight, he made a slight bow and clicked his heels. Abby wore a business suit with a white silk blouse and low-heeled shoes.

"Miss White, I presume. I am your chauffeur, Corporal Steiner." Abby nodded. He looked to be about her age and had hard, penetrating dark eyes. His smile was more like a sneer. "I will take you to our Fuehrer's chalet."

He led Abby to a black Mercedes sedan in the parking lot. Before opening the rear door for Abby, he placed her suitcase on the ground. "I must inspect the contents of your suitcase and purse before we proceed."

"No, you may not," said Abby, speaking German for the first time. "As an invited guest, I resent this intrusion of my privacy. Did your order come from the Fuehrer?"

"No. As one of his personal guards, I must take these precautions."

"Listen, Corporal Steiner, I am an American news correspondent who was personally invited by your Fuehrer. If you touch my personal things, I will not go with you. I'll catch the next train back to Berlin. You can tell your Fuehrer what happened."

The Corporal's face turned a shade lighter. He put her suitcase in the trunk and opened the car door for her. Now the Corporal wondered if he had overstepped his authority. No one had told him that the lady to be met at the station was an American correspondent. Even the chalet servants had speculated that it was a secret liaison behind Eva Braun's back.

He drove in silence and was very guarded when Abby began asking him questions. He did not want any more trouble from this woman.

"Will the Fuehrer be there to greet me?"

"No, I don't believe so. He sleeps late."

"Does he sleep late every day?"

"Yes, I think so."

"Does he stay up late at night?"

"Yes, I think so." *I could be in more trouble.*

That was the extent of their conversation. The Corporal was relieved when they reached the chalet, a gray building with a faceless, heavy steel door marking the entrance. Before opening her car door, Steiner ran up the stairs where a woman dressed in a maid's uniform and a young male valet waited.

"She is an American newspaper writer, personally invited by the Fuehrer. She understands and speaks German very well, so be careful what you say."

Their frowns disappeared, and they greeted Abby with bows, smiles, and welcomes. The valet fetched her suitcase, and both he and the maid led her into the chalet. After the stark façade of the main entrance, Abby was surprised at the ornate foyer. It was a large atrium with a geodesic skylight that allowed live plants and dwarf ornamental trees to gather sunlight. Between the greenery, paintings were hung, which reflected Hitler's taste in bucolic idylls and German Romanticism. Abby guessed they were paintings by nineteenth century European artists, similar to paintings of pastoral scenes she had seen in Berlin's art museums.

She followed the servants up a winding marble staircase to a large, comfortable bedroom on the second floor. It overlooked the small lake and gardens that Hitler had described.

"The Fuehrer told me that he would meet you for lunch in the dining alcove off the atrium at one o'clock" the maid said. "There is a bell cord next to the bed. It connects with our quarters on the main floor. Please pull it if you need anything, madam."

Hitler was standing in the dining room looking out a window. His dog, Blonda, was at his side. "Ah, Miss White, welcome to Dresden. Very good to see you again." He extended his hand and bowed slightly. He wore a tan jacket and dark tie. "I hope Corporal Steiner was on time at the train station."

Abby smiled. "Oh, yes. And he was very proper and accommodating. You can be proud of him."

"That I am. He is but one of several personal guards here. You probably won't see most of them. They have secret observation posts."

"That's reassuring," said Abby. "But I hope they don't observe the inside of the guest bedroom!"

Hitler laughed. "Of course not, Miss White. May I call you Abby?" he said as he held a chair for her at the dining table.

"Yes, you may—if I can call you Adolf."

"Oh, this will be a delightful weekend!" said Hitler. "There is your spunk again! Yes, you may, Abby, but not in front of the servants or guards. It has to be 'Herr Hitler' then."

A maid began bringing in their lunch from the kitchen. "Did you know I am a vegetarian?" Hitler said. "I have my Bavarian chef, Herr Krannenberger, accompany me wherever I go. We will have no meat, but Krannenberger, as you will see, prepares an imposing array of vegetarian dishes, pleasing to the eye, as well as to the palate. I hate to think of the slaughter of animals, you see."

Before he even took a bite, an SS guard brought a servant girl from the kitchen. She carried a plate and fork. Hitler smiled. "My unwilling food taster is here." He put samples of the food he would eat on her plate. She took a step backward and ate the food. There was a long minute when everyone paused. "There, she is still standing, so we can eat," said Hitler.

"Did Corporal Steiner show you any of the sights on your way here?" asked Hitler.

Abby had a mouthful of salad and simply shook her head. "Well, we will take a walk around my little lake and garden, and then take a tour of Dresden."

"Dresden is a beautiful city," Hitler said as they walked through the grounds. "We call it the 'Jewel Box' of Germany because of its baroque and rococo city center. This house is owned by one of my supporters. He has loaned it to me as long I want it—a true Nazi."

After their walk, Hitler's car pulled up in the driveway. Corporal Steiner was the driver. There was another SS guard in the front passenger seat. His dog, Blonda, sat proudly between the two SS men. Steiner opened the door for his Fuehrer and Abby, nodding a greeting, but did not venture a direct look at Abby.

"Go by Dresden Castle first, Corporal, and then go to the Taschenberg Palais." As they were driven around the city, Hitler recited the history of each attraction. Steiner drove slowly, not even risking a look in the rearview mirror. Hitler ordered Steiner to stop at the Neumarket Square.

"Behind that large building on the left is a wonderful vegetable and fruit market where my chef shops almost daily for our food," said Hitler. "I would like for us to walk around this area to view the unique architecture, but it is too dangerous. I would need more bodyguards to do that. Remember when we first met, when that Sicilian fired a wild shot at me at the Olympic site and hit your partner? I was lucky then."

"He was Sicilian, Herr Hitler?" said Abby.

"Oh yes. He had papers on him."

Abby thought. *It was not a wild shot. He was aiming for me. Maybe a last effort by Capone's Mafia friends.*

"I understand your caution. I would rather stay in the car," said Abby. "No matter. This tour is very nice."

Hitler went on, oblivious to Abby's comments. "Oh, they are always trying to kill me, but they have failed. That's because the gods are protecting the man destined to rule Europe and much of the world. Did you know some cowards planted a bomb in our meeting place in Munich just a few weeks ago? I had just left the building when it blew up!" He clapped his hands. "Well, this car is bulletproof and bombproof—built especially for me! And you don't have to worry at the house either. I have an underground bomb-proof shelter leading down a stairway in the pantry. There are escape tunnels from there. The scum will not have me!"

He sat back in his seat and played with his mustache and then pointed to a large theater building ahead. "Being a national figure does have its drawbacks. Several years ago I went unnoticed to the Semperoper opera house up ahead for Wagner's *Tristan and Isolde*. I can't do that anymore."

"The hardships of war," said Abby.

Hitler turned his head toward her, trying to decide if Abby was being factitious or was genuinely sorry for his loss of the opera. Abby stared straight ahead with no expression on her face. Hitler decided she did feel sorry for him.

After dinner Hitler escorted her into his office. Abby noted his desk was huge and utilitarian, but fresh flowers were on all tables. They sat opposite each other in a conversational seating arrangement in front of a fireplace.

"Where is Blonda?" Abby asked.

"She is probably in the kitchen or with the guards. She seems to leave me when she senses there is no danger from a visitor. I love German shepherds. Blonda's mother was always at my side before she died; then her puppy took over. The mother's name was also Blonda."

"Well, Abby, ask me some questions. I want to hear what is on your mind. I think your questions reflect what our adversaries, and even our friends, are wondering about the Third Reich."

"Adolf, why are you so aggressive? Why not be content with healing Germany's economic malaise and helping all of its citizens, not just Aryans? You took over the Sudetenland. What's next and why?

"You're direct as usual, young lady. First let me say, Abby, that your pretty face could be on a German postage stamp! A Nordic blonde! The Queen of the Third Reich!"

He laughed almost uncontrollably, and then turned deadly serious. He leaned forward and put the palms of his hands together as if praying for Abby to understand him.

"I have been aggressive all of my life. Like my Shepherd dogs, I have a lot of wolf in me. It is in my blood! It helped me survive the last war! It helped me survive prison! It helped me lead the Nazi party! It helped me lead the German nation!" With each exhortation, he slammed his right fist into the palm of his left hand; then he paused once again. Slowly, his face turned from beet red to its normal color.

"The Sudetenland is filled with German people. It belonged to us, and we took it back. The Sudetenland people were joyous when we marched into the country."

"I'm sorry, Adolf, I didn't follow your early career and the history of Sudetenland. I was busy getting through school."

Hitler stared at her for a long moment and shook his head. Then he continued.

"Some so-called leaders are slow to lead. They lead from behind." Hitler said. "I am active. I take the initiative and wait for the adversary's reaction. If no reaction, I take another step. And so on. Austria, where I was born, is mostly German, and should also belong in our fold. Germany is hemmed in. We need breathing space!"

A maid came in with tea, wafers, and candy. She poured the tea and left after doing the perfunctory tasting of the food and drink.

"What about the German Jews, Adolf? Will you let them alone?" Abby asked.

Hitler's face reddened again, and he stared at her with half-closed eyes. He set his tea cup on the table. "I will not repeat myself from what I told you at Berchtesgaden. They are not Aryans, and they are troublesome."

He stood, smiled, and raised his hand in a submissive gesture. "I see that I am not getting through to you, Abby. Maybe another time." He gestured toward his desk. "You'll have to excuse me, Abby. I have work to do. I will see you at breakfast tomorrow before you leave. Goodnight."

*I think I was just thrown out.* Abby made her way upstairs to her room and locked the door. She walked over to the window drapes and pulled them open—half expecting to find Corporal Steiner lurking there. Next, she searched the walls of the room and the bathroom for peepholes. Finally, she took an old-fashioned, long-sleeved nightgown from her suitcase. *I'm glad I brought this.* She pulled it over her head and undressed under her nightgown. Then she braced the back of a chair under the door knob, turned on the bedside lamp, and climbed into bed with a book. First, she toyed with the idea of being "Queen of the Third Reich." It didn't last long. Then she tried to read herself to sleep and finally succeeded, but it was a sleep filled with visions of assassins dressed in black.

It was late in the morning when Hitler joined Abby for a breakfast of breads and fruit. The servants were busy around the table, and the same food tasting ritual was followed before eating.

"Herr Hitler, I have been studying the artwork in the foyer. I'm not well-versed on art, but your collection is pleasing and restful to the eyes."

"Thank you, Miss White. Most of them are gifts from friends who know my tastes. I detest most so-called 'modern art.' I considerate it degenerate." He smiled broadly. "Did you know that I have done some paintings myself? I would like to show you my work someday."

Hitler walked her to the door as she was leaving for the train back to Berlin. Abby looked down the steps to the car waiting for her. *My favorite guy, Corporal Steiner.*

"Abby, I haven't given up on you yet," said Hitler. "Would you like to see my Berlin apartment? It's over my chancellery office. It has many rooms. I have some very good paintings there and some exceptional statuary."

Abby looked around. None of the staff were near. "Adolf, I will consider that. Thank you for a most interesting visit. And Dresden *is* a beautiful city."

"Oh, Abby, by the way—I'd rather you not write about your visit here. It's a personal thing that might be misinterpreted, and it's still my *almost* secret place."

He kissed her on the cheek. "Goodbye for now, Abby."

Corporal Steiner was silent on the way to the train station, and so was Abby. Both had had enough of the other.

Abby took her seat on the train and began thinking over all she had learned on her Dresden visit. Warren had told her not to make any notes until she was back in her apartment in Berlin and ready to leave them in his drop box. She tried to list things in her memory on an hour-by-hour sequence of events. When she was satisfied with her summation, she relaxed and started to read her book again, but her thoughts turned to her Wildcat friends. *I need to write to Dan to see how he is doing and if he has heard from Esther and Sean.*

*I still can't believe Karl is now in the Gestapo—such a nice fellow and a brave one. It seems forever since he and Dan saved us from the mobsters in Michigan. Has he turned into a Corporal Steiner or worse?*

As the train changed course, the sun came through her window and blinded her, so she decided to move back to the other side of the train. There were plenty of empty seats on the Sunday train. As she walked back in the car, she noticed a male passenger with his hat pulled down look up at her, and then resume reading his newspaper. Abby looked down as she passed. *His newspaper is upside down!*

After seeing Abby off, Hitler went into his office and sat in his comfortable chair overlooking the garden. It was his favorite place in Dresden to think and plan. He had dalliances with other women besides Geli Raubel and Eva Braun. There was Ema Hanf Staengl, and even an English woman, Unity Mitford. Initially, he'd wanted to seduce this American, but he found her to be a strong, unrelenting woman. Now, he was very serious about making a bond with Abby White on her terms. If he could marry an American, it may help neutralize America's reaction to his plans for Europe. His delusional mind was reeling.

*Winston Churchill's mother was from America. British and American relations grew stronger as a result. European royalty have been marrying off sons and daughters for political and military reasons for centuries. I will continue to pursue that woman. I will charm her.* With that he pounded his right fist into his left hand.

# Chapter Forty

*London—Dan*

The recruitment of Dan O'Gara as a Nazi spy was a feather in the cap for Major Albert Hofer of the SD/SS Gestapo. His boss, Reinhard Heydrich, head of the SD/SS, was delighted when told that Dan had military security clearance. "Good work, Major. This could be our best man yet!"

MI6's carefully prepared fake photographs of the construction of the British radar installations, together with their false locations along the English coast, were readily accepted by Hofer and his associates.

At his next meeting with Gerhard Kuntz, Dan was presented with a list of information needed by the Nazis. It included locations and military strengths of each army base, as well as aircraft factory locations and their monthly production rate of each type of aircraft. "Oh, yes, Dan. We've got wind of the British testing a leakproof aircraft fuel tank. Keep your ears open for that too."

Dan looked at the list. "Come on, Gerhard. You know I have a real job at the *Times*. How do they expect me to drive around England and gather all of this stuff?"

"You've got to be creative, Dan. Once you confirm a location, hang out during your weekends at local pubs chatting up soldiers and civilian employees. You are an authentic newsman with security clearance. Make them feel important and patriotic, and you'll have them giving you all kinds of good information. For more detailed data, seek out a disgruntled person with money problems who has access to the type of information we need. Cultivate that person and eventually offer him money to get information."

Gerhard paused and lit another German cigarette, which immediately gagged Dan. Then he continued.

"Your cover as a newsman is your best asset, along with your Irish charm. We will supply you with payoff money and provide you with good cameras for your recruits to photograph documents.

"Don't look so glum, Dan. We don't expect you to do these things overnight, just one at a time. Of course, we expect you to continue to report on radar installations. We need details on the electronics of the antenna systems. Once you locate the manufacturing site, work on one of the design engineers to get photographs of electronic schematics and mechanical drawings—the business end of the antenna.

"You will be paid big bonuses for this work and, at the same time, get even with the Brits for what they did to your father and uncle and Ireland."

Dan gave a copy of the SD/SS list to his MI6 people in London at a meeting arranged through drop box messages. Mr. Jones was pleased. "Excellent, Dan. We'll provide you with enough real data to continue to convince them of your reliability and loyalty. Military bases are not much of a secret, but aircraft production and radar details will need some careful work on our part to disguise the real things.

"Say, old boy," Jones continued. "Try to chat up your friend Gerhard over a few beers. We are keen to know the chain of command over Major Hofer and the relationship of the SD/SS Gestapo to the military intelligence branch of the Germany army called Abwehr. Dan, we also believe that the Nazis are trying to provide radio transmitters to known Nazi spies already in England. If you hear anything about this, let us know."

# Chapter Forty-one

*Nice—Esther and Jacob*

Esther was delighted to get Abby's letter. She was very interested in what Abby had to say about Hitler's Berlin. The newsroom at the *Nice Phare* was still buzzing with stories and editorials about the recent "*Kristale Nacht*" (The Night of the Crystal) in Berlin and other German cities. Some of the editorials tried to downplay its significance, but Jacob Bernstein's letter from America she received later was frightening.

> Dear Esther,
> I just received the terrible news that my parents and sister were taken from our home in Berlin and "resettled" to a Nazi camp near Dachau, Germany.
> A close friend of my father wrote to me that they barely had time to pack suitcases before they were taken to a railroad station. You may have heard about it in France. But according to Lawrence's letter, the persecution of Jews started when some distraught Jewish boy shot and killed a German official in an apparent retaliation for the forced deportation of his parents. Well, that gave the Nazis enough reason to punish all Jewish people. The S.A. Paramilitary force led mobs in attacking Jewish-owned stores and other businesses. Many synagogues were set afire.
> I am very worried about my family. I went to the Red Cross here, but this is apparently all new to them. They took my information and said they would try to help.

I am now involved in top-secret work for the U.S. government, and I'm not permitted to go to Germany. The State Department is trying to work with our Embassy in Berlin to help me. If you hear anything from your newspaper friends, please let me know.

Your friend always, Jacob.

# Chapter Forty-two

*London—Dan*

Gerhard Kuntz sent a message to Dan requesting that he gather information on the Norden bombsight developed in the United States. "And did the U.S. provide the bombsight to Britain?"

Jones of MI6 told Dan that he should tell the Nazis that he would work on the matter, but it may take some time since the Royal Air Force had very tight security compared to the British army. Jones also wrote, "It is interesting that the Nazis are keen on the Norden bombsight. We know just a bit about it. The U.S. is guarded about its details. We certainly don't have one in our possession yet. Here's what to tell them after a spell. Put it in your own words."

'I chatted up several different Royal Air Force chaps—told them I was writing an article on modern aircraft. They told me the bombsight was an ingenious electrical-mechanical-optical device developed by the American, Carl Norden, over a period of years. They said it had upwards of two thousand precision parts, and supposedly it makes a bombardier's job relatively easy, allowing the aircraft to deliver their bombs with pinpoint accuracy. I don't know any more right now. I don't think the Brits have one yet, but I could be wrong.'

"That should keep up your credibility, Dan," said Jones.

The Nazis were just checking. They had already assigned spies in the U.S. to infiltrate the Norden Company plant in the Queens borough of New York City, but they were working every angle to get data and confirmations on this phenomenal device.

After Dan delivered the information on the bombsight, Gerhard Kuntz sent a message to Dan scheduling another weekend trip to the Nazi site in Wihelmshaven for a training session on new covert tools.

\* \* \*

The training room for agents in Wihelmshaven contained all sorts of clever new methods for transmitting messages, including microdot usage and detection. There were three other student agents. "Now, young men," the instructor prompted, "take a picture of this paper with printing... Now you will reduce it with this equipment to a size of a period... Okay, now you will look at the dot with this microscope."

Dan was amazed. "I can see the original letter!"

Dan was also trained on explosive devices. Gerhard was delighted to show Dan his favorite—a lump of coal that was a bomb.

"This is a canister of explosive with a fuse attached and a molded plastic cover around it. It's been painted black and covered with coal dust from Welsh mines. When it's shoveled into a blazing furnace the fuse ignites and boom! Dan, you can see the fun, can't you? Put a couple in a coal lorry about to deliver coal to the Prime Minister's place at Number Ten Downing Street, or in the coal bucket next to a potbelly stove in a fighter pilot's hut on a British airfield. Exciting, yes?"

Dan nodded and smiled. "I can't wait to try it out."

\* \* \*

Dan settled back in his work at the *Times*, but he became apprehensive when he didn't hear from Gerhard Kuntz for several weeks. Finally, a message came telling him that there would be another weekend training session. "Meet at the same time, same place, and bring your bag. This time it's on radio transmission."

Dan became increasingly introspective. *This is really a dangerous game I'm playing.*

He decided to write his mother, Darcy:

> Dear Mother,
> I hope this finds you well and able to take holidays at the Tralee cottage.
> By the way, before I forget it, I did have the brewery manager send the audited financial results for the past year as you suggested. I'm pleased to report that O'Gara's Brewery is doing

fine. You were right. Your manager is doing a splendid job for the business.

My work at the *Times* is going well. New assignments on military matters are getting more interesting and challenging. Unfortunately, there is a smell of another war in the air. I often get into secret military stuff and wouldn't be surprised if I step on some toes along the way.

I now have access to a firearm in case things get nasty.

Please take measures to protect yourself, especially from strangers.

I'm sorry to have to suggest this to you, but I must. I've asked for a transfer out of this kind of work, but it may be some time before I can extradite myself.

Please give my regards to Cormac and Sally at the cottage. Oh, yes, I did receive a letter from Sean and Esther. They seem to be doing well along with their son, Dan, who Esther says is growing to be a strong young man like his father.

Love always, Dan.

P.S. Remember, be safe.

# Chapter Forty-three

*Wihelmshaven—Major Hofer*

Dan and Gerhard Kuntz took the same ocean-going speedboat through the North Sea to Wihelmshaven. Major Hofer had his retinue of SS men meet the boat and drive them to SS headquarters.

Dan then sensed something was very wrong. Instead of being led to the dining area or training room, he was taken by two SS men to the interrogation room. Gerhard followed. Dan sat and stared into the one-way mirror, and then noticed a side table where there was an array of torture devices spread out on a white tablecloth—clubs, knives, thumb screws, and a variety of whips, some with barbwire tips.

"What's going on, Gerhard?"

"Shut your mouth, O'Gara, and wait."

Major Hofer entered the room, pulling on his leather gloves. He began pacing around the table. Kuntz stood by the door.

"We are very disappointed in you, young man. You are a damned traitor to our cause. One of our other agents in London was on surveillance at an MI6 drop box site when he saw you enter and leave. He didn't know you then, but he followed you on your devious route to the *Times* building and entered behind you. He said the receptionist addressed you as Mr. O'Gara. Our agent returned to the MI6 drop box, read your note about going to Wihelmshaven and returned the note to the box. Don't you stupid people seal your envelopes?"

Hofer stopped pacing, placed his hands on the table opposite Dan, and leaned with a sneer on his face. "So here you are, O'Gara. Are you going to tell us the truth about the data and photographs you gave us, or do you want to make it difficult for yourself?"

"I have nothing to say," said Dan.

"Ha! We shall see," said Kuntz. "I thought you were my best friend. I vouched for you. You signed an official form pledging your loyalty to the Nazi Party. You turned out to be a scummy double agent. You will suffer for this!" With that he walked to the side table, picked up a wooden club, and struck Dan across the side of his head. Blood flowed out of Dan's left ear.

Hofer left the room and returned with another SS man—a very large man with a face of a bulldog.

"This is your jailer, Sergeant Siegler," said Hofer. "He is not a nice man. He will take over from here. We will give you a little time to reconsider your silence."

Siegler grinned, showing big gums and small, crooked teeth. Though Dan was a fairly big young man, Siegler lifted Dan out of his chair and pushed him through the door and down a dark hallway into a bare room with a bright, naked light bulb hanging from the ceiling. The bulb flicked and swayed from air movement when the door was opened, casting long, spastic shadows across the room.

Siegler finally spoke. "Take off all of your clothes and give them to me." Dan complied and handed his clothes over. "Now sit on that chair." Dan sat on the chair and he tipped over, falling to the floor—a three-legged chair. Seigler laughed and left with Dan's clothes. Dan was startled by the slamming of the iron door and another slamming of a metallic iron bolt.

Kuntz told Hofer, "I am ashamed that I brought a spy into our midst. If this gets back to my father, he will disown me. He is a personal friend of our Fuehrer."

"We are all entitled to our mistakes, Kuntz. Just don't let it happen again."

"It won't, sir." said Kuntz. "We told O'Gara that his mother was at risk if he betrayed us. I'm sure he told MI6. With your permission, I will personally take care of her in Ireland, then we can mail a special letter to MI6, warning them that even the families of their double agents will pay."

The concrete floor was cold. Dan propped the back of the three-legged chair under the door knob for balance and sat huddled up against the cold, saying prayers taught to him by Irish nuns in grade school. He said a special prayer for his mother. He heard a noise at the door and stood. Someone opened his cell door and threw in a ragged blanket. He wrapped himself in the blanket and surveyed the room. High on the wall was steam pipe that ran along the back of the cell, and above it a small barred window exposed a patch of gray sky. There was no bed. A dripping water spigot protruded from a wall. A floor drain was next to a waste bucket. The metal cell door had two slits that were opened from the hallway. Dan figured the top one was for observation and the one at floor level was for passing in food. He prayed again.

# Chapter Forty-four

*Ireland—Darcy*

Kuntz and a plainclothes SS man made their way to Ireland posing as Dutch businessmen. Their first stop was the O'Gara Brewery in Kinsale. The brewery manager invited them into his office.

"My family owns a brewery in The Netherlands," said Kuntz. "We are interested in doing a joint venture with your company. We think it would be beneficial for both companies."

"Well, Dutchmen! That accounts for your accent. Sir, I am just the manager here. You will have to talk with Mrs. O'Gara. She's on holiday at their cottage in Tralee."

After they left, the manager telephoned Darcy to tell her to expect a visit from two Dutch businessmen.

Kuntz and his partner drove through the open gate and parked near the front door. They both wore long, black leather coats and black hats. Sally answered the door bell and opened the door. "Yes?" said Sally.

Kuntz smiled. "Are you Mrs. Darcy O'Gara?"

"No, I'm the chief housekeeper. What business do you have with Mrs. O'Gara?"

"We are brewery executives from Amsterdam and wish to speak with her on a business matter."

"Is she expecting you? Did you write or call ahead?

Kuntz frowned and said, "Lady, just get Mrs. O'Gara."

Gerhard Kuntz didn't know that Darcy O'Gara was no ordinary Irish housewife. She had been hardened by years of skirmishes in the fight for

Irish independence and actually participated in chopping down trees and setting roadblocks for trucks carrying British soldiers. She had buried neighbors, her brother-in-law, and nursed her husband after he'd received grievous wounds. Many of her friends had been widowed.

Minutes later, Darcy came to the door wearing a long coat. "I was just going out. What is it, please?"

"Are you Mrs. Darcy O'Gara?" said Kuntz.

"Yes, I am."

At that, the Nazis pulled Luger pistols from their pockets. They had no chance to even raise their guns. Darcy fired two rounds from the revolver she carried in her coat pocket. At the same time, Cormac came from the shadows and blasted them with a double-barreled shotgun.

Sally came running. "I called the Garda." She looked at the bloody corpses, and said, "I'm glad you got them outside—they would have ruined the carpets."

Darcy turned away, her eyes filled with tears. "Now I'm really worried about my Danny boy."

# Chapter Forty-five

*Berlin—The Admiral*

Abby arrived back from Dresden and took a taxi from the train station to her apartment. She made no effort to evade any followers. The Gestapo had to know where she lived by now.

After unpacking, she sat at her desk and wrote down all she could remember about Hitler, his habits, and even details about the food tasting by servants before he would eat anything. She speculated on what might be his timetable for giving Germany more "breathing space." She also made sketches of the floor plan of the Dresden house, including the escape hatch in the pantry.

She knew she couldn't leave her notes in her apartment for a Gestapo search, so she taped them to her stomach before going to the Tribune. She now had a lockable desk at the office with a hidden compartment for safekeeping special items. The bureau chief, James Hoffman, met her at the door.

"Abby, we had an awful incident here over the weekend while you were gone. Janelle Rosenfeld was on the sidewalk out front after leaving the office about noon. Remember Fritz, the office boy? Well, he knocked Janelle down and then beat on her. While she was out cold, he hung a small sign around her neck. In block letters it said JUNDEN. Then he continued to kick her and beat her with his fists. Witnesses saw it happen, but did nothing. The police officers were there, but they let Fritz go. Carol was leaving for lunch, and she tried to help Janelle but was pushed back. Carol said that the people stood around smiling as she was beaten. Abby, there's a terrible trait in the German character—they take joy in the misery of others. In German it's called *Schadenfreude*. I don't know why they are like that. Maybe it makes them feel superior."

"Oh, the poor woman. That's awful. Will she be all right?"

"Yes, I talked to her doctor at the hospial. She told the doctor she wanted to go home to New York. I don't blame her. We'll get along. I'm going over there in a few minutes. Now, come into my office. I need to hear about your trip."

Abby told him very little about her trip to Dresden. "I was asked by Hitler not to write about my visit, but I can tell you that he is one strange person, James. And his artwork in the house belies his fierce temperament—pastoral scenes of sleeping sheep and wandering cattle."

"He's crazy, I'd say. Abby, it's going very bad here. Goebbels's propaganda office has started monitoring all press releases of foreign newspaper offices. I don't know how long we can last under these conditions."

Even before Abby could get her messages to Warren Walters, Hitler had annexed Austria into the Third Reich. It was the talk of the dinner party at the Brazilian Embassy that Abby attended with Claus von Fritsch. They soon parted company at the party—Claus met some fellow officers, and Abby saw Lydia Viazensky's waving hand. Abby liked to hear Lydia's gossip, but she didn't dare to mention her trip to Hitler's Dresden home. *Dear Lydia would have that tidbit all over Berlin*, she thought.

They each took a glass of champagne from a roving waiter and then scanned the huge reception room for familiar faces. Abby saw Warren Walters at a distance talking with another man who was also in black tie. *I would love to go over to him and give him a big hug—he looks so handsome—but I shan't*, she thought.

"Looks like the usual suspects, Abby," said Lydia. "Except now the military are now flaunting their new uniforms with all their ribbons and medals. I do admit they certainly look gallant."

A familiar voice from behind came through to them. "I must say hello to the two most beautiful women in the room."

"Franz!" Lydia said. "I didn't think you could make it tonight."

"Things changed, my dear. We will not sail until Monday."

He gave a slight bow to Abby, "Delighted to see you again, Miss Abby White." He paused. "It's still 'Miss' isn't it?"

"Oh, yes. Maybe I'll be an old maid, but I'm in no hurry. What a beautiful uniform, Admiral, with all your ribbons," said Abby. "It was well worth the wait for the tailor to finish." She touched his decorations on his uniform. "Tell me, what do these ribbons mean? Are we in a war I don't know about?"

He chuckled. "These are from the last war, Abby. I was a junior officer on the SMS *Brandenburg*. It didn't end well for my ship and Germany."

Lydia lowered her voice. "I must tell you, Abby, that Franz and I have been seeing each other." She smiled warmly at Dieter and touched his hand. "I think it's getting very serious."

The Admiral kissed her on the cheek. "Yes, it is, my dear."

It was getting too sticky sweet for Abby. "So, what are you doing now, Admiral? Not sitting behind a desk, I'll wager."

Lydia spoke for him. "Abby, Franz has been given command of a battleship, the *Bismarck*. Our admiral will be captain of one of the largest battleships in the world!"

Dieter laughed. "That only holds until the next one is built larger—which will probably be soon. The German navy is coming on with better ships and more submarines. It's a great time to be a sailor!"

"Abby, I hope you will be in our wedding? Will you?" said Lydia.

"Our wedding! You only said 'It's getting very serious'! My, things happened fast with you two—wartime I guess." She paused. "Yes, I would be happy to be part of your wedding day. When will it be?"

"After we finish sea trials of the ship," said Dieter. "We've installed new and better long-range guns and new technical devices for better accuracy. Got to try them and shake the bugs out."

*More stuff for Warren*, thought Abby.

Dieter saw a ranking officer across the room. "Excuse me ladies, I need to do a little politicking."

"Lydia, I'm a bit dismayed. Why didn't you tell me about your romance with Franz? We are such good friends!"

"My dear Abby, I didn't want to jinx the whole thing. I wasn't really sure of his feelings, or my feelings for that matter, until he proposed to me last Sunday. He even asked my father for his permission before he asked me! I'm sorry, Abby, but you know how these things can go. Still, I should have called you. I'm so sorry. Will you still be a bridesmaid? My sister will be my maid of honor. It won't be a big affair."

"Of course, Lydia. I was only half serious. And maybe a little jealous."

"What about your sweet friend, Claus von Fritsch?"

"I think highly of Claus. He and his family have been very kind to me and were very helpful when I first came to Berlin." She paused and looked at Lydia. "There's just not that romantic feeling there, Lydia. Maybe he's too German and I'm too American. I tried, but there's no electricity between us. Oh, did you know he's being reassigned to Italy as a liaison officer at Mussolini's headquarters in Rome? I will miss him—a wonderful gentleman."

"Ships that pass in the night, Abby. How many people have we met, even as young as we are? Hundreds? Thousands? More? We have acquaintances, work friends, relatives, close friends, and intimate friends. We have very few people in our lives who are intimate friends—ones you can trust with your most inner thoughts and feelings. I apologize again for not letting you know about how serious it was. You are my intimate friend, and I feel very fortunate about that. Please, let's never change that."

\* \* \*

Abby wrote a message to Warren and enclosed her notes and drawings from Dresden. She shook off a tail who tried to follow her from her apartment to the drop box.

> Hello Tall Man/Dark Cave
> I miss you. I was doing fine until I saw you at the Brazilian Embassy dinner party looking so dapper.
> Guess what? Lydia is marrying Admiral Franz Dieter and I will be in their wedding party. He has been given command of a battleship, the *Bismarck*. The wedding will take place after he returns from sea trials of the ship. They have added new long-range guns that need to be tested—according to the Admiral.
> Another bit of info. Before I left Lydia, a young U-boat officer was boasting to us that they are building many U-boats, with the construction site in Hamburg producing the most submarines. And eight bombproof sub pens are under construction along the North Sea and Baltic Sea coast lines. Good data, I trust.
> I hope my notes from my trip are clear. As we parted, the big guy said he wants me to visit his apartment here in Berlin to see his collection of artworks. I'm keeping him at arm's length, but that doesn't seem to bother him anymore. I will accept his invitation unless you advise against it. He seems to talk more openly the more I am with him. This could lead to more important disclosures.

He's a hard person to figure out. Lots of highs and lows. One thing is constant—his hate for certain people , and even countries, that stand in his way. I hope something or somebody will slow him down. Austria is history. Czechoslovakia and Poland will be next, I'll wager. That's what I gathered from his blustering.

Love from the High Mountain

*Excellent job, Abby.* Every week Warren Walters summarized the information gathered by any of the three agents he handled and would send it by air in a diplomatic pouch to the U.S. Intelligence Office of the State Department in Washington, D.C. Warren knew that U.S. Intelligence was now exchanging information with Britain's MI6 in London. MI6 had been contacted by the leader of several senior German army generals who wanted Hitler dead. "Could High Mountain do the job?" asked MI6 and Washington.

The request put Warren in a quandary. *Abby defended herself when attacked by Capone's gangsters, but she is not an assassin. Even if she would agree to kill Hitler, his guards would certainly torture and kill her. How could I let that happen?*

Warren's reply to Washington was purposely vague. "This is a major project that will take time to develop. Does Washington realize that, successful or not, such an action could drag us into a European war that we are trying to avoid?"

This was a brash comment from an underling embassy staff agent, but it hit home. They hadn't really considered the ramifications—it was to be a favor for MI6. Warren's senior in Washington decided that only President Roosevelt could make that decision.

## Chapter Forty-six

*Berlin—Gestapo Headquarters*

After lunch one day, Abby and her friend, Carol Munster, from the *Tribune* office, decided to walk over to 8 Prinz-Albecht-Strass to see the building which housed the dreaded SS Gestapo police. "An ugly building." said Carol. Abby agreed. It was a large, begrimed, four-storied eyesore. Inside was a nest of plunderers, kidnappers, torturers, and murderers. "They're trying to gain respectability among the German military and quasi-military forces." Abby said. "It's not working. They're frightening everybody with their brutality, even the most law abiding citizens."

Like most organizations, the Gestapo had more than its share of competiveness and gossip. The latest story going around the building was about the SS unit in Wihelmshaven. His adjutant told Reinhard Heydrich, the operating head of the SS, the current internal buzz. "Our building is talking about a British MI6 double agent who penetrated our Wilhelmshaven office. The word is that we got him, but two of our agents were killed in Ireland in a stupid attempt at revenge. The action was approved by Major Hofer. Hofer was trying to cover up the story, they say, but it leaked out."

"Incredible!" said Heydrich. "Find out if the MI6 spy was the man who reported on radar stations in England and the Norden bombsight. I recall that he was an Irishman who was supposed to have hated the English. If all that information was false, I'll have to tell Himmler and Marshall Goering. It will be an embarrassment to our organization. Hofer will pay for this!" Heydrich pounded his desk. His adjutant started to leave when

Heydrich raised his hand. "Wait. It occurs to me the Irishman is from a neutral country. There may be some ramifications to consider here. Call the idiot Hofer and tell him not to kill him, but put him in solitary for the time being. He may be a valuable pawn."

Before calling Wihelmshaven, the adjutant returned to his office and began leafing through status reports on his desk. He found the report listing all persons being held by Gestapo units in Germany. Under the Wihelmshaven unit, the name of Daniel O'Gara lept off the page. The notation for O'Gara said that he was exposed as a MI6 double agent by Major Albert Hofer. It went on to say that his cover job was working as a reporter for the *Times* of London and was initially recruited by agent Gerhard Kuntz.

*Oh no! Daniel O'Gara, my Wildcat friend!* The adjutant was Major Karl Kruger who, along with Peter Farben and Hans Strasser, was ordered back to Germany from their spying stint in the U.S.

What the Nazis didn't know was that Kruger was an imbedded sleeper agent for U.S. Intelligence. He was to be activated when they needed him for very special work.

He was recruited rather easily by one William Sullivan of the State Department after an intelligence breakthrough identified the three. The rise of fascism in Germany and Italy was the antithesis of Kruger's sense of freedom in a democracy. Then, too, he had learned to love the American way of life. His decision was finalized by Sullivan's written promise, to be placed on file, granting him immediate U.S. citizenship and a position with the State Department at the conclusion of his service if he desired. His code name was Apache.

*It has to be Dan. How can I help him without exposing myself and negating any mission that the U.S. might plan for me?* He finally picked up the telephone.

"Hofer, this is Kruger in Berlin."

"Hello, Kruger. How can I help you?"

"Heydrich wants you to put the Irishman, O'Gara, in solitary. No harsh interrogation and no killing without approval. Ireland is a neutral country. We may use him as a hostage, or in exchange for one of our agents who Britain has in custody, so keep him well."

There was dead silence.

"You were almost too late, Major. The traitor, O'Gara, was to be executed tomorrow morning since he stubbornly refused to answer questions, even after our most vigorous interrogations."

Kruger reported the close save of O'Gara to Heydrich. "Good work, Kruger. I have been worried about stupid people like Hofer."

He paused. "Kruger, Himmler wants me to travel around and review our new camps and police posts. I have been pleased with your work. Your coordination of settlement trains to our camps has been exemplary. Your judgment is sharp also. Himmler has approved your promotion to Lieutenant Colonel. Another officer will handle the scheduling of deportation trains. Congratulations, Colonel!" He shook Kruger's hand.

"Now you have more authority and can handle serious matters in my absence. I'm confident the office will run smoothly while I travel."

# Chapter Forty-seven

*Nice—Esther*

The telephone rang in Esther's and Sean's flat just after nine-year-old Daniel blew out the candles on his birthday cake. The three boys who were invited as guests didn't notice the ring—they were waiting impatiently for the cake to be cut. John and Maria Foch, Daniel's godparents, did notice the ring while they were ladling out ice cream.
The call was from a friend of Esther's at the *Phare*'s news desk.

"Oh no!" said Esther. "When did it happen? Thank you so much for calling, Helene."

She hung up the telephone and sighed. "Germany has just invaded Poland."

"This is not good," said John Foch. "This could escalate into a terrible war!"

Two days later, after Hitler ignored pleas for Germany to leave Poland, Poland's allies, England and France, declared war on Germany.

Esther was serving dinner that day to Sean and Daniel. "I'm glad you're still a citizen of Ireland, Sean. The *Phare*'s reporters in Paris say conscription for the French army will start very soon."

The German army and air force made short order of Poland with their *blitzkrieg* (lightning war). Norway and Denmark were invaded next, and then Hitler turned his attention to France. Soon there were newsreels in American theatres showing German troops goose-stepping under the *Arc de Triomphe* in Paris. The world was in shock.

\* \* \*

Esther carefully opened a cardboard box that had been delivered by an employee of her father's jewelry business in Lyon. A handwritten letter lay on top of several envelopes and velvet pouches:

Dear Esther,

    I am so sorry what we did to you. Even your mother now wonders whether she made a mistake in sending you away. It was a terrible thing we did. Please forgive us. I'm so happy that the Lyon paper carries your column from Nice, but my tears often fall on the paper.

    Your sister guards your letters sent to her. Yesterday when your mother was out, she showed me a picture of your handsome son—my grandson! Would that things could be different.

    This box contains items for safekeeping. I had my most trusted employee carry it to you. The Nazis are rounding up Jews in Paris for so-called "resettlement." We hear that they are being loaded into railroad boxcars with straw on the floors. I fear that it will only be a matter of days or even hours before they are here in Lyon doing the same. I pray that Lyon will be different, but I doubt it.

    Why is it that Hitler is doing this to the Jews? I have spent the last few years trying to figure this out. I know of no Jews in France who have broken French laws or any other law for that matter. I began as a gem polisher and eventually started my own business. I've worked hard at it for over forty years and have provided good jobs with good pay for all the Company's employees. I have never missed paying taxes or helping my fellow man. What have we done wrong?

    Enough. I'm sorry for bothering you with my thoughts.

    The package contains some portable assets, which will become yours and your sister's if something happens to us. I have been saving diligently for our retirement for many years.

    Protect your family. Try to get out of France if you can and take the package with you. It is too late for us. The devils will probably be down in Nice after Paris and Lyon. Be prepared for the worst.

    You may remember that I have a cousin named Paul Brindle who lives in Staten Island, New York City—his address is 1932 Woodrow Road. He is a good man. If things do get worse, we will contact you through him when things finally quiet down. I pray they will. Again, please forgive us our transgressions.

My love to you and your family.   Father

Esther opened the largest envelope first. It contained a notarized copy of the deed to her parent's house and a bundle of bank certificates issued by French, Swiss, and English banks together with some French, Swiss, and even German currency. There was also a formal appraisal of his company's net worth and a recent appraisal of their house's value. She then untied several small pouches, one at a time. One contained diamonds. Another was half-filled with precious stones, and the third was heavy with women's and men's jewelry. Esther recognized her mother's diamond necklace—a hand-me-down from her grandmother. *Does she know that father sent this to me?*

# Chapter Forty-eight

*Berlin—Abby*

Abby's letter to Dan in London was returned with the notation "Undeliverable." She called an acquaintance at the *Times*. The women said, "Dan O'Gara is missing. He was last seen about a month ago with a German correspondent named Gerhard Kuntz who was also missing. His mother called from Ireland about three weeks ago. She was very upset as you can imagine. Now we hear that Kuntz was killed in Ireland at Dan's mother's house along with another German. We don't know what to think!"

# Chapter Forty-nine

*Wilhelmshaven—Dan*

Dan O'Gara didn't understand what was going on. He was still in solitary, but the countless beatings and torture had stopped. Just three days before, he had lost the end of his left little finger down to the first knuckle. Siegler had tied Dan to an armchair, and then clamped his left hand to a wooden table.

Siegler would ask questions from the list given to him by Major Hofer, like "Who was your handler at MI6?" When Dan didn't answer, Siegler would snip off another little piece of his finger with heavy-duty pruning sheers.

"This is great fun, Irishman. Don't you think so? I really hope you don't confess. This work gives me great pleasure. We'll go to your right hand next, after all of these fingers are gone, and then to your toes."

Change had come suddenly. Hofer was transferred to command a concentration camp in eastern Poland, which specialized in the extermination of the mentally retarded, homosexuals, the aged and disabled—all undesirables for the Aryan Third Reich. His replacement, a Major Osterholtz, read recent orders from SS headquarters in Berlin that included a note on O'Gara. "We may have to release or exchange this prisoner since Ireland is a neutral country. He is to be treated accordingly. You may still use soft interrogation techniques to get names. He did nothing except tell us lies about England's military strength. No felonies committed. International law comes to play here." Osterholtz called in a medical doctor to check on "the special prisoner."

The doctor closed Dan's finger wound with sutures and dressed infected body wounds resulting from whip lashings. After reading the doctor's report, Osterholtz walked to Dan's cell, opened the guard's porthole, and viewed Dan's bony body and ragged uniform. He ordered Siegler to give Dan better food and a bed and "clean him up and get him a clean uniform. I want him well as soon as possible in case of a visit from Berlin. We can still interrogate him, but in a different way. We may still kill him before it's all over, but I don't want Heydrich angry at me. Understand me, Sergeant? If I go, you will go too."

Two days later, Siegler was called into Osterholtz's office. "Siegler, you are an undisciplined, sadistic brute. That's fine with me, but you should know that with certain prisoners you can get more information with honey than with a whip. I have a plan for O'Gara. If this works, Berlin will be proud of us. Listen up. On my tour of the prison I noticed several attractive women. I understand they were taken on an SS raid of a Communist cell in Oldenburg, not far from here."

Siegler took instructions from the Major well. He led the prettiest female to the interrogation room, after she'd been allowed to bathe, clad only in a light coat. "If you can tease this man into answering the few questions on this list, we will be more lenient with you—maybe a work factory instead of the alternative. We will be listening and watching you from our observation room."

Dan was tied into an armchair again, but his arms were free. Siegler pushed the girl into the room and left.

She spoke broken English. "I hear your name is Dan. I am Sasha, ready to entertain you if you answer a few questions for me. You seem to be a special prisoner. They will not hurt you if you speak the truth."

She opened her coat and nestled up to him. "It's probably been a long time since you've had a woman. I'm ready, you handsome man."

She read a question. Dan said nothing. She nestled closer and read another question. Nothing. She sat on his lap and whispered in his ear. "Answer the questions, you fool, or they will kill both of us."

Dan looked sympathetically at the woman "Give it up, Sasha, if that's your real name. I've been near death already. I'm ready to go. I'm sorry."

Siegler opened the interrogation room door. He hit Dan a hard blow to the stomach. "Won't show marks there, Irish." The woman's crying turned to screams as Siegler dragged her by her hair through the door and down the hall.

Osterholtz came into the room. "An admirable example of restraint, O'Gara. Maybe you're a homosexual!" He slapped Dan across the face with his leather gloves. Dan risked a little smile. "Don't gloat, Irishman. I'm not through with you yet." Instead of beatings, they began periods of grueling questioning under bright lights, sleep deprivation, waking him up with a bucket of ice water, and threats of death.

Dan hardened even more. *They can kill me, but the bastards can't make me talk. And as long as they're trying to make me talk, they're not killing me.*

# Chapter Fifty

*Berlin Flashback*

When their espionage ring in Atlantic City was ordered back to Germany, Kruger, Farben, and Strasser met in Berlin with a German colonel who was responsible for reassigning returning spies to other tasks for the Nazis. There were a lot of heel clickings and Nazi salutes exchanged when they filed into the colonel's office. Peter Farben's father, now the head of Daimler Benz's German military vehicle division, helped to get him assigned as an aide to General Halder. Hans Strasser became a head-cracking enforcer for the Gestapo on the streets of Berlin.

Karl Kruger was also assigned to the Gestapo. After Farben and Strasser left, Kruger asked the colonel if there was another post he could take. "Sir, I don't have the stomach for some of the things the Gestapo must do. I couldn't even put my sick old dog to sleep. But I would be efficient and loyal in other work for the Third Reich, I assure you, sir."

The colonel had studied Kruger closely, and then leafed through Kruger's personnel file. "Well, you were journalism major in America, and your father is a newspaper man. Let's see, Goebbles doesn't need anybody in the propaganda office right now, but our SS-Obergruppen Fuehrer, Reinhard Heydrich, needs a personal staff officer to handle records and reports. Let's assign you as his adjutant. It is an important position for the Fatherland."

Kruger had accepted the post. He had heard and read that Heydrich came from a classical music family. His father founded the Halle Conservatory and his mother taught piano there. Heydrich himself was considered a highly skilled concert violinist. *A good man to work under*, Kruger surmised. It didn't take him long to realize that Heydrich, despite his upbringing, was a sadist and enjoyed watching beatings and roundups of Nazi dissenters and innocent Jews. He told Kruger, "I used to get up close when our men crushed skulls. It's like smashing watermelons—great fun! But one time I caught splashing blood, and it ruined a good uniform." He gave his macabre smile. "So I back up farther now."

*I'm a paper-pusher for this monster*, Kruger had thought. *When will they activate me? I need to get out of this goddamn place.*

# Chapter Fifty-one

*Berlin—1941*

Now Karl was now a lieutenant colonel—in charge when Heydrich travelled. *The U.S. intelligence network must know this by now. How can I redeem myself after aiding in these atrocities? Maybe my time will come soon.*

\* \* \*

Warren responded to Abby's information from her Dresden visit and the Brazilian Embassy party:

> High Mountain
>
> You have been right on with your timetable for the aggressive German military moves! And the information on the *Bismarck* and U-boats is priceless!
>
> We would like you to continue to accept big boy's invitations. Anything you can glean from your visits will be woven in the tapestry of intelligence data from other sources. (How about that for prose?)
>
> It was tough for both of us not to blow our cover at the Brazilian Embassy party. I eyed your pretty face once, and then I tried avoiding another look. Not successful.
>
> Back to business. It will be important to know where the Bismarck's home port will be when it returns from this cruise, and its sailing schedule. Hard information to get, but maybe you will hear something at the Dieter wedding coming soon.

You do such good work, High Mountain. Please be careful. We will be moving your drop box as a precautionary measure. Perhaps we can rendezvous soon at some beautiful location. I really miss you.
Dark Cave

\* \* \*

Another invitation by Hitler was delivered to Abby by his personal aide, this time with a tap on the door of her apartment.

"Miss White? A message from our Fuehrer." He clicked his heels and was gone as quickly as he came.

She walked to her desk, examining the envelope. It was addressed by hand with a wax seal on the back embossed with a swastika. She found her letter opener and carefully opened the letter. It was handwritten in German.

Dear Abby,
I have missed your rare beauty and your sharp mind. I hope you can join me for dinner on Saturday, 3 October, at my residence in the Chancellery building. Please arrive at seven p.m. Use the Wilhelm Strasse entrance. The two outside guards will be advised to let you enter. The inside guards will escort you to my office where I will be working. I want you to see where I work, and then we'll go upstairs to my residence for dinner.

Please call my secretary at the number listed at the top of this letter to confirm your acceptance. I do look forward to seeing you again.
Fondly, Adolf

\* \* \*

The wedding between Admiral Dieter and Lydia Viazensky was held at the Ministry of the Navy on Bindler Strasse in downtown Berlin. It was a small wedding as Lydia had wanted, but the German military hierarchy's presence was abundant.

"Lydia, you look beautiful!" said Abby. "Where did you find that lovely dress?"

"It's a very old hand-me-down from a dear aunt who wore it to the Czar's court years ago—well before the awful revolution. I managed to pack it with my things before we fled."

"Now may I ask, Lydia, where did you get all those beautiful diamonds?"

"Oh, from various suitors. I never hated a man so much to give him back his diamonds."

They stood behind a curtain waiting for the clergy to appear. "Abby, peek out there. It looks like a military parade!" The scene was resplendent with officers in medaled uniforms wearing white gloves. Grand Admiral Erich Raeder and Admiral Karl Doenitz were conversing with Admiral Wilhelm Canaris. The most colorful of the bunch was *Reichmarshall* Hermann Goering with his cream-colored uniform. A sash embroidered with gold thread was draped over his shoulder and wrapped around his waist.

Martin Bormann, Hitler's chief aide and office watchdog, told Claus Dieter, "Our Fuehrer sends his congratulations and is sorry he can't attend your celebration. He also wishes you glorious sailing on the *Bismarck*."

Champagne flowed freely at the reception held after the wedding vows. Abby sipped from her glass and listened close by as Goering nudged his rotund body into a group of naval officers chatting with the bridegroom. They moved aside quickly for Goering. "Congratulations, Dieter! My big question is where you will dock that monster of yours. The *Bismarck* will take up a whole harbor!" He laughed at his own joke, and the others nervously joined in.

"Thank you, Reichmarshall. It looks like Hamburg will be our home port. We trust that your Luftwaffe will provide us good air cover if we need it, both in port and as we move about."

"At your service, Admiral, but I doubt if the *Bismarck* itself will need protection. I do think your boys will need protection in the Hamburg bars from all those submariners who also are making homeport there. They are said to be ferocious bar fighters—so ill-tempered after all that time under water. Ha, ha!"

* * *

The Admiral and Lydia's honeymoon at the fashionable Baden-Baden resort in southern Germany was cut short. Raeder ordered the *Bismarck* to sea to interdict and destroy Allied shipping. Lydia sent a letter to Abby with the news and suggested a luncheon date.

Abby delivered information obtained from the wedding and from Lydia's letter to her new drop box. She wrote Warren that she had accepted an invitation to big boy's place. He had placed a message for her in the box.

> High Mountain
>
> You had mentioned to me in a note that your friend and former fellow student, Daniel O'Gara, was missing from the *Times* of London.
>
> I hate to deliver this news, but the British MI6 office notified our Washington office that Daniel was operating as a counter-spy for MI6 and was uncovered by the Nazis. He is in an SS prison at Wilhelmshaven at the North Sea coast. It's been confirmed by another agent. I am sorry to report this to you. Please be careful.
>
> Dark Cave

Abby walked slowly back to her office at the *Tribune*. Her office mate, Carol, asked why she looked so sad. "A friend is in serious trouble" was all she could muster. *I should have said friend and lover.* She closed the door on her office and cried softly. She called Esther at the *Nice Phare* and told her that Dan was mugged by hoodlums in Germany while on an assignment. She was partially truthful; she didn't think it was necessary or safe to tell Esther the whole story.

"Our gallant protector," said Esther to Sean. "How could anyone hurt such a wonderful man?"

# Chapter Fifty-two

***The Chancellery—Hitler***

Abby leaned forward in her taxi and asked the driver, "Why do Berlin buildings look so gray and ugly?"

The driver managed a smile. "Because they are designed by gray and ugly people, you think?"

He pulled up to the Wilhelm Strasse entrance to the German Chancellery. The guards nodded to her and opened massive oak doors. She was led by a junior-grade officer to Hitler's office and escorted to a conversational setting at the end of the large room. "Pleased be seated. Our Fuehrer will be here shortly."

Abby sat in a soft, yielding armchair and looked across a massive Persian rug laid on a honey-colored waxed floor. The rug finally ended under an incredibly large desk. *Is that where he plans his next invasion?* She scanned the room. The vaulted ceiling with frescos was a least twenty feet high, and marble-faced walls had recesses for artwork.

She heard footsteps coming and began nonchalantly studying her finger nails. *I must go to work. Observe, ask, and listen. Keep cool and remember poor Dan.*

"Thank you for coming, Abby," Hitler said as he shook her hand. He turned slightly and extended his arm. "Do you approve of my humble office?"

"Adolf, when did you have time to collect all of this beautiful artwork?"

"Oh, I would never have enough time. Everything was given to me by the loyal supporters of the Third Reich." He led her around the room, telling her what he knew about the various art pieces.

"Very well done. Who designed and decorated this room?"

"Paul Troost was the architect who knocked down the old walls, and his wife, Gerdy Troost, did the décor. I agree. They did a fine job.

"By the way, Abby, I read in a dossier on you that you were a very brave person in your fight against the Capone mob. I also read that your father is a highly respected architect and builder in America and that your grandfather was an innovative builder—among the first to use steel and iron rods in strengthening masonry structures and reinforcing concrete foundations. The technique allowed structures to be built much taller. Albert Speer, my personal architect, and I discussed those wonderful innovations for some time last week."

"My grandfather was a gifted architect despite losing his arm at Gettysburg."

"That's amazing, Abby. An exceptional man."

They sat in a conversational area near his desk.

"Speer and I also talked about inviting your father to Berlin to review our plans for building a *new* Berlin. We have already made a scale model of World Capital Germania. It will be the center of our Thousand Year Reich.

"Just think. Your father and mother and you here in Berlin, and your father being honored for his achievements! Abby, you have remarkable ancestry. I am not surprised—they're all Aryans with Nordic beginnings."

"Adolf, you told me you like it when I speak my mind, so here I go again." She paused and measured her words. "I think your plans are grand, but why must you come up with this Aryan differentiation? My father and grandfather are Americans. We are all human beings first, and then citizens of our countries next. We can do nothing about whether our parents were German, African, or Chinese. Do you see what I mean?"

Hitler's face flushed. Abby noticed a small amount of spittle froth gathered in the corner of his mouth.

"Abby, Aryans are destined to rule the world!"

Just then a black-uniformed, white-aproned maid appeared at the office door. "Mein Fuehrer, dinner is ready upstairs."

"Thank you, Giselle."

Giselle frowned at Abby. Abby frowned back.

There was a uniformed guard at the elevator who buzzed it open, then clicked his heels as Abby and Hitler entered. The elevator opened to a grandiose foyer. The opposite wall of the room was covered with a colorful tapestry depicting dancing nymphs in a pastoral scene. A marble, lace-covered table festooned with flowers was the centerpiece of the room.

Hitler was pleased when Abby said, "Very special."

The dining room table was smaller and more suitable for two people. There were vases of fresh flowers on an antique buffet.

Two girls assisted Giselle in serving dinner. They did the required tasting for poisons.

"This is where I take most of my meals," said Hitler.

"Is your chef, Herr Krannenberger, still with you? This is very good."

Hitler's feathers were still a bit ruffled from Abby's remarks in his office, but Abby thought he was back under control. "Oh yes, he is my only cook, and he comes equipped with a suitcase to keep up with me. Ha!"

"Where is Blonda?" asked Abby. *I've got to get him to relax more and talk. I shouldn't have mentioned the Aryan business.*

"Oh, poor Blonda somehow ate the wrong thing, and she died. Martin Bormann gave me another pup for my birthday, which I call Blondi. She is growing up safely in Berchtesgaden. I may have her here after she is trained."

"I read that Benito Mussolini also has a dog. Adolf, may I ask what you think of Il Duce?"

"This is just between you and me, Abby. He is useful to our cause right now, but I don't care to be near him. He is an arrogant egomaniac. He bristles with self-importance. The runt struts about with his chin stuck out, bragging about his army."

He chuckled and lowered his voice. "In 1935, his Italian supermen had trouble invading and conquering Abyssinia, a small African country whose men fought with spears and obsolete rifles. His soldiers don't compare with my men. No, I won't depend on Il Duce in the long run, but right now he's useful."

He pushed away from the table and rose. "Let's have our tea in the library, Abby. It's right down the hall."

Giselle served cookies and tea, tasting a sample of each, and then closed the door as she left.

Hitler sat opposite Abby and leaned forward in his chair, his hands closed as if he was about to pray. "Now, Abby, please keep an open mind, will you? I have a proposal."

"I always have an open mind, Adolf, but even an open mind is sensitive and resistant to things one can't accept." She smiled. "Just like your feelings about Mussolini."

He laughed. "All right. Here's my proposal." He searched for words. "I know you may not be physically attracted to me at present, so I will entice you a little. I will deposit two million U.S. dollars in a Swiss bank account in your name if you will marry me and stay married to me for at least four years. At the end of the four years the money is yours—no strings attached.

"We don't have to share a bedroom. You know most royals have separate quarters. That will be no problem for me, and I will not invade your privacy unless you invite me."

"Adolf, slow down. What makes you think this is such a good idea?"

"Abby, before you, I had never met a woman with whom I would like to share my life. I would be proud to have you at my side when I review our troops. We would ride together in parades and host dignitaries from other nations at state dinners."

"Herr Hitler, Adolf, we hardly know each other."

"Abby, history tells us that royals of different countries were married often without really knowing each other."

Abby sat back in her chair and looked knowingly at Hitler. "Now things are becoming clearer, Adolf. I sense duplicity here. You want a German-American wedding to keep America at bay. You don't need another adversary. You already have Britain at the front door and the Russian bear knocking softly at the kitchen door."

"See, that's why I need you as my queen. You are quick and well-spoken." He paused and opened his hands in supplication. "Abby, there is that side benefit, which I can't deny, but I believe that America doesn't want its boys in another world war. Here we are, almost two years into war. I've conquered all of Western Europe and fight the British on the sea and in the air, yet America remains neutral. To use your analogy, they also have a belligerent Japan at their back door. Americans still struggle with a deep financial depression, and, pardon me, American men are not warriors like German men. They are content with baseball and bowling alleys.

"I have no quarrel with America—they are an ocean away. I don't like them sending war material to Britain, but our submarines take care of most of that. In a sense, America is in the war already—using Britain as its surrogate warrior."

*I've got to keep him talking,* Abby thought.

"Back to the two million dollars, Adolf. What if you or I die before the four years is up?"

"Ha, you are interested! A good question. I will have our agreement airtight. If I die before the end of the four years and we are still married, you will receive the full amount immediately. If you die and we are still married, the entire amount will go to your heirs in accordance with your last will."

Abby nodded. "But where would you get two million dollars? Wait. Is this a joke?"

"I'm very serious, Abby. We have collected much more than that from the people who have opposed us. The spoils of war, so to speak."

"May we have more tea, Adolf? It helps me to think better."

Hitler rang for more tea. Abby continued after Giselle left.

"Adolf, you have obviously been thinking about this for some time. Now I need time to consider this. Even without America in the war, the present state of your European war complicates your proposal. If you invade Britain, America will certainly use military force to help its ally. As an American and your wife, I would probably be hated by everyone, including the German people."

"Oh no. As my wife, you would share my honor with the Third Reich. The Germans would love you."

"There's also Russia, Adolf. If they are provoked or perceive a weakness in your military strength, they may attack you. What would happen to me if they would succeed?"

"More good questions, Abby. Here's where I stand. For a number of reasons, I've decided to postpone indefinitely my plan, Operation Sea Lion, to invade Britain. Maybe we will never invade them. They are an admirable Aryan Nordic society. I could live side by side with them."

He paused and drank his tea. "We have signed the Nonaggression Pact with Russia. If we must make war with them it would be a one-front war without having to invade England. Our soldiers would make short work of those inferior Communist pigs. We would only have to kick in their door, and their whole rotten structure would collapse.

"We also are close to signing the Tripartite Pact with Italy and Japan, again for additional solidarity against the West…Does that calm you down a bit, Abby?"

"Wait a minute, Adolf. Italy and Japan are not Aryan nations. Aren't you being hypocritical by joining with them?"

"They are of use to me now. I may need the Japanese to tie down large Russian forces in Manchuria and Siberia, but they will not be a part of the Thousand-Year Reich."

"I'm beginning to understand. But I need to spend more time thinking about this. I should leave now."

She smiled, rose, and touched Hitler on the shoulder. "What an evening. I just thought I was coming for dinner."

Hitler escorted her down to the Chancellery door. "There's a car waiting outside to take you home." He kissed her hand. "Goodnight, my queen."

\* \* \*

Dark Cave
There is snow in the mountains.
Tall Mountain

# Chapter Fifty-three

*Nice, France—Resettlement*

The telephone rang. "Esther, this is Sophia Jordan. We met briefly at the *Lyon Press* before you moved to Nice. Remember me?"

"Yes, of course, how are you?"

"Not good. There is now a Nazi in charge of Lyon named Klaus Barbie. Yesterday our sources told us he issued a secret order to the SS a few days ago to round up all Jews in Lyon. A priority list included the rich and more prominent Jews. I'm not either of those, but I'm getting out of here tonight.

"I called to let you know that your family was arrested and taken away at dawn today."

"Oh, no!" It was just as her father had predicted. "My sister, too?"

"Yes, that's what their neighbor said. She's a friend of mine. She overheard the commotion at the Frankel's door. The SS gave them fifteen minutes to pack one suitcase each. They were told to pack all their valuables so that thieves wouldn't steal them while they're gone. We wonder if that wasn't a ruse so that they can steal from them later. Easier than spending time searching for hidden treasures in the house and things buried in the garden.

"One of our reporters who hangs around the railroad station said that the early morning group was loaded on boxcars bound for resettlement camps.

"I'm sorry to tell you all this, Esther, but I thought you should know. We hear that Nice will be next. You'd better get out. You are a well-known person with your newspaper column. Esther, there are already traitors in our midst trying to gain favor with the Nazis. Be careful. I must go now. Good luck."

\* \* \*

Sean had lost his job when the French shipbuilder closed. The shipyard workers were ordered into the army to try to stop the German invasion. Sean's Irish citizen papers saved him. He came home after a day's job search to find Esther sitting at the kitchen table staring at a blank wall.

"What's wrong, Esther?"

"Sit down, Sean." She reached over, held his hand, and told him about the telephone call from Lyon.

"I feel guilty. I've tried to cry for my family, but I can't raise the tears. After ten years they almost seem like strangers." She paused and squeezed his hand. "But they are my family." Then she cried. Sean rose, pulled her gently from her chair, and hugged her.

"Sweetheart, we've got to get out of here. I heard the same talk from the men at the bar where I stopped for lunch today. A truck driver from Lyon said the Germans were slowed down by the Resistance just south of Lyon."

When bedtime came for Danny, he was reluctant to go to his room. He sensed something was not right. "Can I sleep with you and Daddy in your big bed?"

"Of course, darling. Now go to bed with sweet dreams. Daddy and I want to talk for a while."

"Sean, I'm not going to be led off like a sheep bound for slaughter like my family. Why don't we join the Resistance? We know how to fight. We proved it in Ireland." She smiled. "At least you did—but you did see that I can handle a gun."

"Hold on, now. What about Danny?"

"I've thought about that. I'm sure the Fochs will keep him. They love him like a son. Their house on Lake Castellane is just far enough away. Our neighbors will think Danny disappeared with us. Besides, everyone will have their own worries about the Nazis in town. Sean, Marie is a retired teacher, so she could tutor Danny while we are away."

"You've really been planning for this, Esther."

"Yes, ever since I received my father's warning letter and his package. My thoughts have been scrambling over this. I didn't want to worry you about it, but now I must.

"Sean, we could leave most of Father's money and jewels with the Fochs and have some earmarked for Danny's care. We'll take enough with us to buy our way into the Resistance. I'm sure they need money to buy food and arms. My father would approve.

"I heard around the newspaper office that a stronghold of the Resistance movement nearest us is in the Vercors mountain area south of Grenoble and north of the Drome River. What do you think about my idea, my love?"

"I know we don't have much time, but let me sleep on it."

Sean woke up, sat on the edge of the bed, and rubbed his face awake. Danny was in the bathroom He looked over his shoulder at Esther. "Hey, I'm out of work. Might as well do something constructive—like killing Nazis!"

Esther made telephone calls while Sean packed; then she came into the bedroom to help. "John and Marie said they would be delighted to have Danny live with them. I told them we would be there tomorrow morning.

"I also called the news desk at the *Phare*. Told the news editor that I was interested to know about the Vercors Resistance fighters and needed some names. The editor said that the group called *Marquis due Vercors* is most active, and their leader is thought to be one Jacques Lavin. He is said to be a great leader with great motivation. His father, a fierce Resistance fighter, was arrested and taken to the Hotel Terminus, SS Gestapo headquarters in Lyon. Barbie, now called the Butcher of Lyon, personally beat him, skinned him alive, and put his head in a bucket of ammonia. He died shortly after. Do you think Jacques Lavin might be motivated? The editor didn't know any other names. Lavin's the man we've got to find, or someone else in charge."

"Okay. Good calls. You finish packing while I work on our route."

Sean was bent over a map spread on the kitchen table. "Look here, sweetheart. I think our best bet is to drive up secondary road 85 through Digne, Saint-Bonne, and enter the Vercors region from the east. It'll be slower through the Alps, but safer. Agreed?"

"Good plan. Let's bring along enough food to last for a while. You pack our guns and what ammunition we have. I'm taking a French flag and a white flag in case we need them."

\* \* \*

John Foch had counterfeit identity papers ready for Esther. "I have my sources. It's the least I can do for the cause. Show this to the Germans should they stop you. You are now Aimee Allard to them. I took an old photo of you from the *Phare* file. It's a bit fuzzy. Sean's papers from neutral Ireland should be good. Remove any references on you to Nice and your old job there. You are now two lovers wandering the Alps—heading eventually to Aimee's home in Geneva, Switzerland. You live out of your car, camping. That's why you have all of your clothes and the food. I would take off your wedding ring, Esther, and give me all your personal papers, letters, and anything that identifies you as Esther Frankel. I stole a license plate off a car and changed yours just to be safe. Please go through all your things. We will save them for you."

He looked at them quizzically. "You don't have guns on you or in your car, do you?"

"Yes," said Sean.

"A sure way to get arrested and summarily shot. Leave them with me. The Resistance should have guns for you.

"If, for some reason, we must move, contact my longtime attorney, Claude Belanger, here in Nice. Memorize his name—don't write anything down. Claude Belanger. And leave address books with us."

Out of earshot from Danny, John said, "I don't have to tell you this is very dangerous. You may not come back."

Marie sat dabbing her eyes. "They do what they have to do, John." She rose and embraced them both. "Your Danny will be safe with us. His red hair provides additional protection."

# Chapter Fifty-four

***Southern France***

Esther and Sean left at dawn while Danny slept. They told Danny the night before that they would be away for a time to do research for a special story Esther had to write. Danny had few questions—the Fochs were like grandparents.

They drove the route that Sean had planned and passed one manned German anti-tank gun carrier parked near Saint-Michael, but they were not stopped. They had practiced joking and laughing and looking straight ahead.

"This is really beautiful country, Sean," said Esther, as they navigated the vineyard covered foothills of the Alps. "I remember from my grade school history book that this road is called Route Napoleon. He and his army once marched from Marseille to Grenoble along this road. It was a mountain path then, of course."

"That had to be a killer march," said Sean.

They proceeded through a gorge called Gap and were passing Saint-Bonnet when they were stopped by a German road block. A half-dozen soldiers surrounded their Citroen. A young lieutenant motioned them to get out of the car.

He studied Sean and Esther. "Papers?"

Two soldiers faced them with rifles held hip-high while the rest searched their car.

"Where are you going?"

"We are driving around to see this part of the French Alps," said Esther. "Have never seen them before. Headed toward Grenoble. That'll be another new one for us."

"Where then?"

"I don't know. Just having a fun tour. Probably head on to my family's old place in Gstaad."

Sean said, "We both got laid off from our jobs, so we decided to see the countryside."

The lieutenant addressed Esther. "What is the name of the big lodge in Gstaad?"

"The Gstaad-Saanenland. Have you been here?"

"Yes, a very nice place."

The car searchers nodded to the officer.

"All right, you are free to go."

At the village de la Mure they left Road 85 and drove west into the Vercors region using side roads. Their Citroen then traversed switchback dirt roads up the foothills, and then the vineyards gave way to scruffy grasses and pitch-pines.

# Chapter Fifty-five

***Vercors Plateau, France***

They slowed for a roadblock of logs. Esther held her small French flag out the window and waved it. Several armed men appeared out of nowhere.

"Here we go again," said Sean.

Esther smiled. "I think these are the people we've been looking for."

"I hope so. They could be bandits."

"Who are you and want do you want?" said a short man with hairy arms like a black bear. He wore a blue beret cocked sideways on a nest of curly black hair. He lowered his gun as he gave a cursory look at the inside of the car.

"We want to join the *Maquis du Vercors*," said Sean.

"Now why would you want to do that?" The other men laughed.

"My wife's family was arrested by the SS in Lyon two days ago. We believe they were taken by train to some secret camp." The laughter turned to a murmur.

The leader nodded. "All right, step out of the car and show me your papers while we search your car."

"Their car looks okay, Jacques—some food, clothes, and sleeping bags."

"Your forged papers are well done. What is your real name, lady, and where are you from?" Satisfied with Esther's response, he looked at them for a long moment.

"Do you realize what you're doing? This is very dangerous work. You could die."

"This isn't the first time we've been told that," said Sean.

Esther said, "We understand. We still want to do our part against the Boche."

Jacques nodded. "You are convincing so far. Blindfold them, Charles, and take them to our camp. Bring along their car. We might need crazy people like these two." He laughed, and the other men joined in.

They were led through woods for several hundred yards, challenged by two sentry posts along the way. When their blindfolds were removed, Sean and Esther found themselves surrounded by a large group of armed men and women.

"A couple of volunteers from Nice," Jacques announced. "Can any of you vouch for them?"

"The woman looks like a columnist in the Lyon newspaper," said one man. He was seconded by a woman.

"Is that true?" asked Jacques.

"Yes, I did interviews with people on the streets. We lived in Nice. I'm from Lyon originally. My husband worked at the Nice shipyards."

"We can use a writer for our underground newspaper," said Jacques.

Ester took a half step forward and raised her voice. "I can help, but I came here to fight."

A tall woman with a bandolier of ammunition wrapped across her chest and a red bandanna wrapped around her head elbowed her way through the group. She walked over and looked down at the diminutive Esther. She had a sharp face with a pointed nose. *She's going to peck me*, thought Esther.

"What would you do, little woman, get on a stool and scratch a German's face with your manicured nails?"

Esther moved very close to the woman. "I bet I could scratch your eyes out from here, big woman."

The group of fighters laughed heartily until Jacques raised his hand.

"Enough! Danielle, let's give them a chance. This woman said she just lost her family in Lyon to Klaus Barbie's SS. We will confirm that. Relax, everyone. Back to business."

\* \* \*

Sean and Esther were soon assimilated into the Marquis. The group was dedicated to making life miserable for the invaders. Jacques told them the men and women of the Resistance came from all economic levels and political leanings of French society, including academics, students, aristocrats, priests, liberals, anarchists, Gypsies, and Communists. "They submerge their differences to kill Germans." Jacques said.

Jacques pulled Esther aside a day later. "Your story checked out. Our informers confirmed that your family was taken by the SS and separated at the train station. Your father was sent to Mauthausen-Gusen, but your mother and sister were sent to Ravensbruck, a camp for women. They reported that your father was killed last week. I'm very sorry." Esther slid to the ground and wept.

Esther and Danielle seemed to have resolved their differences, but there was still an underlying dislike of each other. "I think she's jealous of your shortness and vice versa," Sean said.

"She's a Gypsy, Sean. As hated by the Nazis as we Jews. We have that in common—we will be fine."

Sean and Esther showed their efficiency with firearms and were taught how to set timers on both dynamite and plastic explosives, set booby traps, throw hand grenades, and kill silently with a knife.

Esther blanched when they were given cyanide capsules to evade torture if captured. "One of us must survive to take care of Danny."

They kept their currency in money belts under their clothes, using some of it to buy better firearms than the group's standard inventory of captured German rifles and old English Endfields. They both chose the same make of 9 mm submachine gun—the MP40 Schmeisser, and the same Luger sidearms.

"Good choices," said Jacques. "I think you will be good additions to a team I'm putting together to take out a military train."

# Chapter Fifty-six

*Wittenberg, Germany—Abby*

Warren agreed to Abby's request for a meeting and sent her two sets of round-trip train tickets. She was to go to the Savighy Place train station and board a train bound for Magdeburg, then get off the other side of the train just before it started to move. She was instructed to go two tracks down and board a train headed for Leipzig. The Germans prided themselves on their exact adherence to departure and arrival train times. Abby made the two-minute difference in departure times with time to spare. She got off the train at the small university town of Wittenberg with two school-age girls and waited inside the station until the train left to make sure no one else jumped off at the last minute.

Abby took a taxi to the Hotel Walheim and found the bar. Warren was talking with the bartender. Abby kissed him on the cheek and sat next to him on a bar stool. Warren ordered her a drink and then listened as the bartender moved away.

She spoke softly "Warren, I can't do this anymore. That man is crazy as a fox. I'm beginning to understand Hitler's techniques. He uses his wide range of temperament to scare people, or gently persuade them if he wants something bad enough. You never know what to expect. This time he was logical and even charming." She told him of the whole evening at the Chancellery apartment, ending with Hitler's offer of two million dollars to marry him.

"Are you serious, Abby?"

"Absolutely. He said he would have secret legal papers prepared that I could take to an attorney that both he and I trusted. A Swiss bank account holding the money would be confirmed."

He shook his head, still in disbelief.

They moved from the bar to a corner table in the restaurant.

After they ordered dinner, Warren began making coded, shorthand notes while they talked. He went over every item, writing as Abby recalled minute details and the emphasis that Hitler provided. From Abby's memory he even recorded Abby's description of Hitler's Chancellery office and drew an approximate floor plan with entrances, exits, and elevators; including the layout of Hitler's spacious apartment above his office.

They finished their dinner with brandy and coffee. Warren looked around. They had the restaurant to themselves.

"Abby, do you realize the significance of the intelligence information you are giving me and the Western allies? Hitler's real intentions regarding Britain and Russia together with a planned pact with Japan and Italy? It's a bonanza! And Abby, your marriage to Hitler will be the greatest intelligence coup in history."

"What are you talking about, Warren? I told you I was through. Do you really believe I would marry that megalomaniac and put myself in mortal danger?" She paused. "Wait a minute, are you joking with me?"

"No, I'm serious, Abby. I'm speaking for the U.S. government. You said he vowed he wouldn't touch you—that the marriage would be for political purposes."

He reached out and held Abby's hand. "Four years is a short time. You will be the greatest American heroine since Amelia Earhart. And just think what a great start we will have with all that money!"

Abby pulled her hand away, sat back in her chair, and squared her shoulders. "This is a Warren I didn't know existed. How can you suggest this if you really care about me? What has gotten into you?"

"Hey, I'm also in danger just being with you. We deserve to be rewarded for all our work and risks taken. The time is *now*. I learned last week that the State Department's lead role in intelligence gathering will be eliminated. All info will soon be handled by the new Office of Coordinator of Information under one William Donovan, a buddy of Roosevelt. I will be just a paper pusher. Remember, I told you I was waiting for the right moment to break away from the crowd and be someone. This is the right moment for me—and for you too. This is our chance for fame and fortune! Not that it matters, but my mother would be proud of me."

"So you want to 'be someone' at the probable expense of *my* life?"

He leaned over and lowered his voice. "We are partners, remember?"

Abby cocked her head to the right and stared at him. Warren sensed he was losing her.

"Abby, this is so much bigger than the two of us."

Abby's eyes welled with tears. "And I was beginning to think the opposite. That nothing was bigger than our loving relationship."

"If you don't do this, Abby, you will be doing a great disservice to your country and the poor countries being ravaged by Hitler." He gathered himself. "And remember, you signed a contract with the U.S. government to be our agent."

Abby rose from the table. "Thank you for letting me see this self-seeking side of you. Don't ever try to contact me again—tonight, tomorrow, or ever."

She leaned over him. "By the way, that two-year agreement expired last month."

Warren watched her leave, then banged his fist on the table and yelled for another drink. *She can't do this to me!*

# Chapter Fifty-seven

*Col de la Bonette, France*

Esther shivered in the breaking dawn and snuggled closer to Sean. They were concealed among huge boulders overlooking railroad tracks, waiting for their target. Even though it was June, there were patches of snow hiding behind the shade of the boulders.

Seventy Resistance fighters had climbed two thousand feet to intercept a train headed south to Nice, which they knew to be laden with ammunition and German soldiers. Their platoon leader, Danielle, had taken Esther and Sean under her wing. She was close by. "Stay down and be ready to fire. When I start firing, shoot anything that moves. Can't take prisoners. Can hardly feed ourselves. Leave the wounded. This train is supposed to be carrying a large amount of supplies for the invading pigs. We'll take some of it for ourselves."

Danielle sensed how tense they were. "Hang loose, you two. Hey, Esther, where did you pick up this Irishman?"

"It's a long story. Sometime over a campfire."

Transport trains were favorite targets of the Resistance. They soon figured out that removing bolts from the rails was far more efficient and safer than planting explosives. Sean had helped unbolt connector plates on the outside rail. Danielle had supervised the work. "The train will pick up speed coming down the mountain. This should derail the whole train."

The sound of the train changed as it braked coming down the ravine. Esther could make out soldiers manning a twin-mounted heavy machine gun on the car behind the engine. She and Sean took the safeties off their MP40 submachine guns. The front wheels of the engine hit the gap in the connector plates and they watched the engine veer off sharply to the downhill side of the mountain. When the German soldiers in the open troop cars saw what was happening, they jumped from the train only to be met by withering fire and hand grenades from the Resistance fighters.

After all the railroad cars had obediently followed the engine down the mountainside and the firing subsided, Danielle yelled to Sean and Esther, "Let's go down to pick up as many rifles and ammo as we can carry uphill to our pack horses. Don't let the wounded shoot you."

They slid down the embankment firing at survivors who were taking aim at them. Esther steeled herself for the gruesome task by thinking of her parents and sister. Then one SS officer rose up and pointed his Luger at Sean. Esther turned her machine gun on him and gave him a burst of bullets in the chest. The man stared in surprise at Esther and tumbled down the mountainside.

The wounded were moaning and cursing at them. Esther could manage only two bloody rifles in addition to her own weapon. Danielle led them up a switchback trail to waiting pack horses.

The leader, Jacques, joined them. "Where did all these draft horses come from?" Sean asked.

"They're on loan from local farmers. They send us food and help like this."

Sean and Ester walked to the Resistance hideout with one of the farm boys named Paul, a fourteen-year-old. "Why do you take risks like this, Paul?" Esther asked.

"This is no risk, Madame. You are taking the risk. I can't wait 'til I'm old enough to fight with you."

A surviving German soldier crawled up mountain from the attack and saw the German weapons being loaded on the draft horses and mules by unarmed men and boys. He lived to report it. Two days later an SS detachment rounded up all men and boys over thirteen in the farming community. They made them dig their own graves, and then shot each in the back of the head. The women and surviving children were forced to cover the bodies with dirt. The SS also shot and killed all their horses and mules.

Jacques called his Resistance fighters together. "A woman heard a soldier address the leader of the SS killers as 'Major Striker.' He is a coward who is afraid to come after us here. Instead he massacres unarmed villagers. We will come upon him sooner or later and will have a special ceremony for him and his bastards. Save your anger 'til then. Right now, it's our duty to provide the survivors with food, sympathy, and encouragement. It's not going to relieve their grief, but we must try."

Esther turned to Sean. "Sean, that Paul was only a few years older than our Danny. We must talk about this."

# Chapter Fifty-eight

*Berlin—Early 1941*

Abby figured she couldn't abruptly stop her bizarre relationship with Adolf Hitler even though her spying days were over. His unpredictable temper could create a danger for her. She needed to ease out of his life without offending him.

The opportunity came faster than she expected. A courier appeared at her apartment door delivering another envelope with a wax seal embossed with a swastika:

> My Dear Abby,
>
> I apologize for the delay in getting back to you. The battlefields have taken my attention lately.
>
> I realized the other day that you have not been to my home in Berchtesgaden, the Berghof. I recall that you stayed the whole time at the hotel with the other press people. Also, you didn't have the experience of going up to my tea house on the summit of Kehlstein. Some English people call it the Eagle's Nest.
>
> Can you break away for a long weekend on next Thursday, the 24th? I will have my trusted aide, Greta Schonberg, escort you. She will be in a sedan that will pick you up at your place at six p.m. You will have excellent accommodations on the overnight train to Munich. A driver will meet you and Greta for an easy drive to Berchtesgaden.

I plan to be there early that week for a meeting with my military staff and will welcome a break from those ugly men to see your pretty face. I will show you the life you can live as my partner. The people are treating me like a god. Now I need a goddess for the people to adore. Please call my secretary to confirm the weekend.

Fondly, Adolf

Abby deliberated on her options and finally set her plan.

\* \* \*

A silent Greta Schonberg sat next to Abby in the Mercedes on the way to the train station.

Abby tried to think positively. It was good to get out of the city. She had told James Hoffman at the *Tribune* bureau of her weekend travel plans. He shook his head in his concern. "Be careful, Abby, Himmler and Heydrich do all of the killings with the tacit approval of Hitler."

As they went south, the foliage of the trees changed to limitless shades of red, orange, and greens. The colors and terrain reminded Abby of fall weekend trips with the family to Brown County in southern Indiana, where beautiful hills rolled down to the Ohio River. *I want to go home*, thought Abby.

# Chapter Fifty-nine

*Berchtesgaden—The Berghof*

Goebbels had suggested pilgrimages to Berchtesgaden to honor their leader. Hundreds of tourists now crowded its streets, all hoping to get a glimpse of their Fuehrer.

"Do you see that fence and guardhouse, Miss White?" Greta asked. "Our Fuehrer recently decided to restrict access to his home so that he could rest better and hold his conferences without the crowd noise."

The household at the Berghof was alerted to receive the American journalist whom Hitler seemed to favor. They gossiped when Eva Braun left the Berghof for the weekend.

Hitler greeted Abby at the door. "Always a pleasure, Abby. I hope the trip was satisfactory."

He gave her a quick kiss on the cheek and shook her hand vigorously. Greta and the house staff watched with interest. They had never seen their leader treat a woman with such respect.

After Abby was settled in her room, Hitler took Abby on a tour of the huge house.

"I met with my military staff this week in this room. They're now on their way home to their families for the weekend."

The conference room was large with several areas for small group discussions. Precious Gobelins, large tapestries woven in Paris, adorned the walls. Together with a unique coffered ceiling, the hangings served to make the room a more manageable size. Abby tried to imagine the planning for mass destruction and killings that went on in the room a few hours earlier.

Hitler's private study was lavishly furnished. The conversation center was at the end of the white pine-paneled room. A massive white marble table was surrounded by light green sofas and printed flowered overstuffed chairs. Before Abby commented, she looked around for snooping household staff. Seeing none, she said, "Very nice, Adolf. This is a welcoming room. A different motif from your rooms in Dresden and Berlin."

"Yes, Martin Bormann used a woman designer from Salzburg. A fresher look, like mountain air. I am very relaxed here. Maybe it's because it's only a few miles from my native Austria.

"Now let me show you my private bunker." There was a door in the central part of the house that led two floors down to a furnished apartment. "It's enclosed by three feet of concrete, and it's self-sustaining—all systems are separate," Hitler said. "Bormann is very thorough."

"Let's go up. I want to show you the view from the balcony before dinner."

From the balcony that wrapped around the house, Hitler pointed out the chalets nearby. "That's Bormann's over there. He is kind of the sentry post for all of us. Goering's is up there."

He smiled at Abby "You can see how protected you would be if you lived here."

"Adolf, I need to talk to you about that."

He looked at his watch. "Later, Abby, dinner is waiting."

Hitler was a moody person—highs and lows. At dinner he was in a good mood and seemed to want to stay that way. He sensed something from Abby and didn't want to hear it. He was the same way with his generals. "I don't believe what you're saying. Confirm! Confirm! Tell me good news."

At the dinner table Hitler asked Abby, "Can we talk about your 'real West'? Have you ever seen real cowboys?"

"Yes. Once our family had a vacation trip to Wyoming and the Dakotas. We rode horses and met real cowboys. They were dusty, sunburned, hard-working men and boys. Not like those in western movies with their sparkling outfits and white hats. The 'real' West was the wild, *wild* West. My grandmother was a homesteader in northern Kansas. She had to fight off renegade Indians."

"Ah. So that's where you got your spunk! Abby, tomorrow will be a fun day. In the morning we will take a short drive to Lake Konigssee and cruise the lake. In good weather it's my thing to do. Then we'll return for a visit to the *Kehlsteinhaus*."

Before retiring Hitler took Abby for an uphill walk to the Obersalzberg tea house. A contingent of SS men in street clothes followed at a discrete distance.

"I try to do this walk every day after lunch. It's good for the digestion and helps me to sleep soundly. I should be doing it more after dinner like this."

\* \* \*

Even on the lake cruise, Hitler dressed semi-formally with a double-breasted light brown jacket and brown tie. He also wore one of the two Iron Crosses he'd won in World War I.

As the boat cruised by St. Bartolomae's Chapel, Hitler straightened up in his seat.

"Abby, I was raised a Christian. Sang in a boy's choir. Can you believe that? But when I was a teenager my little brother died. He was a loving, dear boy. That loss and my years in the trenches, stepping over dead men, turned me into a cynic. I have nothing to do with the Church now. For the most part they are leaving me alone, so I will leave them alone."

\* \* \*

Abby held her breath on hairpin turns on the way up the mountain to the *Kehlsteinhaus*—the Eagle's Nest. They left the sedan well below the summit and walked into the interior of the mountain. A surprisingly large elevator waited to take them the last 400 feet to the summit. "The Eagles Nest took more than a year to construct. Martin Bormann presented it to me as a gift on my birthday."

Bormann knew of Hitler's claustrophobia, so he made the elevator as large as possible. He gave the elevator a twenty-foot ceiling and covered the walls with Venetian mirrors. Abby and Hitler sat on an ornate, velvet covered bench with polished brass arms. The operator nodded and smiled, then moved the controls. As the slow ride to the summit began, Hitler reached for Abby's hand. His clammy hands were shaking badly.

"Can you make this go any faster?" asked Hitler.

"No, sir. Its design doesn't permit me to do that." said the operator.

Hitler whispered to Abby, "I know that. I just hate confined spaces. My father once locked me in a closet for a whole day and night. I don't do this ride often."

"May I ask what you did to deserve such treatment?" asked Abby.

Hitler squirmed in his seat. "I was just a little boy. I poured some gasoline on a cat and set it afire to see what would happen. My punishment was justified."

The rooms in the Eagles Nest were spartan with mostly bare concrete walls. There were several guest bedrooms, a kitchen, a guard room, and a large main room called the "tea room." The tea room was dominated by a massive fireplace of red Italian marble.

"That was a gift from Mussolini," said Hitler.

"That was a fine, generous gift," Abby remarked.

"He is still a pompous, strutting frog. Abby, let's go out on the balcony with our tea."

They sat at a table shaded by an umbrella near the concrete railing.

"We are now more than 6,000 feet above the valley. Luckily, your visit brought an unusually clear day. Look around you. Over there is Austria; that mountain mostly behind us is in Italy; the tall one on our left is in Switzerland; and, of course, we have a beautiful view of Germany in front of us."

He reached again for Abby's hand. "Abby, if you consent to be my wife under the contract I had prepared, you would be queen of Germany, Austria, France, Poland, the Netherlands, and many other small countries. This will all be yours," he said, waving his arm out to the expanse. "You will be honored, respected, and envied by all as Queen of Europe."

Abby rose from her chair and walked over to the railing. She resisted a smile as she thought, *This reminds me a little bit like the scene in the New Testament where Satan offered the world to Jesus.*

"Oh, Adolf, you paint such a beautiful picture. I have been sorely tempted, but just this week I received a cable from America, which makes all of this untenable right now. I didn't know whether to cancel this trip, but I decided I should meet with you in person to explain my dilemma. I wanted to talk with you about it yesterday at the Berghof, but there was no time."

Hitler's face was flushed and frowning.

"It is from my sister, Jane. Would you like to read it?

"No. Read it to me."

> My Dear Sister Abby,
> In my last letter I told you that Mother and Father are very ill. It has gotten worse very quickly. Mother's cancer, which we thought was in remission, is spreading again. The doctor said there is little he can do except to relieve her pain. Our father's congestive heart failure condition has worsened. He has trouble

going from bed to wheelchair. His doctor says it is a matter of time. We are all weary from caring for them. They ask for you often. It has been years since they have seen you. Need I say more? Please come home. We all need you.

 Your loving sister, Jane

"Adolf, you see I can't do what you propose—at least right now. I am honored that you would consider me for a companion, but I must go home."

Hitler slumped in his chair, staring at the concrete floor.

"Adolf, please try to put yourself in my position. What if you hadn't been in your beloved Germany, maybe working in India or China, and your family needed you…?"

"Enough. I hated most of my family. They were mean people except my mother who didn't pay much attention to me. I couldn't wait to be out on my own.

"Abby, you go home and tend to your family. Who knows? Maybe things will go quickly for you, and you'll return soon. A good correspondent wants to be where history is being made. Right?"

\* \* \*

The train ride back to Berlin was punctuated by long periods of silence, then polite chatter would resume between Abby and Gretchen.

Gretchen wished she could talk to Abby as a girlfriend, but her assignment was only to escort Abby. The Sunday train was more crowded. She did not try to engage Abby in serious conversation—someone may be listening. If she could, she would tell Abby about the kitchen talk at the Berghof. It was buzzing about Hitler's obvious affection for Abby, yet they slept in separate rooms. They all wondered why.

Abby was lost in her own thoughts. She was grateful that her sister, Jane, had read her urgency and had responded with a cable that worked. Her parents were getting older, but were in good health.

# Chapter Sixty

*Berlin—Lydia*

The Tribune's Berlin bureau chief, James Hoffman, stopped by Abby's desk. "Abby, while you were returning yesterday, a good friend in the German press told me in confidence that the battleship *Bismarck* had been sunk by the British in the Atlantic about four hundred miles west of Brest. France. More than two thousand men were killed. We can't print that, but didn't you have a German naval officer for a friend who was on that ship?"

"Oh, my! Yes, that's Admiral Franz Dieter, captain of the *Bismarck*. I must see my friend Lydia Viazensky—I mean Lydia Dieter. They were married shortly before he had to go to sea."

Abby met Lydia for lunch. They sat in a quiet corner booth. "Abby, I can't believe it happened. My dear Franz died at his post. For god's sake, Abby, we were just married. We should still be on our honeymoon!" Then the tears flowed. "God, how I hate wars."

"I'm so sorry, Lydia. He was a wonderful, kind man."

"One of the few surviving officers called me from a hospital in Spain. A rescue ship from Brest pulled him out of the water. He said that the *Bismarck* received a heavy bombardment from British ships and planes, and Franz was on the bridge when he was killed instantly by a shell." She pulled out another tissue from her purse. "His call meant more to me than the short note of regret sent by Admiral Raeder. You remember the admiral from our wedding reception?"

"Yes, I do. He was probably embarrassed and depressed by the loss of his new battleship and all of those fine men, Lydia, and didn't know what to say."

"It was such a short marriage. I'm still in shock, Abby. Do you think they could send his body home for a decent burial?"

"I just don't know. He might have been buried in the sea that he loved. I would call Doenitz's office to find out." She reached out across the table and held Lydia's hand. "My dear Lydia. How awful! And now I must tell you that I will be leaving soon for the United States to visit my family."

Lydia's eyes open wide. "Well, that's more bad news… You must hurry back, my dear friend."

She moved forward in her chair and spoke softly. "Abby, I am pregnant, and my husband is dead. I don't know what to do. I would eventually like to marry again, but men are reluctant to marry a woman with a child." She put her head down and whispered, "I've found a doctor who'll relieve me of the baby, and I'm thinking that's what I should do. What do you think, Abby?"

Abby sat back in her chair and thought before answering.

"Lydia dear, I once had a decision to make like yours. I was an inexperienced eighteen-year-old freshman in college and succumbed to a visiting football player and got pregnant. That was the most stupid thing I've ever done, so far. The man disappeared. I didn't even know his last name. I went home and confided in my mother. She was a nurse and is very levelheaded. She suggested a convent in Wisconsin that welcomed unwed mothers. She had heard that they had couples waiting to adopt babies. That's what I intended to do, but I was saved from making that move by an early miscarriage.

"My dear Lydia, you are the widow of a brave admiral, and you are a beautiful woman. You are of royalty, and Franz was an exceptional leader of men. Your son or daughter will be of royal lineage. Don't do it—have your and Franz's baby. You will have many suitors, believe me. A good man would welcome your baby."

Two days later Lydia called Abby. "I'm so thankful we had a chance to talk. I'm taking your advice—you are a wonderful friend.

"Oh, Abby, got a bit of gossip I forgot to mention—this time about you. I was at an Italian Embassy party before Franz died. One German Major, Otto somebody, with a little more drink than usual, whispered to me, 'Is it true your friend Abby White is seeing our Fuehrer on a regular basis?'

"I told him you were a professional writer and were doing a series of articles on him. Am I right, Abby?"

"You're right. As terrible as he might be, Hitler is an international figure, and I'm an international foreign correspondent. That's my job. Thanks, dear friend, for saying that to him." *Damn. The talk of the Italian Embassy. I've got to get out of here.*

James Hoffman had no problems with Abby's trip to America. Of all his staff, he thought Abby was the most dedicated and talented. She had been recognized several times for her award-winning dispatches, resulting in a promotion to Senior Bureau Correspondent. Her interviews with Hitler, de Gaule, Petain, and Mussolini also won awards. She was the leader of the U.S. correspondent team covering the 1936 Olympics in Berlin when, much to Hitler's chagrin, the U.S. team led by the black Jesse Owens beat most of Hitler's "super Aryan" Germans. Hoffman cabled the home office of the *Tribune*. "She's taking a two-month leave. I would give her six months. I just hope she returns."

Abby had a local press contact in Wilhelmshaven whom she paid to bribe a kitchen worker at the Gestapo prison for news of Dan. According to reports, Dan was now being treated reasonably well by his SS jailers. She also knew that the neutral Republic of Ireland Embassy in Berlin was unsuccessful in obtaining his release.

Getting to the United States was more difficult now that Germany was at war with Britain. She found that she had to travel through German-occupied France by train to neutral Spain and catch a passenger ship to the States. All ships flying the flag of neutral nations had to take a longer southern route to avoid the possibility of being mistaken by German U-boats as a belligerent.

All went well—until it didn't.

# Chapter Sixty-one

*Vercor Plateau Area, France*

Sean and Esther were selected along with fifty other veterans of the French Resistance to set a trap for the SS. British planes dropped supplies, including medicine, to the Resistance at night in agreed-upon drop zones. Lately though, the SS had broken their radio code and seized the supplies before the Resistance could act. The undermanned Resistance pick-up crews had to back off a fight.

The deception now was to send coordinates and a drop time to the British with a sign-off that cancelled the message. The SS didn't detect the cancellation signal and readied a patrol to pick up more booty. The drop zone was a clearing near a dense wooded area. The Resistance fighters buried themselves in the woods well before the supposed drop time.

The Resistance leader, Jacques Lavin, split up Sean and Esther for the fight. This was to be their last skirmish, and Jacques didn't want both killed. They planned to return to Nice, pick up their son, and escape. Esther was moved down the line with Danielle, and Sean stayed with Jacques.

"Relax, Sean. They won't be here for an hour or so." They sat with their backs against a fallen tree that would serve as a defense barrier.

"So, Sean, why did you marry a Jewish girl when you once told me you were a born Christian?"

"Jacques, I don't have to explain my actions to anyone, but the sake of passing time, I'll talk some." He shifted his seat on the ground to look directly at Jacques.

"My reasoning goes beyond religion or so-called ethics and prejudices. My wife is a kind, lovely lady who is also very tough—as you have seen. I see her as a good person, a good mother, and a smart, able companion.

"There is a common misunderstanding that Jewish people killed Jesus, who was also a Jew," said Sean. "It was the Roman governor, Pontius Pilate, and his soldiers who tortured and crucified Jesus. They *were* instigated and pressured by the Jewish high priests who were jealous of Jesus' popularity with the people. The apostles and disciples loved Jesus, as did the thousands of other Jewish people who flocked to hear his teachings. Many died for him." He paused. "So, that's my rationale regarding the Jews, Jacques. And Esther is my beloved wife."

"My God, Sean, I never heard of it that way. I'll have to think about that."

Sean reached for his machine gun. "Think about it later. Here they come. Three trucks. Now let's kill some invaders."

Jacques passed the word down the line and then focused his binoculars on the enemy climbing off the trucks. "They're all SS, Sean. Wait. There's another truck coming on our right flank with more troopers. Maybe we've been betrayed?"

"Don't think so," whispered Sean as he pointed. "Look how nonchalant they are."

The first squad of about a dozen walked slowly in the full moonlight toward the drop zone with their weapons slung loosely over their shoulders. Their voices travelled easily over the flat terrain. "Major Striker, your orders, sir?"

"Let's see if we can catch some of the cowards this time. Move everyone into that copse of trees over there. Park the trucks near the back and cover them with brush. The foolish bastards should be here soon. Save a few for questioning if you can. Kill the rest."

The SS walked along the side of their trucks as they advanced directly toward Danielle's and Esther's hidden position in the woods. "This is going to be fun," one trooper said to his partner as the trucks moved off to go around the back of the woods.

Two Resistance snipers were ready. Their firing would signal all to fire. They lay on the ground covered with brush, but with an open view of the approaching SS. A coin toss had decided who would take out the ranking officer. Now the winner dialed his scope carefully and focused his crosshairs on Major Striker's forehead.

*Let them come closer*, thought Jacques.

The SS troopers were only fifty yards away from the woods when one of them yelled, "I think I see movement in those woods."

"It's a trap," Striker said to his lieutenant. He barely finished "trap" when they both were dead. Striker took a bullet in his forehead. His lieutenant had raised his head just enough to take a round through his mouth that went out the back of his head. Heavy machine gun fire from the Resistance turned the drop zone into a killing field. The SS troopers fired wildly at unseen targets. One wild bullet struck Danielle in her head and killed her instantly. Esther held her in her arms and cried. The flanking SS force saw they were outnumbered and tried to retreat. Jacques and Sean took down a number of them as they fled. Only a few managed to climb aboard a truck moving out in second gear.

Jacques stood silently over Danielle's body, and then walked out in the field. He found Striker's body, took a white bag out of his pocket, and drew his field knife out of its leather sheath. The mirror polished surface of the blade reflected the full moon.

"Sean, you don't have to see this. Block the view from the others." He plunged his blade in Strikers chest, opened it up, removed his heart, and put it in his bag.

The next night, two men, pretending to be drunk, staggered up to the guard of the Gestapo headquarters, the Hotel Terminus, in Lyon. While one distracted the guard with foolish questions, the other set a small black box on the steps, and then they staggered off, singing as they went. An enclosed note read: "For Klaus Barbie. Here is what happened to one of your men, Striker, who murdered unarmed men and boys. Striker had no heart then, and he has no heart now. A gift for you. It is our warning. You may be next?"

Reprisal was swift. The next day, fifteen Lyon residents were selected from the streets at random and were executed in a public square.

The day after the trap of the SS, Jacques called all his fighters together.

"It is a sad day. Our beloved Danielle gave her life for a free France. She was a true fighter—daring and resourceful yet caring enough to always protect her comrades. Let us pause a moment in silence to honor her." The moment passed. Then someone in the rear started singing the French

National Anthem, *La Marseillaise*, and the rest joined in, singing very softly.

"Another report I must tell you," Jacques said. After the parachute drops had been compromised, the Brits told our southern group, through another radio frequency, that they could land in the dark if they would clear a vineyard. Instructions included time and location together with the placement of torches for the landing strip. Well, loyal villagers were clearing the vineyard when two truckloads of SS and *Milice* appeared, shot the workers, and pulled eight men from their homes and executed them. Again, we were betrayed."

His eyes swept around the group. "If there is a spy in our midst, we will find you out soon.

"On the brighter side, we now must honor two of our best warriors, Sean and Esther. They are leaving after faithful service to our cause to collect their only child and disappear."

He called Sean and Esther forward and tried to enclose them in his short, muscled arms. "They are a wonderful, happy couple whom we will miss." He paused and smiled again. "When I think of their names I can't help but think this should be the start of a joke. Did you hear the one about the big Irishman and his pretty Jewish girlfriend who go into this Italian bar...?" The fighters laughed, and then gave Sean and Esther a hip-hip-hurrah. This time, Jacques received the hugs from Sean and Esther.

* * *

Jacque's crew pulled the tarp from the O'Connors' car and got it running again. They searched the couple and the car thoroughly to remove any connection to the Resistance. It was Aimee Allard and her Irish lover traveling again as tourists, looking for good spots to visit and enjoy. Again, they were stopped by a German roadblock, questioned, searched, and released. "I hope our luck doesn't run out before we get back to Nice." said Esther.

# Chapter Sixty-two

*Nice and Escape*

Young Danny had grown taller and sturdier in their absence. After many kisses and hugs, Danny lost his feeling of being deserted. His hiding place in the open with the Fochs worked well. John Foch said, "No one is concerned with a red-haired ten-year-old boy. They have their own problems since the Germans occupied Nice."

John had bad news for Esther. "Some of the smaller concentration camps still keep records of inmate's comings and goings. The French underground smuggles out copies of the listings. The Ravensbruck records show that Mira and Estelle Frankel of Lyon died two months ago of 'unknown' causes. The conditions there are said to be brutal. I'm so sorry, Esther."

After seeing all the slaughter while with the Resistance, the deaths of her estranged family had little effect on Esther. *I'll cry someday, but not right now.*

John and Maria urged the family to move on. "There are many with new eyes, looking for ways to gain favor with the Nazis," said John as he returned the cache of valuables her father had sent to her months ago. It was a sad parting for the Foch and O'Connor families.

John had given them a route to the port of Marseille on the Mediterranean and had them memorize the names and addresses of loyal French they might need along the way. They then bribed their way for passage to

Lisbon where they stayed with Spanish friends of the Resistance until they boarded a Swedish freighter headed west to Panama with a stop at Dublin, Ireland.

# Chapter Sixty-three

*Ireland—The O'Connors*

With tears of happiness, they made their way down the gangway in Dublin with Danny in tow. "We're safe now," said Sean.

They were met at the train station in Cork by one of Sean's brothers. That night the O'Connor clan, with all of Sean's brothers, sisters, and his parents had a rousing party with bagpipes to welcome Sean, Esther, and Danny.

Darcy O'Gara was at the party, and Sean and Esther finally had the opportunity to visit with her. Dan's imprisonment had taken its toll on her. "I have no news about Dan. The Irish Embassy in Berlin seems powerless with the Nazis. I pray every day, but I realize that I may never see my Dan again."

While staying at a rental house near Kinsale, Sean and Esther talked at length and finally decided they would go to America. "A new start for us and Danny," Sean said. Esther wrote to her uncle, Paul Brindle, in New Jersey. He replied:

> Dear Esther,
> I am so sorry to hear about my brother, Mira, and Estelle... Come to America with your Sean and Danny. We will be your sponsors and sign your affidavits. I have enclosed

necessary paperwork. Let us know your plans, and we will meet your ship.

Esther's dream wish with Abby on the *Bremen* was coming true. *Now, who shall I be in America? Aimee or Esther O'Connor?*

# Chapter Sixty-four

*Wilhelmshaven—Dan*

Almost every day at dawn, Dan heard the crack of rifle fire coming from the courtyard of the jail.

*I will be led out there some morning, and then the other prisoners will hear the crack of fired bullets, and then the quick smack of the bullets hitting my body, and then they'll wonder if they will be next.*

He had been in solitary for months. He was using a small stone to scratch days on the wall below his bed, but Siegler caught him, beat him with a stick, and rubbed off Dan's record. Seigler wouldn't talk to him except to taunt him. Dan had talked once to Major Oberholtz and once to that women prisoner who'd tried to seduce him to gain favors. It hadn't worked. Dan told them nothing.

As a diversion, he would lay on the floor at his cell door to listen for sounds in the hallway. He would often hear muffled screams and crying. *At least I'm not totally alone.*

Dan once read a book set in the Middle Ages about a solitary confinement prisoner who slowly went mad. *I've got to keep my mind working.* He spent hours going back to his time at Northwestern, reflecting on subjects he'd studied, teachers, and fellow students. He tested his memory on how each teacher delivered subject matter, and even how each dressed. He tried to remember details of campus buildings and the library layout.

Next, Dan would visualize his internship days at the *Tribune* and the fun time the interns had had at the Chicago speakeasy. Then there was the

Saturday lunch in Evanston when he and his fellow interns made plans to get a firsthand crime story.

It was painful to remember that St. Valentine's Day when their lives were changed forever. He would stop there, saving more recent times for later, and go back to Northwestern days, searching his memory for more details.

One evening he heard the food door open. He got on his knees to see who delivered his food. All he could see was a slender hand—most likely a woman's. *Interesting. Another bit of information to file away.*

As he ate his watery mashed potatoes, he noticed a buried piece of paper. The note said, "Swallow this after reading, or you get no more. Abby sends her love."

Now Dan spent every waking hour thinking about the message. *How does she know I am in here?*

His mental exercise was now "Abby sends her love." He rolled over his remembrances of her and their times together—the hillside picnic overlooking Dingle Bay; the après ski moments with the Wildcats at Gstaad and their night together. Then he began speculating. *Does Abby now realize that she does love me, or is it her way of giving me hope? I wish she would have said, "All my love. Waiting for you," or something like that. Maybe she's remembering our good times together—maybe not. Well, why shouldn't she?* Round and round.

"Okay, Irish, Major Oberholtz said you need a little sunshine. On your feet," Seigler said one day. He handcuffed him and led him to the courtyard where he tethered him with a ten-foot chain attached to the top of a steel pole. "Say woof, woof—our Irish Setter," which was followed by a parting blow on his back from his truncheon. "I'll be back in an hour, doggie boy."

The sun blinded him at first, but then it was wonderful to feel its warmth. A swivel attached to the top of the pole allowed Dan to walk in a circle around the pole. He looked around as he walked. There was a small tree in the corner of the courtyard. Its green leaves were turning brown and curling up, getting ready to fall. Next to the tree was a wooden wall set into a concrete base—a backstop for rifle bullets. It was covered with blood stains. Some stains were fresh and bright red. Other stains had dried to a dark red, almost black. The sandy soil at the base of the backstop had been splashed with blood that was crystallizing into an eerie mosaic pattern.

Dan's attention was drawn to the tree. A red-crested bird landed on a branch. A real bird. Dan smiled for the first time in a long time. The bird sat on his perch, looked around, focused on Dan, and then flew up and away over the top of the building. *It probably smelled death here.*

Siegler led him out to the yard at the same time every day. As he walked around in circles, Dan wondered if other prisoners were given the luxury of an hour outside. He moved small stones with his feet to create a tiny ridge from the pole to the end of his chain, away from where Siegler attached him. He stepped carefully over his creation. Each day he would examine his work. Nothing ever disturbed it. *Interesting, something to think about*, mused Dan.

Before his note from Abby and his daily outing privilege, Dan had planned various ways to kill himself. When first thrown in solitary, Dan did push-ups and running in-place to try to keep in shape. After weeks and months, he gave up hope and let his once-strong body begin to atrophy. *What's the use?* Now he walked as fast as he could around his circle and stopped periodically to pull on his chain to strengthen his arms.

Suddenly the daily outings stopped. There was no explanation until Dan found another message buried in his food. "Siegler was killed while raping a female prisoner. He bled like the butchered pig that he was. Thought you would like to know."

"Damn right I would like to know. Wonderful!"

Two days later, the phone rang in Oberholtz's office. "This is Kruger. I hear that one of our sergeants was killed at your place. What happened?"

"Oh, good morning, Colonel. Yes, Sergeant Siegler was in a women's cell searching for contraband when his throat was slit wide open by one of the women wielding a homemade weapon—a tin can lid embedded in a piece of wood. The two women in the cell were killed, of course."

"That's not the way I heard it, Oberholtz. I want a full report from you on my desk in three days. We can't afford to lose good men. This worries me… I don't think your jail is under control, Major." Kruger sighed over the phone. "You have an international prisoner named O'Gara there who is very valuable to us. I want him transferred immediately to headquarters. Have him on the train to Berlin tomorrow with two guards. Lieutenant Rath in Building Two will sign for him. Do you understand these orders, Major?"

"Yes, sir. And I will have a full report to you about the Siegler incident."

"You'd better."

Kruger hung up the telephone and smiled. He had been waiting for the opportunity to discredit Oberholtz and get Dan to Berlin so he could at least look after him and monitor his treatment.

# Chapter Sixty-five

*Berlin—Chancellery Apartment—November 1941*

Hitler was not in a good mood. His valet, Heinz Linge, woke him as usual with the latest reports from the battlefronts, then bowed slightly and left since Hitler preferred to dress himself. He glanced at the reports as he shaved. Nothing had changed since last night. Soviet troops had shown resolve and had retaken Rostov, and the attack on Moscow was slowing to a halt in the Russian winter. Temperatures were dropping below zero, and the German troops lacked winter clothes—the high command expected them to take Moscow weeks before. In Africa, Rommel's army had taken a beating from British forces, and had retreated from Cyrenaica to El Agheila.

He usually was very cordial with his servants and cooks. This morning he ate his toast and fruit dish in silence. *Things are not going well,* he ruminated. Beside the recent battlefront setbacks, now Abby White will be in America for a while. *I must stay positive. Her parents may be dead already.*

He took the elevator down to his office. His adjutant was waiting as he exited. "My Fuehrer, good morning. Reichfuehrer Himmler is waiting outside your office."

Himmler had been an aide to Hitler since the early days of the Nazi Party in Munich—a former chicken farmer who finessed his way to lead the dreaded SS. In 1934 Himmler took over Goering's Gestapo. He was now in charge of all secret police and concentration camps.

An obvious sycophant, Himmler praised and flattered Hitler, much to the disgust of other top Nazis like Goering and Bormann. He had blind loyalty to Hitler, an unwavering belief in him and the Third Reich. He showed his allegiance by killing more and more Jews and other so-called enemies of the Third Reich.

Still, Hitler was never impressed with the appearance of Himmler. This came to mind again as Himmler rose from his chair outside of Hitler's office. His military stiff posture appeared forced. He had the looks of a clerk with his pinched face and thick, round steel-rimmed glasses. He was the antithesis of Hitler's poster board Aryan superman.

"My Fuehrer, I am sorry to bother you without calling for a meeting, but I must talk with you about a very sensitive matter."

"All right. Come in and close the door." He told his adjutant to hold his calls.

Hitler sat behind his desk and motioned Himmler to a chair. "What is so important, Himmler? Have out with it, I have a heavy schedule."

Himmler scooted forward in his chair, leaned forward, and spoke softly. "Sir, it's about your friend, Miss Abby White, the newspaper correspondent."

Hitler's face flushed. *How dare he mention his good friend, Abby.* "Himmler, what are you doing? You are to concentrate your efforts on our enemies, not my personal friends. I want this clear to you! Understand? I will hear no more from you about Miss White. You are excused."

Himmler's face turned even paler. He rose from his chair, saluted, clicked his heels, and walked toward the door, but then stopped. "My Fuehrer, I would be in dereliction of my duties if I didn't report this to you. We believe that Miss White is a U.S. spy."

Hitler rose slowly from his desk chair. His mouth stayed open as he searched for words. "You're insane, Himmler! The lady is a news correspondent and a good friend of mine. I will hear no more of this. Any news writer will be looking for good stories and appear to be nosing around. You are badly mistaken, Himmler. Go back to arresting Jews and Communists."

Himmler walked toward the desk. "Please let me tell you what my office has found."

"Himmler, I will give you five more minutes. Sit down."

"We have established that she is very close to a Warren Walters of the U.S. Embassy who we believe is head of U.S. Intelligence in Berlin and handler of several spies we have identified. The network uses drop boxes around the city to exchange messages. Miss White has been seen and photographed using those drop boxes."

Hitler's face reddened. "You have been taking pictures of my friends without my approval? She is an American citizen. Maybe they're personal messages concerning her ailing parents in America."

"Why then, my Fuehrer, would she go to the trouble of meeting Walters at locations outside of Berlin? We have pictures of them on overnights in Furstenberg and Wittenberg."

"That's enough, Himmler. I need to call von Rundstedt about Rostov. We have a war going on, you know. Get me those pictures and include dates and time of day they were taken. You have a weak case for accusing her of spying."

Himmler left, and Hitler began pacing around the room. *A spy?* He began thinking about all that he had told her about his military plans and his personal thoughts. *I did tell her many things. It was to give her confidence in me as a leader and a husband. Have I made a fool of myself?*

The next morning Himmler returned with pictures of Abby and Walters walking a path in the woods at Furstenberg and others from their visit to Wittenberg. He also brought pictures of Abby leaving a drop box location and Walters leaving the same location later that same day. He stood behind Hitler at his desk talking about the pictures with the smile of a cat that just caught the mouse. "Sir, she could have poisoned you."

Hitler's hands started shaking so badly that he dropped the pictures. "Himmler, I know Miss White is planning a trip to America to visit her parents who are deathly sick. Have our agents in Chicago find out if her parents in Indianapolis are near death. I want a quick report."

Himmler soon reported that John White and his wife appeared to be well and active. Her father went into his office every day, and her mother was very active in civic affairs. Now Hitler became furious. "She said she had to go to America because of her dying parents. She is a liar and a traitor. She may never come back. We must arrest her before she escapes."

"Yes, sir. On what charges should we arrest her?"

"Espionage, of course! Spying for the Western Allies!"

"Sir, this can be a delicate issue. As you said, she is an American citizen. We already have strained relationships with Washington after our U-boats torpedoed and sank one of their destroyers, the *Reuben James*, in the North Atlantic."

"Look, Himmler, you're the one who brought the Miss White case to me. The U.S. hasn't gone to war over the loss of their ship, and they're not going to war over the arrest of an American correspondent." He walked over to his window, and then turned around. "Himmler, arrest and kill Abby White! Now! I want her to have a very painful death for the trouble she has caused me. There are many ways to kill. I want that woman to die of multiple little things. And I will want a movie of her last days in pain, like you did when you hung those Communists with piano wire last month. Now do your job! Find and arrest her! You're dismissed."

# Chapter Sixty-six

*Berlin—SS Gestapo Headquarters*

After Himmler ordered Abby's arrest, he sat in his third-floor office thinking. Then he called his major deputy, Reinhard Heydrich, who was on the road again, checking on more newly opened concentration camps. "The Fuehrer has ordered me to arrest one Abby White for espionage. You may know of her as a correspondent for the *Chicago Tribune*. We have good evidence that she has been spying for U.S. Intelligence through their Embassy here in Berlin. I will have some of our men pick her up tonight."

"I do remember her, sir."

"This is a special case, Reinhard. Besides being a citizen of the neutral U.S., she is well-known for her work around the Embassy set and by other highly regarded people in Berlin. She also has been good friends with our Fuehrer over the years. I can tell you that he had great affection for her until he saw our evidence. Now he calls her a liar and traitor and wants us to eliminate her with extreme prejudice. He even wants us to take movies of her punishment and death. Reinhard, I'm not sure his mood will last. He changes his mind frequently as you know."

"Yes, sir. I'm just curious, why did he call her a traitor?"

"I don't know. Maybe because she betrayed his affection for her. I don't know. So, we must treat her with care until time has passed. I don't want us to kill her, and then have the Fuehrer relent and then order us to release her. He might be very upset with us if that happened. Then again, with his focus on the battlefields, he may forget all about her. Then we can do what we want with her. Our photographs show a very pretty young lady."

Heydrich chuckled. "I understand, sir. Yes, I agree we must wait. I will call Kruger. I will make it clear to him regarding her treatment and will follow up when I return."

Kruger was shocked when Heydrich told him that the American correspondent, Abby White, was to be arrested for spying. *How in the devil did Abby manage to get herself in such a mess?*

Kruger knew she was at the *Tribune* bureau, but didn't try to contact her over the years since it might comprise his sleeper position in the SS. Abby heard that Karl was a now a leading officer in the SS headquarters in Berlin. She was afraid of the SS and what Kruger may have become.

*Now I will have Dan O'Gara at one end of this prison and Abby White at the other. Ironic! All the surviving Wildcats from the Capone era are here except for Esther. I wonder if she's dead. Maybe she'll be the next to join us.*

# Chapter Sixty-seven

*Berlin—Abby's Apartment*

Abby was excited as she finished packing. It was years since she had been home. She checked her purse for the second time. Her train route from Berlin went through German-occupied France to Paris where she would transfer to a limited express train taking her into neutral Spain to the port city of Lisbon. On the second day there, she would board her New York-bound ship.

Next, she checked her newly issued U.S. passport and her approved transit papers needed at country borders. She was satisfied she had everything and moved to her small kitchen, poured a generous glass of Chardonnay, and thought, *I wonder if I'll ever see Berlin again.*

A loud rap on her door startled her. She kept the chain on her door and peaked out. There was a middle-aged man in a dark suit holding a paper in his hand. Two SS police in uniform stood behind him.

"Yes, what do you want?"

"Are you Abby White?" His smile was cordial, showing two gold-caped front teeth.

"Yes."

"Open up. You're under arrest."

*I've been had.* Abby was stunned, but her face showed defiance. "Show me your credentials."

The man frowned and fished out a small case from an inside breast pocket. He showed his Gestapo badge with his picture. "Now open up, or we will open it for you."

Abby took the chain off the door and opened it farther. "You must be mistaken. I am an American citizen and a *Chicago Tribune* news correspondent."

The agent put on his reading glasses, shook the papers in his hand, checked the apartment number on the door, then read, "Abby White, at this address, is to be arrested and taken to Gestapo Headquarters. The charge by the Third Reich is espionage." He put the papers in his breast pocket. "You will come with us now. Take only your purse and coat. It is a cold November night. We will be searching this place later." He showed his gold teeth again. "We already have a key from your building superintendent." A door across the across the hall was opened and closed quickly.

Abby's purse lay on a table near the door. He nodded to the SS police. "Search that and her coat."

"Don't you touch my purse," Abby said. She reached for it, but the second SS man stopped her. He pulled out Abby's treasured Beretta.

"Well, look there," said the agent. "Why are you carrying that?"

"For my personal protection."

"You don't need this now, Miss White. We will protect you now." He pocketed the gun.

"All right, I will come with you to get this matter resolved quickly. I must be at the train station early tomorrow morning."

The agent smiled. "I think you will miss your train."

Abby sat in the backseat of a sedan between the two SS policemen. As the car approached the large gray building, she thought of the time she and her office mate, Carol, out of curiosity, walked to the notorious Gestapo building on their lunch hour. She never dreamed she would be seeing it again—this time from the inside, under arrest.

# Chapter Sixty-eight

*Gestapo Headquarters*

The trio escorted her through a rear entrance to a room where the duty officer, Captain Mach, sat behind a massive table. Abby glanced down a hallway. *Jail cells.* The sign over the hallway entrance read "Women's Section."

The agent gave the arrest papers to Mach who signed the transfer portion indicating acceptance of the prisoner and handed a carbon copy back to the agent. Then the arresting crew left.

"Three men to bring you in! Are you that dangerous, or just an important person?"

"Sir, there is a huge mistake here. I am an American citizen with press credentials. I have interviewed your Fuehrer several times. He will vouch for me. Please call his office."

The captain turned the pages of the arrest papers and smiled. "It says here that our Fuehrer ordered Reichfuehrer Himmler to arrest you. We must obey his orders." He pressed a button on his desk and a tall blonde woman with close-cropped hair came through a door. She wore a brown flared jacket with large buttons and a matching long skirt that touched the top of her shoes. She did not smile. "This is the international guest we were expecting, Fraulein Schnell. Take her, search her person, give her a change of clothes—you know, the usual—and put her in cell eight. Miss White, when have you last eaten?"

"I'm not hungry. Please contact the American Embassy and the *Chicago Tribune* bureau office. Mr. Hoffman is the bureau chief. Here, give me a piece of paper and a pencil."

She so surprised the captain that he obeyed. "Here is Mr. Hoffman's number. You can look up the Embassy's number. Let them both know my whereabouts."

Mach stiffened his posture in his chair and recovered his authority. "In due course, Miss White. In due course. Take her away."

Fraulein Schnell took Abby by the arm and led her down the hallway. When they were out of earshot, the guard said, "Where did you learn German, Miss White?"

Abby turned her head toward her. Now there was a friendly smile on the guard's face.

"In school in America and on my job here in Berlin."

"You speak it like a native. I would never know you're American." She stopped. "Here's your cell. It's a nice one as far as cells go. See that steel door down at the end of the hall? You don't want to go in there. When they open it you can usually hear screaming. I told them I could not work in there. In you go. Now I have to search you. Take off all your clothes and sit on that stool."

She searched Abby from head to toe and every orifice in-between. Abby shivered and covered herself as best she could with her hands and arms. Schnell started with her hair. "You'd be surprised how often we find dangerous things in a person's hair. One guard lost her eye when a prisoner used a sharp hairpin on her."

She moved down Abby's body. "I hate to do this search, but I have my orders. I once found a tiny one-shot pistol hidden in you-know-where. *Richtig, stimmt,* you look clean. Put on this underwear and smock. I will put your clothes and coat in the storeroom up front.

"Are you sure you're not hungry. Breakfast is a long time away."

"All right, I'd better eat something."

"I'll bring something shortly."

Abby looked around the cell. A metal bed frame with a thin mattress and blanket. No pillow. A toilet and washbowl. A small metal table with a wooden stool. A smoked glass window with a wire barrier.

Abby's meal consisted of a boiled potato, sauerkraut, a small wrinkled apple, and bread and water.

"Most prisoners don't get a good meal like this, Miss White." She whispered, "You are to be treated with special care." She pointed to an open slot at the bottom of the cell door. "Slide your tray through there when you are finished. Lights go out at ten o'clock. Breakfast at seven. I understand you will be interrogated tomorrow morning. Good night."

Abby lay on her mattress. *I've got to convince them that the whole thing is a mistake. I doubt they will buy it, but I've got to try. What was I thinking when I accepted Warren's proposal to serve as a spy? Not very smart.*

An SS lieutenant sat across from Abby in a chilly interrogation room. Abby thought he look sickly. He was a small man with a small head that poked out of his high-collared uniform jacket. His pasty face wore rimless glasses. He took his cap off, revealing a balding head. "I am Lieutenant Raff, Miss White. We will have a little session here."

He looked her over. "What a come-down for you from when you graced all the embassy parties in your fancy dresses. Now you wear a drab prisoner's smock. Not very chic!" He laughed as if were a good joke.

"You socialites don't remember or care who was guarding you. I was in charge of security at our Embassy parties. You were friends with the von Fritsch family, right?"

Abby nodded. "Lieutenant, it was a number of years since I was at those embassies. Why are you still a lieutenant?"

Raff shifted in his chair, visibly upset. He rose without answering and spread pictures on the table, turning them to face Abby.

"Now, let's get down to business. You are charged with espionage by the highest authority in the Third Reich, our beloved Fuehrer. Do you deny these charges?"

"Yes, of course. Has the American Embassy and the *Tribune's* Berlin bureau been notified?"

"Yes. I hear both have protested your arrest." He gave Abby a crooked smile. "Let's see how far that gets them."

He sat back down and motioned to the pictures. "So, Miss White, it looks like you spent many hours at several locations with Warren Walters, the U.S. Embassy man who we have identified as the handler of special spies. How can you deny these pictures?"

Abby examined the pictures. "You people have been very busy. Why aren't you at the Russian front fighting a real war?"

Raff smiled. "I was told you are gutsy. Again, can you deny these pictures?"

"Of course not. Warren was my boyfriend for a while. We met in out-of-town places for romantic interludes. I would think your agents' reports confirm that."

"Why did you use his drop boxes?" Abby shook her head and smiled. "It was a little romantic game we played, leaving love notes for each other."

"Why did you stop seeing him?"

"I finally realized that he was not the man for a long-term relationship."

Raff got up and paced around the table. "Let's change the subject. Why did you lie to our Fuehrer about your parents being deathly ill?"

"How did you know about that? It was a very personal talk between me and your leader."

"Our Fuehrer told Reichfuerhrer Himmler that."

"Adolf had a romantic interest in me that I didn't share. I made up that story so I could break it off without hurting his pride. I was also afraid of his mercurial temperament."

Raff banged his fist on the table.

"You blaspheme our Fuehrer with your self-importance! How dare you call our Fuehrer by his first name? He could have any woman in the world. You lie again!" He rapped on the mirrored window in the room. An SS sergeant came through the door. "Sergeant Rudolf, this woman has blasphemed our Fuehrer and has insulted me. She is a spy and a clever liar. Take her to the interrogation room in the women's section. Put her on the steel table and lock her down. I will join you shortly."

Abby was led back to her section and down the hallway towards the steel door. She couldn't stop shaking. The sergeant opened the door and pushed her inside. The room was like that in a horror movie she saw when she was in high school. Chains with shackles hung from the ceiling and other chains were fastened to the walls. At the end of the room was a wooden table with manacles fastened at one end. At the other end two manacles were tied to ropes that were coiled around a drum with a hand crank. Abby gasped and felt nauseated.

She was shackled to a stainless-steel table that reminded Abby of an autopsy table she also had seen in a movie. The table was slanted so that blood could flow down to a hole in the table and then to a drain in the floor. Raff came into the room. "Good work, Sergeant. Now take off her sandals and fetch that birch rod over there. I want to teach this bitch some humility."

Raff stood over her with arms folded. "All right, society bitch. What military information did you pass to Walters?"

"I don't know what you're talking about." Abby herself was in disbelief at what was going on. *I'm an American girl from the Midwest. What am I doing here?*

He motioned to the sergeant. "Give her ten good strokes on the bottoms of her feet, then stop for more questions."

Abby gritted her teeth and took the beating without a word, but tears flowed down her cheeks.

"How's your memory now?" said Raff. Abby stared at him through her tears and said nothing. Raff signaled the sergeant to begin again when the door opened.

"What the hell are you doing, Raff?" said Captain Mach. "We were instructed to treat her with care, not beat her."

"But she insulted our Fuehrer and me."

"You stupid oaf," said Mach. He ordered the sergeant to drop the birch rod and undo Abby's shackles.

Mach looked at Abby's lacerated, bleeding feet. "Sergeant, get a stretcher and another man and carry her back to her cell. I will get a doctor to treat her. Raff, we all may pay for your stupidity. Don't you touch that woman again. I will deal with you later." He left to get a doctor, and on the way thanked he Fraulein Schnell for her alertness.

Abby's wounds were slow to heal. After heavier bandages were used she was able to walk around her cell. The staff of the women's section was not to tell of "Miss White's accident when she stepped on broken glass." Still, the truth of the matter was disclosed to Lieutenant Colonel Kruger in his office by a cleaning woman who was beaten by Raff when she accidently broke his favorite coffee cup.

Kruger dismissed Raff from the SS for failure to obey orders. He called an officer friend in the regular army and had Raff sent to the subzero Russian front. Captain Mach was chastised by Kruger, but not demoted. Kruger still resisted the impulse to visit Abby in her cell. He prepared a report on the incident and filed it away as November slipped into December, 1941.

Heydrich called Kruger. "Reichfuerhrer Himmler and I won't be in the office for a bit of time. We are meeting with several manufacturers around the country to evaluate their plans for a more efficient way to eliminate the undesirable vermin. The army is complaining that we use too much ammunition to shoot the deplorables, and killing them with carbon monoxide in the back of trucks is too slow and messy. The engineers are suggesting a system using Zyklon B gas to kill a building full of the scum at one time, and then use large crematoriums to get rid of the bodies. Isn't that exciting? We have a conference planned at Wannsee on 20 January.

We're calling the conference 'The Final Solution to the Jewish Question.' Everything all right there, Karl?"

"Yes, sir. Had to discipline some staff on a minor matter, but no jailbreaks since you left."

Heydrich laughed. "That's a good one. 'No jailbreaks.' Karl, I know you'll continue to handle things well in our absence. Call me if you need to."

Kruger was authorized to read all of Heydrich's incoming messages in his absence. He sat upright when he read a top-secret message from Hitler's office. "The Japanese have advised me that they intend to attack U. S. military bases in the Pacific in the very near future. I assume our heroic partner will attack the Philippine islands."

Kruger's considered what would happen next. *The U.S. will declare war on Japan. Japan's partners, Germany and Italy, will then declare war on the U.S. It will be a world war with everyone picking sides. It will get wild. I must think on this more.*

Kruger walked to his apartment on a busy street, hunching over against a cold wind. He was pulling up his coat collar and his SS cap down when he was bumped almost head-on by a tall man. "Sorry, sir," the man said. Then he mumbled, "Your pocket," and disappeared into the crowd. Kruger reached into his coat pocket and felt paper. He waited until he locked his apartment door to read the note.

> Kruger—
> We know it's been years since we have enlisted you as an undercover agent. It is our fault for not staying in touch. We now have an urgent need for your services. We must know if you still wish to be an agent for America and consent to act for us.
> We understand if we have lost your loyalty to us over time. We will never disclose your past affiliation with us. If you are still with us as an agent ready for assignments, please stand under the clock in front of Shultz's Department Store at 1800 o'clock next Friday, the 17th, for three minutes. We will provide more information later.

Karl appeared under the clock as requested. The following day another note was placed in his pocket by a passerby.

> You are activated, Apache. We know your position and situation. We want you out of there along with your prisoners, White and O'Gara. Develop and execute a plan to motor north to Rostock, then turn east to the coastal town of Bad Doberan. There is only one inn in the town. You will be expected there on 9 December at 1800 hour. We will have agents there to meet you.
>
> If you can't execute your plan, set off a fire alarm in your building at 1200 on 8 December. We'll hear it. Good luck.

# Chapter Sixty-nine

*SS Headquarters—December 1941*

Kruger noted that Hitler's guess at the Japanese communiqué was almost right. Japan made a surprise air attack on Pearl Harbor, Hawaii, from aircraft carriers on December 7, and then attacked American bases in the Philippine Islands ten hours later and invaded the islands on December 23.

The SS building was buzzing with the news. Captain Mach called a meeting of his staff. "I believe Japan will next attack Russia in Manchuria, and the Russian pigs will have to send troops there. That should leave us free to take Moscow." They were applauding Mach's talk when Kruger walked into the room. The cheering stopped when they saw a different look on Kruger's face. "Captain Mach, step outside with me, please."

"Yes, Colonel."

"Mach, sit down and listen closely. I have received disturbing information from our counter-spy network. A British assault team plans to parachute tonight outside of Berlin, make their way into the city, and storm this building before dawn. Their mission is to rescue our prisoners, Abby White, the American spy, and Daniel O'Gara, the British spy, before we can interrogate them properly. If they can't get them out, they are to kill them. The spies must know more secrets than we thought they did. Reichfuerhrer Heydrich wants me to handle this personally because of its new importance. We need these prisoners alive.

"Captain, you will handle preparations for me. The raid is apparently scheduled for dawn tomorrow. I want an unmarked sedan filled with petrol at the Women's Section entrance at midnight tonight. The driver is to be armed. Have him bring a submachine gun for me. Bring the prisoners White and O'Gara to the entrance in street clothes and coats. Is this understood, Captain?"

"Yes, of course. But, Colonel, let *me* get them out of here. Your place is here."

"I have considered that, Captain, but I must obey direct orders from Heydrich. Besides, I've been an administrative person, pushing papers. You are a veteran who can fight. You know this building very well, better than me, and any replacement we might bring in now." He paused and lowered his voice. "Mach, there may be a traitor in our building who has given them a layout and cell locations of our prisoners. Get to the switchboard and allow no calls to go out. The raiders and their spies must think they have the advantage of surprise, but you'll be ready to stop them in their tracks. Plan your defenses. Trap them. Try to save at least one of the attackers for interrogation."

Kruger looked at his watch. "Get one of your junior officers out here now. I want to have him take me on a fresh tour of the building I might see something that can help you before I leave. Now let's get on with it, Captain."

Dan O'Gara was still held in solitary, but the beatings had stopped, and even the interrogations had slowed. He did hear screams from the hallway as prisoners were dragged from their cells for interrogation or execution. The killing yard was away from Dan's cell, and the sounds of rifle fire were distant and muffled.

The other sound that always chilled his bones was the click-clicks of guard boots in the hallway. *Who are they coming for now? Me?*

"Lieutenant, open the viewing port on prisoner O'Gara's cell. Then walk down a bit. I don't want to scare him to death with two of us surprising him.

Kruger moved to the viewing port. "O'Gara, come here." Dan moved to the door and looked at the man in the SS officer's cap. "Hello, Dan. Listen, don't act like you know me." He paused. Dan looked like a different person—skinny with hollowed eyes. "I'm Karl Kruger, your old Wildcat classmate. Don't yell or say anything."

Dan took another look at the man and stepped back with his mouth opened in awe.

"Dan, Abby White is a prisoner here too. I'm getting you and Abby out of here with me at midnight tonight. Act surprised when they bring clothes for you and take you down to an exit. I will be there along with Abby. Okay?"

Dan was stunned. "Abby is here?"

"Yes, she was arrested for spying."

"Okay, I'll be ready."

The lieutenant stood at ease down the hall. "All right, Lieutenant, take me over to the Women's Section." Along the way, Karl checked the few external windows, pretending to check their security. They came down the stairs to the steel door at the end of Abby's hall. He ordered, "Open it up."

He looked around the room. "Does this room have any other entrances I can't see?"

"No, sir."

"Good. Lock it up. Now, down the hallway to the American woman's cell. I want to see how she is after her accident. Knock on her door and wait before you open the viewing port. We are still gentlemen, aren't we, Lieutenant? Again, move off while I question her."

"Yes, Colonel."

Karl looked inside at Abby. "Come closer, Miss White. I'm Colonel Kruger, in charge here." He checked the hallway to make sure the officer had moved off. "So, how are they treating you, Abby?"

"Better. When will I be released?"

Karl moved his face closer to the opening. "Abby, don't yell or act surprised. Look at me. I'm Karl Kruger, your Northwestern classmate. I've been a U.S. sleeper agent for years, just now activated. We will get out of here tonight at midnight with Dan O'Gara. Can you walk with your wounds?"

"Yes."

"Good. They will bring you street clothes soon. See you at midnight."

Abby's knees weakened, and she had to sit down. *Is this some evil trick to kill us as escapees? He's been a Nazi for a long time.*

As midnight approached, Fraulein Schell brought Abby's clothes from storage and helped her dress. "I'm sorry for your beating, Miss White," she said and then led her to the front door in handcuffs. Dan stood by the door with his own guard. At first, Abby thought it was someone else. The man in handcuffs had a tangled black beard and hair down to his shoulders. Clothes from another prisoner hung loosely on his frail body. He leaned against the wall, peered at Abby, and then looked away. His eyes were spiritless and half-closed.

"Dan, it's Abby. What have they done to you?"

Dan shifted his stance, but said nothing. The guard put a heavy coat over Dan's shoulders, and said, "He has been a troublesome prisoner."

At midnight Karl approached the group gathered at the exit door. He carried a black briefcase. Abby and Dan just stared at him. "Everybody looks ready to go, Captain. Who is our driver?"

"Sergeant Rudolf, Colonel, a good man. He waits outside."

"All right." He pulled Captain Mach aside. "I found one window unlocked on the second floor. Check all windows and the roof doors. They may use the fire escape to the roof and go down from there. Check everything personally. Good luck."

"Colonel, may I ask your destination?"

"No, Captain. The raiding force may capture and torture you to find out where we're headed. Our Reichfuerhrer would not be happy."

The handcuffs on Abby's wrist hurt when Sergeant Rudolf pushed her into the back seat next to Dan. Abby eyed Rudolf. *Wonderful, the same monster who beat me.* The Sergeant opened the front passenger door for Karl, and then climbed into the driver's side. He asked the Colonel in a low voice, "What are my orders, sir? I was not given any by Captain Mach."

"Head northeast toward Wittstock. I will give you directions as we go. Be alert for trouble, Sergeant. Watch for cars tailing us. Be ready to shake them off. These are valuable prisoners as you should realize by now. You watch the roads. I will watch them."

Karl put the submachine gun, a Bergmann *machinenpistole* on his lap. "Sergeant, where is your weapon?"

"In my heavy coat pocket, sir—the coat on the floor."

"Stupid man! How were you trained? Were you planning to ask our attackers to wait until you find your pistol? Stop the car. Find it and put it next to you on the seat." Rudolf was sweating visibly when he finally got himself together.

Abby didn't risk any conversation, but she scooted closer to Dan, touched his hand and gave him a smile. He looked at her, nodded, and stared straight ahead.

The city streets of Berlin were in semi-darkness in response to enforced blackouts because of British air raids. Then the streets gave way to a completely dark highway. They drove slowly for several hours. The only talk was from Karl. "Rudolf, keep your eyes on the road. You're drifting around." After passing through Whittstock, Karl saw a chalet on a hillside off the road. Even though it was almost three in the early morning, there was a light in a window. *Somebody's up*, thought Karl.

"Turn left at that side road, Sergeant. See that house on the hill? Drive up to the front door."

An outside house light went on.

"Sergeant, give me the keys to the prisoner's handcuffs."

The sergeant smiled. "You want to let them go to the bathroom. I'm ready too."

Karl took the keys and opened his car door. He walked around the car to the driver's side, taking the safety off his machine gun as he walked. "Out of the car, Sergeant, with your hands in the air. Leave your pistol on the seat and give me the keys to the car."

Rudolf did as he was ordered. "What's going on, sir?"

The homeowner came out of his door with a shotgun at the ready— a gray-haired man ready to defend his home.

"Sorry to bother you, sir," Karl said. "This man is an imposter, a spy posing as an SS trooper. I believe he was about to attack me and release the prisoners. Do you have a room without windows where we can lock him in temporarily?" Karl saw him glance at the back seat. "We are transporting these prisoners to a safer location." The man saw the handcuffs and nodded.

"Come this way with him, sir. We have a lockable room in our basement with no windows. Bring in your prisoners too. It's too cold to leave them. My wife, Gilda, can watch them. She's got her own gun."

Gilda held her pistol on Abby and Dan while they took Rudolf down the basement.

"So, what did you two do? You don't look like criminals."

Abby smiled and said. "We were making love in a public place."

"Oh, that's not good," said Gilda.

As they were going down the stairs, Rudolf started to speak. "You shut up, or I'll use this on the side of your head," said Karl. "Or maybe you want me to shoot you? Take off that uniform, you dirty spy, including your shoes, and get in that room."

The homeowner held his shotgun steady on Rudolf, then pushed him in the room and locked the door. "Good idea, Colonel, he wouldn't get far in this cold weather in his underwear."

"Sir, you are doing a great service to the Third Reich," said Karl. "I will personally recommend you for a citizen's medal."

The man beamed. "I was in the first war in France. I know how to use this gun."

"Excellent. I thought you had been a soldier because of your bearing. Now keep him in there and don't listen to his lies. He is very clever—had me fooled for a while."

With the uniform and boots in the front seat, Karl shook the man's hand. "I'll be off to find a military post."

"Colonel, the town of Wittstock has nothing, but there's a road checkpoint about ten kilometers north of here." He saluted. "My name is Fritz Munster. You know, for the medal?"

# Chapter Seventy

***Northern Germany—Road Block***

Karl was behind the wheel and heading north again. After a mile, he pulled over to a rest stop. It was deserted.

"Dan, the old man back there said there's a check-point up ahead. A colonel driving this car could arouse suspicion. I'll pull over to have you change into Rudolf's uniform and then take the wheel. His clothes should be a decent fit."

Abby looked at Dan. "Karl, I don't know if he's okay to drive. He's in bad shape."

Karl gave him water and rubbed some on Dan's face. "Dan, you've got to change clothes and drive this car. You can do it. You *must* do it if you want to escape."

Dan looked at him and nodded.

Dan wiggled out of his street clothes in the back seat with Abby's help. She finally brought a little smile to Dan's face with; "You know, Dan, I haven't seen you in your underwear for quite a spell."

She tucked in his long hair and smoothed down his beard as best she could, then they made the switch at the wheel. Abby put on her handcuffs again. "There it is up ahead. I'll do the talking," said Karl.

Dawn was washing away the dark of night as they rolled to a stop. A half-dozen Wehrmacht troopers manned the checkpoint. A sergeant walked over to passenger's side, and Karl lowered his window. "Colonel, what bring you out here to this desolate place at such an early hour?"

"Sergeant, we are transporting an important female prisoner to a safe place for interrogation. There are people who want to silence her, so be alert. They may have followed us." Karl gave him transit papers, which Karl had signed—with a forged signature of Heydrich to boot.

"Colonel, did you lose a prisoner? This says a man and a woman."

"Oh, at the last minute the man became deathly sick, and I had to leave him at SS Headquarters."

The sergeant looked at Dan, the driver. "You should be ashamed of yourself, Corporal, with that shaggy beard."

Karl got out of the car. "Sergeant, this man just returned from the Russian front on furlough. I drafted him to drive this car since we're short of drivers at headquarters. I'll get him clean him up later.." He moved closer to the sergeant until he was nearly in his face, and then lowered his voice and spoke sternly.

"Sergeant, this is a top-secret mission. Do not discuss this with your men. It could result in serious trouble for you with Reichfuerhrer Heydrich. We must move on. Open the gate!"

The sergeant stepped back, saluted, and waved to the soldier in the booth. The gate arm went up, and Dan drove through.

"Good work, Karl!" said Abby. She reached over and patted him on the back.

"Even the army is afraid of the SS, my dear Wildcats."

\* \* \*

A while after Karl left with Abby and Dan, Fritz told his wife, "Gilda, I'm thinking they won't be here 'til tomorrow to pick up the imposter or spy or whatever he is, so I think we should feed him."

"All right, I'll warm up the leftovers from lunch. It's probably more than he deserves."

Fritz carried the food tray down the steps with Gilda following and unlocked the door. "Coming in with food." Rudolf put his shoulder hard into the door, knocking Fritz and the food tray to the floor. He then jumped on him, beating him with his fists. Gilda raised her pistol and fired two bullets into Rudolf's brain. "Get up, Fritz, we have a mess to clean up. You okay?"

After cleaning the basement and covering the body, Munster and his wife drove to the roadblock. The guard shift had changed, and another sergeant was in charge. He approached the car, and the Munsters opened their windows. "Sir, we need your men to pick up a body of a spy we have been holding for the SS.

"What are you talking about, old man?"

Munster got out of the car, bristling. "I am not an 'old' man! Just twenty years ago I fought in the Great War when you were still in diapers, sucking on your mama's teat."

"All right, sir, I'm sorry. What is this all about?

"We were holding a spy who dressed up as an SS—holding him for the colonel who said he would pass through here."

The sergeant gave him a blank look. Gilda got out of the car.

"Well, anyway, we were going to give him some food in our homemade cell when he attacked me," said Fritz. "While we were fighting, my wife, Gilda here, shot him in the head two times and killed him."

Gilda moved up to the sergeant. "He deserved it. I took my time to fix a nice plate for him, and he knocked it all over the basement and broke one of my heirloom plates. And, oh yes, he was beating on poor Fritz here."

The sergeant sent men to the house. In the meantime, he questioned the Munsters at length. Eventually, he called his superior who called Berlin. Captain Mach took the call at SS Headquarters. "I don't know what really happened up there, but Colonel Kruger must have his reasons—he is on a top-secret mission. I will send a patrol car up there."

# Chapter Seventy-one

*Karow—Lunch Stop*

"This somehow reminds me of the 'good old days' in Michigan when we escaped from Capone's men," said Abby.

Dan, still in the mental aftermath of terror, started talking. "I hope we're as lucky."

The snow had melted on the highway, and they made good time going through the rugged lake country of northwest Germany. They stopped for lunch in the small town of Karow. "It looks okay, let's go in," said Karl. The husband and wife, owners of the small café, were in awe of the SS colonel and bowed many times as they both took their food orders.

The wife whispered in the kitchen while preparing their food. "Why is that woman wearing handcuffs, and why does that soldier have all that hair?"

"No talk. Get them their food and let them go. Don't ask them any questions, woman, they're SS," he hissed.

## Chapter Seventy-two

*Northern Germany—Karl's Confession*

Abby squeezed Dan's shoulder as he drove and smiled at Karl. "I never thought I'd ever see you two again. It's like make-believe. Karl, do you think we can get some wine tonight to celebrate?"

"Abby, if there's a bottle of wine in Bad Doberan, we'll find it and we'll celebrate."

They slowed down to avoid attention and paced their speed to arrive in Bad Doberan at the agreed time. Karl turned his body in the front seat to look directly at Abby and Dan. "I need to tell you both about what I had to do in the past years to keep my sleeper assignment. When we first arrived in Berlin from our Atlantic City location, I was assigned to the SS. I managed to get posted to SS Headquarters and avoided being sent to the SS street force that rounded up Jews and beat up unarmed men and women. But my duties turned out to be worse." He cracked his window a bit and lit a cigarette.

"I had to oversee the scheduling of trains to take Jews and other 'undesirables' to concentration camps spread over Poland and Germany, and then later I had to go to the train stations to supervise the loading of the trains. Often men and boys were loaded in boxcars headed one way, and women and girls to another camp. Sometimes they waited until the train arrived at the camp to select the fittest for work details, and then marched the rest to the gas chamber buildings for 'shower baths'— doors were sealed and poisonous Zyklon B gas was forced through the 'shower' heads into the room. The dead were removed from the rooms by other prisoners who were forced to load the bodies into the crematories.

"One night I had to stay over at Auschwitz on an inspection tour. I was asleep in the commandant's building when I was awakened by horrible cries. The next day I learned that they had run out of Zyklon, and children had been hurled into the furnaces alive."

"Karl, stop!" cried Abby.

"I can't," Karl said.

"When prisoners arrived at the concentration camps, some were selected as guinea pigs for medical experimentation. These were direct orders from Hitler. One weekend, Heydrich sent me down the Dachau camp to review high-flight research. I had to look through the observation window of the decompression chamber when a prisoner inside would stand a vacuum until his lungs ruptured. He went mad. He beat the walls with his hands and head and screamed in an effort to relieve pressure on his eardrums and chest."

"Karl, please stop," said Abby. "We all did things we didn't want to do to carry out our assignments."

"Abby, I hear you, but my work was despicable and unrelenting. I was an integral part of the mass murder of innocents. I tried several times to get transferred to Goebbels' Propaganda Office or anywhere, but Himmler said I was too valuable to the SS. I was promoted to Lieutenant Colonel. My father and mother and siblings were very proud of me.

"I had given up hearing from U.S. Intelligence. From 1938 on I believed they had forgotten about me.

"Then my transformation began to take place. When the Wehrmacht armies swept through France, the Netherlands, and North Africa, I was swept along in pride for my native Germany. I began to *really* listen to the speeches by Hitler, Goebbels, and the like, and started to wonder if these 'victims' *did* cause all of the problems. I began to enjoy strutting around as an SS colonel and looked the other way at the disgusting atrocities of the Nazis. I *was* a Nazi. I was afforded all the amenities given the SS officers: wine, women, and a lot of parties. It was a heady experience. People would step off the curb into the gutter as I approached and then nod and smile and lower their heads as if I were the devil passing by and they didn't want to offend me. I fantasized—if Hitler kept winning, I could rise to the top next to Himmler. My father and mother would be ecstatic!

"I had almost lost my soul when I learned of your imprisonment in Wilhelmshaven, Dan. It slowly brought me back to the real world. It took me awhile, but I finally got focused again. Then *your* arrest, Abby, and a contact by U.S. Intelligence, got me planning for this. That's when I started microfilming hundreds of secret Nazi documents." He raised and patted his black attaché case. "There are details of the SS's and Wehrmacht's current strengths, weaknesses, and locations, and locations of all the concentration camps."

He threw his spent cigarette out the window and lit another. "I carry a heavy burden of guilt for what I have done, either by commission or omission. Somehow I must make amends the rest of my life." He stopped talking and stared ahead.

There wasn't much Abby could say or do except to commiserate with him. "This nightmare will soon be over, Karl," said Abby. "Then we'll all be free of this god-awful experience."

They drove slowly through the street of Rostock, and then turned east to Bad Doberan, a tiny resort town on the Baltic Sea. "If you sailed a boat north of here you'd be in Denmark," said Karl. "It's only fifty kilometers from here. It's off season, and water is cold, but it's not frozen. That's not an option anyway—Denmark is German-occupied territory now."

They had paced their driving to arrive at the designated hour. Abby took off her handcuffs and put them in her pocket, "I hope I don't need these anymore."

"So, Karl, how in the hell do we get out of here?" Dan managed.

"We'll soon find out."

# Chapter Seventy-three

***Bad Doberan, Germany—Baltic Sea Coast***

"This town can't be more than four square blocks, but it's so quaint and pretty. Look at those street lights," Abby said. Lighting the way in soft yellows were replicas of antique ship lanterns. Most of the shops were closed for the season.

"My family visited here when I was a child—great memories," said Karl.

"There's the inn," Abby said.

Dan parked in front, and they walked in with Karl leading the way. Two men were sitting in the lobby. The men were large with weathered fishermen's faces, and they wore heavy knit sweaters and Greek fisherman's caps. Even though Karl's party was expected, the two men were startled when the uniformed SS, Karl and Dan, came through the door. They stood with guns raised. Karl raised his arms in surrender and said, "I think we're on time."

"What is your code name?" asked one of the men.

"Apache," said Karl.

"Good," said the man as they lowered their weapons. The visitors were led into a sitting room behind the registration desk

Karl smiled, pulled off his leather gloves, and said, "I'm Karl Kruger. That's Abby White, and he's Dan O'Gara."

"As expected. Very good," said one man. "You don't need to know our names right now. The owner and his wife are preparing food for you. Please give me the keys to that car. We have to hide it. In that closet you'll find fishermen's clothes for the men and a nice fall outfit for the lady." The man smiled at Abby. "I don't know if you'll like the style, Miss, but I know it will keep you warm."

He looked at Dan. "I'll bring some shaving things and hot water for you, young man."

Dan looked in a mirror for the first time in months. "God, I'm ugly." He needed scissors to cut off his beard before he shaved.

The inn owner knocked on the door. "I'm Hans. My wife, Bella, and I own this place. Dinner is ready in the kitchen." Hans was short and round and graying.

Bella was ladling vegetable soup from a large kettle. Bella was shorter and rounder and jollier than Hans. There was a long wooden table with benches in the center of a large kitchen. A wood-burning fireplace gave off warmth and light.

"Have a seat, friends," said Bella. "We have a nice dining room, but it's more private back here."

"Oh, it's so cozy in here," said Abby. "And the soup smells wonderful."

Hans joined the group after locking the front door. The two men who greeted them earlier came in through the rear kitchen door. "I'm Emil, and he's Fredrick. May we join you?"

"Of course," said Abby.

Looking at Abby with her braided blonde hair, ski sweater, and ski pants, Emil said, "Miss, you look like a northern German woman."

Dan ate like the half-starved prisoner he had been. His eyes watered a bit. "The best meal I've had for a very long time."

After Hans and Bella cleared the table they joined the group. Emil seemed to be the group's leader. "You know by now this is a very risky business, but in your case, our brave visitors, you are well worth it. Our men in Berlin gave us the rundown on you." Emil pointed around the table. "A deeply embedded American agent with the SS who led your escape from Berlin. An American woman who is not only a respected news correspondent but also an excellent U.S. agent and an accepted confidant of Hitler before her arrest and torture. Then we have the Irish counter-spy for the British who spent many months in SS prisons enduring torture without breaking. We are honored to help you all survive and escape. The information you'll provide will be invaluable in bringing down the Nazis."

Hans went into his pantry and brought out three bottles of his best wine. He looked at Abby and Dan. "Karl said he promised you wine to celebrate." They filled their glasses, raised them high, and cried "Salute" in several languages. When they ran out of "Salutes" and wine, Emil closed the evening. "You will stay the night in rooms generously provided by Hans and Bella. Tomorrow we will move you to another location where you will be taken out of here for good. Don't ask any more questions because I won't answer them."

Hans picked up the talk. "We have observers with radios on the main roads leading into town. We don't want to fight unless it's absolutely necessary. Do you all have weapons?"

"Not me, sir. The SS stole my Beretta," said Abby.

"Frederick. That top cabinet on the right. Get that handgun and ammo for the lady."

"I'm okay. Took the Sergeant's pistol," said Dan.

"Did you get the submachine gun and ammo out of the car?" Karl asked.

"Yes, a fine addition to our firepower," said Emil.

"Okay, let's get some rest," said Emil. Sleep with your clothes on, including shoes. Put the safety on your weapon and sleep with it—it's your best friend."

"Emil, can I take a short walk down to the docks?" asked Karl. "My family took several holidays here when I was a small boy. I have fond memories of Bad Doberan."

"Okay, but don't be long, and talk to no one."

Karl pulled on a stocking cap and coat and walked down to the docks. *What a wonderful time we had here*, he thought. He sat on a bench lost in thought. Finally, he walked to the lighted dock office. He knocked and entered. "Sir, may I use your telephone for a call to Berlin? I'll pay you in advance?" He made one phone call.

# Chapter Seventy-four

**Bad Doberan—Karl**

"Hello, Mother. It's Karl."

"Karl, my beautiful boy. How are you, Son?"

"Oh, I'm fine, Mother. Everything okay with the family?"

"Yes, but your father is on a business trip to Munich. He'll be sorry he missed your call. Your brothers and sisters are fine. We're all so proud of you, our Colonel! Have you met Himmler and our Fuehrer yet?"

"Himmler, yes, but not Hitler." He paused. "Mother, I called because I'll be out of touch for a while on a special mission. Please forgive me, but must go right now…Goodbye, Mother. I love you."

He made his way back to the inn and lay awake in his bed.

After the hall lights went off, Abby went to Dan's room and knocked softly on the door. "Dan, I need to talk with you."

He let her in and gave her a warm hug and then looked at her face. Her lips were quivering and her body shaking. "Dan, I confess. I'm terrified again. Can I stay with you tonight and stay near you tomorrow? If I die, I want to be near you when it happens."

Dan's Irish lilt was gone. His voice was deep, almost guttural. "Stay, Abby, but I'm not sure about myself and what protection I can give you. My mind is full of demons, and my body is weak. It's hard to think clearly."

Abby thought, *I have no idea of all he's been through.*

They lay together fully clothed and dozed. In the middle of the night Dan sat straight up in bed and said, "No! No!" Perspiration ran down his face. Abby wrapped her arms around him and reassured him. "It's all right, Dan. It's all right."

They were finishing their breakfast coffee around the kitchen fireplace with Karl, Frederick, Bella, and Hans when Emil rushed in. "We've got to move on. One of our spotters radioed that a military staff car followed by a truck full of SS were seen south of Rostock. They could be here in Bad Doberan in a couple of hours if they're on our trail. We need to get into the truck parked at the back door. Get your things together and leave no traces in your rooms. Hans, get rid of those SS uniforms and Miss White's old clothes. Bella, wash up those extra dishes and shelve them. Empty all waste baskets and take the trash far away."

They climbed into the rear of a bakery delivery truck and sat on a blanket covering the cold steel floor. Emil drove the truck with Frederick in front with his machine gun, and they headed east out of Bad Doberan, away from Rostock.

Karl speculated as they were bounced around in the truck. "Remember the old veteran, Munster? He probably got nervous when nobody came to pick up Rudolf and likely drove to the roadblock to find out what was going on. I bet Munster was very upset when he found out he was duped and there would be no hero's medal for him. And I'm sure Heydrich has been notified by now—he has to be furious. And he has to be very worried if Hitler asks for Abby, or to see movies of her dying. Heydrich told me about Hitler's orders." Abby shuddered. *They won't take me alive again.*

# Chapter Seventy-five

*Island of Poel, Germany*

Emil headed the van toward Wismar, and then took a side road north, crossing a bridge to the tiny island of Poel. There was just one house on the island, a rustic seaside house with a barn. Emil parked the van in the barn. 'The owners are in sunny Spain," said Emil as they walked to the house. "They're anti-Nazi and may stay there indefinitely. They've given us full use of the property for a safe house and exit route from Germany. We've taken out several British airmen who were shot down and rescued by us. We'll stay here for a spell."

Abby helped Frederick start a fire and prepare a meal. Emil moved furniture to reveal a hidden radio transmitter.

"All right," said Emil. "The pickup is tonight at 0200, Frederick. It's one short flash when we push off. They'll respond in turn."

"Who's 'they'? When are you going to tell us what will happen?" asked Karl and echoed by Abby and Dan.

Emil got Frederick's nod of agreement. "All right. You'll be taken out of here by the British submarine, HMS *Storm*. We have a motorboat tied to a pier near here. We'll head out at 0145. The *Storm* will surface at 0200. You will climb up a ladder to the deck and drop down a hatch. At 0210 the sub will submerge. They'll submerge without you if we mess up—too much risk of being spotted by strollers on the mainland who can't sleep."

# EPILOGUE

"Don't scare them, Emil," said Frederick. "The captain of the *Storm* knows this may be the most important cargo of his career."

They were dozing by the fireplace in their life jackets when Emil woke them. "Dammit, Frederick, I think someone has informed on us. They've arrested Hans and Bella. Our man, Joseph Mueller, on this side of Bad Doberman said a military sedan followed by a military canvas-covered truck was seen heading our way. Joseph is coming in his speedboat to help us. We've got to get these people to our boat and out to sea."

"Emil," said Frederick, "you know the boat and the signaling routine better than I do. The demolition rigging at the bridge was my work. I'll stop them there."

"I'll help you," said Karl.

"You're too valuable to risk, Karl. You're coming with us," said Emil.

"No. Frederick can't stop them by himself." said Karl.

He picked up his machine gun and headed for the door with Frederick. They walked quickly toward the bridge. "Karl, there are two steel poles that we'll place in the brackets across the entrance to the bridge. The troopers will have to get out to lift them off. They'll be exposed. That's when I'll detonate the mines buried in the ground." He pointed. "You lay low on the right side. I'll be on the left with my detonator. Start firing while their ears are still ringing from the explosions. We should be able to kill most of them and then run back to the house. We have an escape tunnel in the big bedroom that leads to the boat dock. There's a trapdoor under the throw rug. See you there."

They saw two sets of headlights approaching on the road to the bridge about a mile away. "Let's get to our positions, Karl. Rub some dirt on your face. Lie down and cover up with brush."

Karl took his position on the ground, but then stood. "No! I can't do this. I can't kill my comrades!" He turned and ran toward the house. He burst through the door as they were leaving for the boat. "Hands up! Drop your weapons! All of you!"

Abby cried, "Oh, Karl!"

Karl looked at Abby and Dan. "I can't betray my Fatherland and family. I know the SS. They would torture and kill everyone in my family. The troopers will be here soon. Pass me my briefcase and stay away from your weapons."

Joseph Mueller had arrived from his speedboat and heard Karl from the kitchen. He came around the corner with his gun at the ready. Karl raised his machine gun, but Joseph shot first. Karl was dead before he hit the floor.

# Epilogue

"Let's go! Now!" yelled Emil. Abby picked up Karl's briefcase, and they ran for the boat.

The SS vehicles pulled to a stop before the bridge, and an officer jumped from the sedan. "Get those poles off," he ordered. Armed troopers jumped from the rear of the truck. An officer saw Frederick rise to depress the plunger on the detonator and shot him in the shoulder. Frederick fell on the detonator and mines exploded under both vehicles. Most of the troopers were killed instantly or taken out of action. The survivors hit the ground and looked for targets. Finally, it was quiet. "This is the only enemy we can find, sir," said a sergeant. The officer walked over to the wounded Frederick. "Save this man for interrogation," said the officer. Just as he said that, Frederick pulled a small two-shot Derringer from his inside vest pocket and shot the officer in the face, and then put the muzzle in his mouth and pulled the trigger before the SS troopers could react.

Emil, Abby, and Dan heard explosions and gunfire as the boat slipped out of the cove into the open sea. Abby and Dan huddled under a tarp in a sudden, chilling downpour. Then the sea opened up in front of them, and the HMS *Storm* surfaced like a huge whale, dark and menacing. Several sailors were out of the conning tower hatch in seconds, throwing a line to Emil and pulling the boat alongside.

"What will you do, Emil?" Abby asked.

"We have several hiding places up the coast," he said while helping Abby and Dan up a Jacob's ladder into the waiting arms of the sailors. "Good luck!" Emil yelled. Abby and Dan disappeared down the hatch, and the *Storm* submerged as quickly as it had surfaced.

The sub's captain soon stepped away from the periscope to welcome them aboard. The crew wrapped the two in warm blankets and gave them hot tea. "There were supposed to be three of you. What happened?"

"Our friend, Karl Kruger, helped us escape from Berlin, but didn't make it," Abby said.

MI6 agents met the *Storm* in a sub pen in Holy Loch, Scotland. A British Navy doctor examined Abby, then Dan. He wrote in his report to MI6:

> Miss White's wounds from her beating are healing nicely. Her mental condition is also good considering what she has been through in the last several weeks.

Mr. O'Gara will need time to recover both physically and mentally. I found that he has suffered through many months of torture, starvation, and humiliation.

His body scars show that he was beaten severely and often, poor lad. I recommend that he receive psychiatric treatment wherever he goes from here.

In the morning, they were spirited across the countryside to MI6 Headquarters in London. Abby and Dan sat in the rear seat of the sedan holding hands. "Dan, I will never let go of you again. I love you. I want to marry you if you'll have me."

Dan slumped in his seat and looked at her with tired, cavernous eyes. "That sounds wonderful, Abby, but I'm not ready for anything right now. I'm still living in that cell, listening for foot falls in the corridor. My mind is in a weird place.

"Abby, I owe you my life. I was going to kill myself before I got your message. I saved pieces of cloth to make a rope. My plan was to keep pilfering cloth until I had enough to throw the rope over the steam pipe in my cell and hang myself… Maybe after these debriefings we can go to Ireland and I can rest and get back to normal."

"My dear Dan. I know you've been through so much more than I. I want to be with you as you heal and forever after that."

# Chapter Seventy-six

*London—MI6*

Jones of MI6 met with them in his office. He moved out from behind his desk and shook their hands, "Hello, Dan, welcome home. And I presume this lady is the extraordinary Miss Abby White? You two have had a whirlwind of terrifying experiences. I'm honored to have you both here." He paused. "Before we get started, I want you to meet someone, Dan. I understand Miss White is already acquainted with him." He pressed a button on his desk, and a man entered the room. The man hung back a bit, acting sheepishly.

Dan was tiring of this cloak and dagger business. "Who *are* you?"

Jones answered for him. "This is Warren Walters, an American intelligence agent who handled a number of agents in Berlin from the American Embassy. He managed to slip out to Switzerland before they closed the net on all Embassy personnel."

"He was my contact at the Embassy, Dan," said Abby. "Hello, Walter." She resisted the urge to ask, *How's your mommy?* Instead she said. "Did your friends in Bern take you in?"

"Yes, the Bexel's. You have a very good memory, Abby."

Warren stood as straight as he could, looking very official. "Abby, I'm so sorry for what you had to go through. We pressed hard for your release, but Himmler wouldn't budge. That's when we decided to activate Karl Kruger. I got the ball rolling with Kruger and pocketed the escape plan on him on the street after he agreed to escape with you. He was a good man. Actually, we lost track of him for years. After we declared war on Germany someone in Washington was sifting through the files and found Karl Kruger's agreement to be an embedded agent for the U.S. We tracked him down to the SS in Berlin. We were lucky he was still willing to serve."

He looked at Abby and Dan and shook his head. "The underground in northern Germany just reported that he was killed on the island of Poel. I'm so sorry."

Abby took Dan's hand and squeezed it hard, and then she wiped away tears. "He saved our lives in Berlin. *He was a good man—overwhelmed by conflict and guilt.* He may be dead, but he left a treasure of information in this briefcase. I think it's filled with enough Nazi secrets to keep both of you busy for quite a while. Karl was a true hero."

Jones invited them into an adjoining conference room where coffee and tea were served. Abby sat at the table, but then pushed away. "Please bring in a stenographer. We will wait."

A stenographer positioned herself at the table. Abby continued, "Before any debriefings, we want signed and notarized statements from each of you representing your governments. Neither of us are military personnel. Our contracts with both of you expired months ago. The first statement will provide Dan back-pay from the British government for time and salary lost while in SS prisons, plus $15,000 for the physical and mental damages he suffered. The U.S. State Department's statement will provide $5,000 for me. We will wait in the outer office until the statements are prepared for our review.

"Two more things," said Abby. "This mass of Nazi intelligence data prepared by Karl Kruger must be recognized. I want another signed statement from the U.S. that at the war's end, the government will provide a bronze plaque for the Northwestern University library. It will say, 'In remembrance of Karl Kruger, Class of 1929, for meritorious service in the United States Intelligence Service during World War II.' I suspect that's what they'll call this war. I don't care what they will call it as long as it's not the 'The Third Reich Victory.'

"Also, we'll need a statement from Walter that the U.S. will provide military transportation to the U.S. for both of us after a period of rest and recuperation in Ireland. Do you agree with all of this, gentlemen?"

Jones looked at Walters, and they both nodded.

"Good. We'll wait until the statements are ready for our review," Abby said. "Can you have our tea brought out to the outer office?" She took Karl's briefcase with her.

# Chapter Seventy-seven

*Tralee, Ireland*

Darcy stood on the steps of the house, backed by Cormac and Sally as usual. "Come here, we need hugs," she said to Dan and Abby. Then she pulled away and looked them over thoroughly. "You two better have good excuses for being gone so long… Oh, my Dan, so much weight lost—we'll fix that."

They moved into the house. "Just in time for tea and just in time for a little surprise," Darcy said. Esther, Sean, and Danny came out from the kitchen. "We're still waiting for a ship to America, but we're in no hurry now that you're here," said Esther. There were hugs and tears all around, followed by hours of each relating their experiences.

It took two months for both Abby and Dan to recuperate, but one Saturday there was a wonderful Irish wedding on the bluffs overlooking Dingle Bay. Esther was Abby's maid of honor, and Dan's best man was Sean. Dan whispered to Abby before the cleric began, "Ever us."

The End

# Epilogue

**Abby White O'Gara and Dan O'Gara** made their home in Chicago. Abby became a senior editor for the *Chicago Tribune* and won a Pulitzer Prize for a series of articles on the Cold War. Dan preferred the outdoor life after his time in SS prisons and owned and operated ferry boats on Lake Michigan. Dan was in port enough for he and Abby to have three children.

**Darcy O'Gara** eventually sold the brewery in Ireland and traveled the world, spending many days visiting with Abby and Dan's family in Chicago.

After traveling the Eastern seacoast in America, **Esther Frankel O'Connor** and **Sean O'Connor** settled in New Jersey. Esther stayed home with Danny and his two new sisters and wrote a novella and other pieces about their experiences with the French Résistance. Sean and Esther invested some of her father's bequest in buying an auto agency. This lead to a nationwide chain of auto agencies called O'Connor's Fine Cars.

**Warren Walters** retired from a low-level position in the State Department. He lived with his mother until she passed away, and then he married.

Esther's friend from the *Bremen*, **Jacob Bernstein**, joined scientists Oppenheimer and Feynman and others at the Los Alamos Laboratory in the final assembly and testing of the war-ending atomic bombs used on

Japan. He later was chairman of the physics department at Purdue University, his undergraduate alma mater.

**Lydia Viazensky Dieter**, the Admiral's widow, had a baby boy fathered by the Admiral. After the war ended, she married **Claus von Fritsch**, Abby's old friend, and had two more children. Claus became a leader in the post-war West German government. Lydia was again a fixture at embassy dinner parties.

## *Historical Figures*

Infamous Gangsters

**Al Capone,** leader of the Chicago Outfit and Chicago's South Side Gang, was arrested and convicted of federal tax evasion. He served time in Alcatraz and died at age 48.

Capone's competitor, **Bugs Moran,** who headed Chicago's North Side Gang, died at 63 in Leavenworth Federal Prison.

Nazis

Just ahead of the advancing Russians **Adolf Hitler** married his long-time mistress, **Eva Braun,** in his Berlin concrete bunker located twenty-eight feet beneath the city streets of Berlin. They then both committed suicide by poison. Hitler first tried his poison on his German shepherd, Blondi. Hitler's maniacle aggression resulted in more than sixty million deaths world-wide.

Hitler invited **Joseph Goebbels** and his family to join him in his bunker in the final days. Goebbles and his wife, **Magna Goebbels,** committed suicide after fatally poisoning their six small children.

**Heinrich Himmler,** SS mass murderer, was caught in the uniform of an enlisted man trying to flee. He escaped the hangman by killing himself with a cyanide capsule.

Czech soldiers parachuted into Prague and ambushed **Reinhard Heydrich,** Himmler's hatchet man, as he rode in an open car. He died of his wounds on June 4, 1942. The Germans took savage revenge—1,331 Czechs, including 201 women, were immediately executed.

**Hermann Goering** killed himself in the Nuremberg prison with a hidden vial of cyanide just two hours before he was to be hanged. Ten other top Nazis were hung until dead on October 16, 1946. Hundreds of lesser Nazis who committed atrocities were tried and executed.

# Acknowledgements

Most helpful, most encouraging, and indispensible was my editor-in-chief, my wife, Nancy. Her efforts and patience in this three-year endeavor were immensely valuable.

Our friend, Louise Larson, read the first drafts and made excellent observations.

The staff at Dog Ear Publishing was instrumental in preparing my manuscript for market-ready publication.

# Suggested Readings

Bair, Deirdre. *Al Capone—-Life, Legacy, and Legend.* Nan A. Tales/Doubleday, 2016.

Batvinis, Raymond. *Hoover's Secret War against Axis Spies.* U. of Kansas Press, 2014.

Churchill, Winston. *The Gathering Storm. Second WW, Vol.1&2.* Simon/Schuster, 1948.

Chicago Historical Society. *Encyclopedia of Chicago.*

Duffy, Peter. *Double Agent.* Simon/Schuster, 2014.

Einstein, Albert. *Out of My Later Years.* Citadel Press. 1956

Evans, Richard. *The Third Reich in History and Memory.* Oxford University Press, 2015.

Geiss, Josef. *Obersalzberg. The History of a Mountain from Judith Platter until Hitler.*
 Geiss Verlag, 1980.

Glass, Charles. *Americans in Paris. Life/Death under Nazi Occupation.* Penguin, 2010.

Hitler, Adolf. *Mein Kampf.* Franz Eher Nachfolger, 1925.

Keegan, John (Editor). *Who Was Who in World War II.* Crescent Books, 1984.

King, Howard and Kelly. *The Roaring Twenties.* URL, 2006.

Macintyre, Ben. *Agent Zigzag.* Broadway Paperbooks, 2007.

Millard, Candice. *Hero of the Empire, W. Churchill.* Doubleday, 2016

Padfield, Peter. *Himmler.* Henry Holt & Company, 1990.

Perry, Douglas. *The Girls of Murder City.* Viking, 2010.

Persico, Joseph E. *Nuremberg–Infamy on Trial.* Penguin, 1995

Plenk, Anton. *Obersalzburg and the Third Reich.* Plenk Verlag, 1982.

Piekalkiewicz, Janus. *Secret Agent, Spies. WWII.* William Morrow & Company, 1969.

Rees, Lawrence. *Hitler's Charisma. Leading Millions into the Abyss.* Vintage, 2012.

Shirer, William. *The Rise and Fall of the Third Reich.* Simon/ Schuster, 1960.

Snyder, Timothy. *Black Evil. The Holocaust as History and Warning.* Crown, 2015.

Sulzberger, C.L. *American Heritage History of World War II.* American Heritage. 1966

Vassiltchikov, Marie. *Berlin Diaries 1940—1945.* Vintage, 1988.

www.ingramcontent.com/pod-product-compliance
Lightning Source LLC
LaVergne TN
LVHW091534060526
838200LV00036B/599